The Dance

By Suzie Carr

Cover photography: Amanda Robertson

Also by Suzie Carr:
The Fiche Room
Two Feet off The Ground
Tangerine Twist
Inner Secrets
A New Leash on Life
The Muse
Staying True
Snowflakes
The Journey Somewhere
Sandcastles

Keep up on Suzie's latest news and projects:
www.curveswelcome.com

Follow Suzie on Twitter:
@girl_novelist

For you, Fee Fee. Your light inspires and amazes me.

Acknowledgements

This book is a result of the combined efforts of many people. With your generous guidance and expertise, I learned a great deal about honeybees, love, friendship, forgiveness, and communication. Steve and Kathy, your generosity has opened up a whole new level of awareness in me. Thank you for welcoming me into your bee apiary and home. Your love for and devotion to honeybees is touching beyond words, and I am so grateful you allowed me to experience that magic for myself. Dr. Marla Spivak, I will forever be in awe of your work, and am grateful you took the time to direct me to *Bee-Time: Lessons from the Hive* by Mark Winston, the book that set my research into motion. To Amanda Robertson, your artistry is awe-inspiring. Thank you for the gift of the magnificent cover photograph that captures the true essence of *The Dance*. To Diane Marina and Dorina, as always thank you for being my sounding board during those critical early periods when I have just an idea floating around my head, one that you both help me to sculpt into a story worth telling. To my editor, JoAnne, thank you for always giving my work your keen eye and generous care. To Jennifer, Deborah, Felicia, Angela, and Alak, thank you for the gift of your time, honesty, and insights. You helped me turn this idea into a piece of work I am proud to share. Thanks for that confidence! And to my Sunshine, thank you for teaching me how to love, let go, and trust in the process of this magnificent life.

Carr—The Dance

Prologue

Jacky Applebaum always knew *her inner circle* – as she lovingly referred to them – was a mismatched bunch from the very start. Jacky stood at the wayside of their bunch, too cautious, too impatient. That night marked their fifth year anniversary as a viable dog training and daycare facility, and many came to help them celebrate.

Jacky hovered over the dessert table, wavering between the pecan tart and the flan. From her vantage point, she caught sight of Marie, her best friend and business partner, defending her stance on RVing over hotel stays to Greg, one of the lead trainers whose face turned a deeper shade of red with each octave Marie climbed. Marie loved a good debate. She was loyal, but not a pushover by any stretch of the imagination. She had a knack for spotting fake and showed no qualms toward pointing out inconsistencies. Greg's face verged on blood red as Marie continued her rant, waving her hands and pointing her finger as she enjoyed dipping into her rebuttal. People didn't mess with Marie. She owned the room with all of her six-foot height and sharp-focused eyes. Though she might've appeared drill-sergeant tough on the outside, on the inside, a soft core of sincerity and love flowed.

Hazel, Marie's *friend*, stood beside Marie looking every bit as uncomfortable as she would if standing in a box full of spiders. Her eyes darted back and forth between Marie and Greg, and her lips did that twitching thing they did every time Marie heated up into a good debate. Hazel was the most balanced of them all in the Inner Circle, always sweeping up after Jacky and Marie's quarrels and smoothing over any residual rough edges with quiet grace. She always appeared and disappeared on a whisper.

Jacky glanced at a reflection of herself in the mirrored wall. She wore her light-colored hair down and flipped up the ends slightly to create body. Even in the dimly lit room, she could tell her hair needed new highlights to spruce it back up to its sunnier look. Not exactly a priority, though.

She looked back down to the desserts and chose the flan. She spooned some into her mouth. Scanning the room, she spotted Sophie, her step-daughter, talking with a couple of her giggly friends. She wore a dress way too short and a tad bit on the see-through side to be appropriate. Sophie could charm her way into and out of anything. Her friends adored her. They watched in awe as she began to direct a waiter to refill the water pitchers on every table. Sophie was charismatic and brimming with innocence, in a subtle and contagious way, always mesmerized and excited about something or another. Her deep dimples and spunky spirit kept Jacky on her toes, running every which way to keep her entertained.

Drew, Jacky's wife, snuck up behind her, placing her chin on Jacky's shoulder. They stared at their daughter for a moment in silence. "She's so bossy," Drew said.

Jacky reached down and took her wife's hand. "Just like her momma."

Drew smirked and gulped a mouthful of wine.

Jacky then stole the glass from Drew and also gulped back a hearty mouthful.

In a few short weeks, they'd celebrate eight years together. All in all, the years had been kind, overflowing with laughter, teasing, and half-baked attempts at discerning the purpose of life. After all that time, Jacky never tired of lounging in bed on Sunday mornings reading *The Sun* and planning the next twenty-year trek through time. Teasing Sophie, petting their dog, Rosy, and filling the flannel bed sheets with biscuit crumbs had punctuated their past, present and undoubtedly their future. And Jacky couldn't be any happier.

Little did Jacky know, however, that life would soon take a reckless detour, one triggered by two heavy and regrettable words.

Chapter One

It all started with Jacky asking Drew to pass the salt. She passed the pepper instead. "Where are you tonight?" Jacky asked, pushing the pepper shaker toward Sophie.

Sophie, in all of her thirteen years of age, put down her fork and folded her hands under her chin, steadying in for the analysis. "Yeah, Mom. You're not here. I mean physically, yes, but you're playing with your spaghetti."

"I've got a lot on my mind." She darted from Jacky to Sophie like a cornered stray cat bracing for attack. "Cut me some slack."

"Okay chill out." Jacky reached over the silk flower arrangement and grabbed the salt. She disliked the arrangement with its fake daisies and leaves. They collected dust and reminded her of a waiting room in a doctor's office. They couldn't grow live ones, though. They never remembered to water them. So, they chose plastic over dead leaves.

Drew played with her broccoli florets, pushing them around the plate with clumsy strokes.

Jacky stopped twirling her spaghetti. "We're just concerned. That's all. You've been running around looking exhausted for days now."

"Days?" Sophie cut in. "More like months." She shoveled a pile of spaghetti into her mouth.

Drew fiddled with a chunk of parmesan cheese now. "I could really use an extra hour each day. Just one additional hour would do me wonders." She shook her head, fighting herself on the inadequacy of a twenty-four hour day.

3

Since Jacky met her, Drew operated at blazing speed. She always bounced around activities and work like a restless Boston terrier, sniffing and scurrying about. But that night, something distracted her. Her overstimulated brain skipped on the edge of a groove. She never played with her food. She normally devoured it.

"So that's it?" Jacky sipped her lemonade. "You're just busy and overwhelmed?"

She twirled a lone spaghetti strand. "That's it, babe." She looked up and forced a smile. "I just need a good night's sleep."

Stress oozed from every fine line on her face. Or was it sadness?

"Well, let's talk about something not work related then," Sophie said. "I have to do a presentation for school. Maybe I could talk about my family. You know, how you met and all that." She pushed a meatball out of the way. "By the way, Ashley and her mom became vegetarians. We should consider it too. Ms. Kendall saw a video about how cattle meat is processed." Sophie scrunched her face. "It's disgusting."

Jacky wrapped her hand around Drew's wrist. "We need to get her different friends."

Drew's face flushed deep red. "Don't be silly."

"I'm joking, sweetheart." She tickled her side, and Drew squirmed and squealed.

"I'm not going to stop until you promise to drop the bad mood."

Drew's laughter filled the kitchen, warming up the drabness instantly. Even the fake flowers took on a livelier glow.

"Okay," Drew squealed. "Yes, okay, it's gone."

Jacky stopped, and took in the beautiful twinkle resting in Drew's light eyes. Even with her strawberry blonde hair pulled back into its messy bun, she looked stunning.

Drew laughed, and covered her mouth. Oh how Jacky loved when she did that. For a momentary span of time, her wife revealed that sweet, quiet side she adored; a monumental shift from the dueling side of that personality where confidence coated every move, slight or bold.

Jacky eased back against the chair, enjoying the return of their familiar lively vibe. She took a long, restorative breath. "Did I ever tell you how I fell in love with your mother the first day I met her?" she asked Sophie.

"Oh, juicy material for my presentation." Sophie scooted up. "Tell me."

Jacky regarded the half smile on Drew's face. "Well, we met at a Walk for Paws event on an unusually cold October day."

"How cold?" Sophie asked. "I need details."

"Forty something degrees."

"In Maryland?"

Jacky nodded. "So, I was prancing around in a circle with a dancing Calhoun named Dixie when I noticed your mother videotaping me."

Drew raised her eyebrow. "You make me sound like a stalker."

"Well, Mom, in all fairness, you can be sometimes. I mean you hide in bushes to get the right shot."

Drew did. As a photographer, Drew circled the state for the next big story. She hid in bushes and behind cars. Hell, she once even scaled a fire escape to get a bird's eye view of the mayor in a parade.

"So anyway," Jacky said, eyeing her beautiful wife, "she hopped over a pair of Yorkies to get to me. She carried this big video camera on her shoulder."

"On her shoulder?" Sophie asked. "They're so scrawny."

"Hey," Drew pointed her finger at her daughter. "You've got the same ones, so zip it."

"So, yeah, your mother came bolting at me with that camera. She had that look she gets when she realizes she's ten minutes late for *American Idol*."

"Like this?" Sophie stretched her neck and began wagging her head like a chicken.

"Exactly."

"I do not look that way." Drew folded her arms across her pink Nike t-shirt.

"Yeah, you do, Mom."

Drew shot Sophie a twisted smile.

5

"So your mom comes up to me with her head all wagging and neck stretched like she's pecking for feed."

Drew leaned back with a scowl, and Sophie all but spit out the lemonade she just sipped.

"She puts a mic in front of me and starts interviewing, all business-like. 'We're here with our own local Dog Whisperer, Jacky Applebaum. Ms. Applebaum, tell us how you got started.'" Jacky mimicked Drew's reporter-style voice.

"What did you say?" Drew nudged. "Go ahead tell her what happened."

"For the first time in my life, I couldn't get my tongue to work. It got stuck in the back of my throat. She mesmerized me with that delicate smile."

"Aw." Sophie wiped some spaghetti sauce from her mouth with the back of her hand. "Love at first sight, then?"

"Sort of," Jacky said.

Drew slapped Jacky's hand. "Sort of?"

"I'd call it puppy love," Jacky said. "The next night. That's when I fell in love. I fell right down that abyss, and I've never been able to get of it out since."

Drew picked up her glass. "It was the Mai Tai."

Jacky gazed into Drew's baby blue eyes, remembering back to their first date. "The Mai Tai, huh?"

Drew nodded.

The Mai Tai did help to calm Jacky's nerves that night. The very fact that Jacky had conjured up enough nerve to even ask Drew out still astounded her. Gripped by the idea of Drew disappearing from her life, though, Jacky stepped into boldness. Right there in the training circle at Walk for Paws, as Drew turned to walk away, Jacky grabbed for her arm and blurted out the invite to meet up for drinks the next night.

Jacky chuckled at the memory. "We can't credit the Mai Tai. The bartender watered it down."

"Then, what? Her smile again?" Sophie asked, rolling her eyes.

"No. Not the smile either."

"Geez," Sophie sighed. "What the hell can we credit?"

"Watch your mouth, young lady." Drew squinted at her.

"Fine. What the heck can we credit?"

Jacky tossed her napkin on the table. "The Crab Rangoon."

"The Crab Rangoon?" Drew laughed.

"Yup. The way you ate them with reckless abandon stole my heart. You ate with such gusto. I'd never met a woman who ate with such passion and disregard for utensils as you. From that first fervent bite, our journey began. From there it blazed the open road."

"Really?" Drew mouthed at her.

Jacky nodded on a wink.

"How can this be the first time I'm hearing this story?" Sophie slurped another mouthful of spaghetti.

"You never asked, kiddo."

~ ~

Later that night when Jacky returned from a walk with Rosy, their Retriever Spaniel mix, she noticed the freezer door open. She closed it and walked up the stairs to Sophie's room. She knocked and opened the door. She discovered Sophie sprawled out on her bed and on the phone.

"Did you go into the freezer for anything after dinner?"

"Hang on, Ashley." Sophie tore off her earphones. "No. Why?"

Jacky sighed. Drew left it open again. "Don't worry about it, kiddo. And don't stay up too late."

Sophie stuck her earphones back in. "Oh my God, I know. Did you see how he looked at you?"

Jacky closed the door on her giggle.

She ventured down the hall to their bedroom. She entered their spacious room and landed her eyes on the ruffled bed. Drew already tucked herself under the blankets, with her back to her.

Jacky sat on the edge of the bed, taking in the soft shadows all around her. The faint scent of lavender played on her senses, dulling the subtle pulse of annoyance that plagued her only moments ago. "Are you awake?"

"I am now," she mumbled.

Jacky climbed under the covers and stared at the back of Drew's head. Her bun resembled a small animal's nest the way it matted and twisted. She feathered her hand down Drew's shoulder and arm. "You left the freezer open again."

"Mm. Did I?" She stiffened under her touch.

Jacky dropped her hand. "Unless Rosy can do a new trick."

Drew tightened the fluffy comforter around her. "Sorry. It won't happen again."

Jacky remained silent watching her wife cocoon herself. She placed her hand on Drew's shoulder again. "You need to slow down."

"I'm fine."

Drew was always fine. She piled to-do items onto her plate until it overflowed, drowning out their family time. If a new assignment across the state didn't tempt her, she flung herself into a new activity or class. She craved adventure, circling the state of Maryland with her video camera and tripod to capture the heart of living and breathing new experiences.

Jacky undid her ponytail elastic, allowing her scalp a break from the tight pull. She ran her fingers through her hair, then looked around their bedroom again. She knew Drew was an adventurist the moment she met her. She just never understood how lonely being married to one could be until they sank into the routine of life together.

Sophie didn't veer far from being an adventurist, too. She mirrored her mother not only in looks, but in her primal pursuit of exploration. By age five, Sophie had already taken a ride on a helicopter, explored part of the Appalachian Trail on horseback, and recorded her very first snorkeling expedition in a documentary where she educated and entertained her audience on the importance of safety and fun, as good as a five year-old could.

Would they ever slow down and take a breath? "Why do you do it?"

Drew rolled over. "Do what?"

"Try to escape through more and more commitments."

"I left the freezer open and suddenly I'm escaping and taking on too many commitments?"

"Are you?" *It's a legit question.*

Drew groaned.

"I'm just concerned," Jacky continued. "Last week you forgot to turn off the outdoor lights, the week before that you left your car running in the driveway, and three days ago you forgot to take the bag of milk and eggs out of the trunk."

Drew cradled Jacky's hand and grinned. "Maybe you're right. Maybe turning forty has changed me into a tired old woman."

Jacky relied on that upward curve of Drew's mouth far too much. She reacted to it like a child to a puppet. It catapulted her from the brinks of upset to bright sunshine in a matter of nanoseconds. "What does that make me then?" Jacky joked.

"A tired older woman by six months, I suppose."

Jacky pulled out Drew's messy bun and ran her fingers through the layers. "We need a vacation."

"Soon," she whispered. "I promise."

She traced her finger along Drew's warm lips. "It's been so long," Jacky whispered, hinting her desire.

A dramatic pause ensued.

"Maybe tomorrow? I'm tired, babe."

"Of course." Jacky lowered her finger and rolled over. It had only been four months. What would another night hurt?

Jacky cradled her head against the pillow and stared off into the dark night. In the shadows of the hours that passed, Jacky lay in a tangle of restless thoughts.

Comfort and routine had long ago taken over the early thrills and adrenaline rushes of their first years. Dinners grew cold on the counter, laundry piled up in the corners of their bedrooms, and suggestive kisses turned into quick pecks on the cheek as one of them rushed out of the house for an all-important meeting or activity.

One day, Drew kept promising. *We'll take a nice vacation. We'll tuck ourselves into a mountain-side resort where entertainment will consist of roasting marshmallows over an open fire pit and hiking the great outdoors in search of peace and stimulating conversation about the future, outer space, and the purpose of life. Trust me,* she'd say.

Jacky tossed and turned. She trusted in Drew's plan to take that vacation, and hopefully in so doing, they would be able to get everything back on track again.

The next morning, Jacky woke to an empty bed. She rose, petted Rosy, and then checked the bathroom, the kitchen, and the living room.

She ventured back upstairs and peeked in on Sophie. She found her talking on the phone to Ashley again. "Hey, have you seen your mom?"

Sophie pulled her earphones out. "She's not here?"

"Maybe she's out back." Jacky headed back down the hall and toward the stairs.

"I have an eye doctor appointment in like an hour," Sophie yelled out to her. "I hope she's here."

Once in the kitchen, she headed over to the back door. Angry raindrops pounded the pavement, but despite that, Jacky lifted the blinds, hoping to see Drew outside sneaking a cigarette under the patio umbrella.

Nothing.

She turned back to face the empty kitchen. The freezer door hung open again. *My God. Would it kill her to pay attention to something other than everything outside the house?*

Jacky picked up the cell and called her.

"Where are you?"

"In the car. I've got a meeting, and I'm running late."

"You didn't even say goodbye."

"I woke up late. I just ran out and figured I'd call you in a little while to explain. Kate needs me at the dojo because they've got an army of kids coming in for a preview day. If I'm not there, she's going to have to deal with them by herself."

Another item added to her full plate. "You left the freezer open again."

"Ugh. I'm sorry." Pause. "I was just in a hurry."

Her excuse broke through their bloated dam and choked Jacky's reserve of compassion. "You're always in a hurry."

"Please don't turn this into a lecture."

"A lecture?" Anger curled up Jacky's spine, flicking its poison.

"I'm sorry I left the freezer open," Drew said. "I've just got a lot on my mind."

"Like a dojo full of strangers?"

"Not now, Jacky. Please let's not fight today."

Her newest obsession, the dojo, and her friend Kate, Ashley's mother, always took a front stance to their family. The smelly rubber floor and grunts of wannabee martial artists won. They infiltrated her home, tossing her peace and balance out of the way as they dug in and took over.

Jacky heard the shower running. She still covered her mouth so Sophie wouldn't hear their inevitable argument. "What about your daughter?"

"What about her?"

"You forgot, didn't you?"

"What did I forget this time?"

"Her eye appointment?" Jacky pinched her leg to vet some of the anger. It continued to torment her with its grueling flicks.

Drew sighed. "Fuck."

Silence.

"Can you take her? Please?"

Unbelievable. "I've got clients lined up. I can't just cancel them."

"Please," she begged in her desperate voice. "This is important."

"Everything's always more important than us lately."

"That's not true, Jacky. Please don't believe that."

"You're obsessed with the dojo."

"I enjoy it," she hissed.

"First a hobby, that's how it all begins with you. Then, the hobby evolves into this all-encompassing fiasco where everything gets put to the side. You're there more than here. And when you come home, you're all stressed out and taking it out on us."

"Not now, okay?" Drew begged. "I'm running late. I'll call you later to discuss it."

The anger fought its way into her words. "You ran out of the house without saying goodbye. You just dumped your responsibilities into my lap again. Admit it, you didn't forget about your daughter's appointment."

"I did forget."

"Well, that's even the more troublesome." Her breaths quickened to the point her lungs hurt.

More silence.

"Drew, you're constantly asking me to cancel my day to take Sophie here and there. I can't do this anymore. You're running out of the house forgetting to shut freezer doors and to take your daughter to medical appointments. Something has to give."

"I didn't have time to wake you up with a fucking cup of steaming coffee and the newspaper, so now something has to give?"

"Excuse me?"

"You heard me," she snapped. "My life is careening out of control, and I just need you to give me a break."

Give *her* a break? *What about me?*

Clients relied on her, and that sat a little higher up the ladder of importance than some karate kick. How dare she shovel this on her? "For the past six months I've been the only one cooking, cleaning, and driving Sophie to every cheerleading practice, every student council meeting, every friend's slumber party, and what do you do? You come home and treat us like your life is more important than ours."

"Stop being such a bitch."

Jacky's blood pressure flared. She paced the floor, nauseated. "You can come home and take your own daughter to the eye appointment."

"My daughter?" Drew asked.

Jacky's temples throbbed. "Yes, she is *your* daughter!"

"Well, thank God for that," Drew screamed.

"Fuck off," Jacky yelled so loud the entire neighborhood must have heard. She hung up, then flung the phone.

Jacky stormed around the kitchen counter, kicking and punching through the squally debris to find something, anything to latch onto that made sense.

"What's happening?" Sophie asked.

Jacky turned around to find Sophie dripping and draped in a towel.

"I'm sorry. God, I'm sorry." Doused in shame, Jacky steadied against the counter. "I thought you were in the shower."

Sophie swallowed. "Clearly, I'm not." She turned and walked down the hall toward the staircase.

Jacky stood under the heat of the kitchen lights, embarrassed. The longer she stood, the more the shame dug at her.

She needed air.

She reached for Rosy's leash. "Come on girl. Let's go for a walk."

A few minutes later, Jacky resumed normal breathing and thought back on her fight with a clearer mind. How could Drew not see that her reckless, chaotic life affected all of them?

How would they ever fix this?

Perhaps Marie could help them reconcile by being that third person. If Marie didn't agree with something, she'd let them know. Marie took no sides, even when it came to Hazel. Marie couldn't tell a lie if her life depended on it. Maybe if Hazel's life depended on it, she could. But, certainly no one else's.

Yes. She would sit Drew down that night after dinner and suggest inviting Marie and Hazel over for a barbeque and mediation that weekend.

When Jacky arrived back at the house, Sophie was gulping milk from the carton. Jacky stopped short of reprimanding. Sophie suffered enough damage for one day by hearing her tell her mom to fuck off. "I'm going to take you to your eye appointment. Are you ready?"

She shrugged. "Yeah, sure. You can just drop me off, and I can take the bus to school from there."

Jacky put her arm around Sophie's shoulder. "Nah. I'll take you." She'd call Marie from the car and tell her to cancel her first few dog training clients of the day.

Sophie put the milk carton back and gathered up her book bag. "I'm ready."

~ ~

A couple of hours later, they returned home to grab Sophie's lunch tote from the kitchen counter. Rosy leaped at them, excited and ready to walk.

"I'll take her for a walk. I could use the air," Sophie said. "I'm already late for school. What's another half an hour?"

Jacky slid the leash off the hook in the hallway. "I could use some air, too."

Sophie shot her a frown. "Fine. Just let me tinkle."

Jacky bent down and pet Rosy. "She hates me."

Rosy stared blankly at her.

"I don't blame her. I cursed out her mother." She leaned her forehead against Rosy's snout. "You need a breath mint, pretty girl."

Rosy licked her nose.

Just then, someone knocked on the front door. Jacky snuck over to the window to get a peek. Two policeman stood on her front stoop.

Her heart dropped.

Somehow, she managed to open the front door. One of them asked, "Jacky Applebaum?"

Jacky froze.

Sophie walked up to Jacky's side.

14

Rosy moved in, sniffing the officers.

"Can we come in?"

Jacky nodded and moved aside, and they entered.

A heaviness dropped on the room, snuffing all remaining light and freshness.

They stood in the foyer and removed their hats. The beefier of the two inched forward. "We're sorry to have to inform you," he said with a softness that didn't match his size, "Drew Applebaum was in a fatal car accident this morning."

As the policeman spoke, the room blurred. She found Sophie's fragile, cold hand and cradled it as the police explained the details. Somewhere in between their sobs, Jacky heard about the bystander who had reported the accident happening around nine o'clock that morning.

A bigger lump formed in her throat.

Nine o'clock. Just about the same time she had carelessly flung those two regrettable words at her wife.

~ ~

A fierce shock took over immediately, leaving Jacky in a state of numb disbelief. She attempted to push through the shockwaves to save Sophie from drowning in the tumultuous wake of their sadness, but to no avail. Sophie wanted to be alone. No amount of food, hugs, or attempts at talking would bring Drew back to them.

On the morning after Drew's death, Sophie stood before Jacky. "I don't want to be here right now," she said on a whisper. "I'm going to Ashley's for a few days."

Jacky cradled Sophie's wrist. "Kiddo, please don't go."

A small cry escaped from deep inside Sophie. "I need my best friend right now."

They stood staring at each other, each lost in a battle with their new cruel reality. If Jacky allowed her to go, would that hurt or help Sophie? Would Ashley offer Sophie better comfort than she could?

Of course she would. Ashley was a good friend, and someone Sophie trusted. If anyone could keep Sophie's heart safe in the coming days, Ashley could.

Jacky nodded, vying for strength and confidence in her decision. "Okay, kiddo."

In the days following, Jacky sent Sophie text messages, and she'd respond in one-word answers.

Marie urged her to continue to give Sophie room. So she did, but not without reminding Sophie that she was there for her if she wanted to talk.

The night of the funeral, at Ashley's insistence, Sophie finally agreed to go home with Jacky.

As they entered their empty home, Jacky reached out for Sophie's arm. "Can we chat?"

She shrugged, slipping into the safety of her new and justified silence.

Jacky never prayed, but she prayed in that moment. She prayed to a God she didn't know for guidance. She couldn't have Sophie hate her. "I never meant what I said to your mom that morning. The words just came out. We were fighting." Jacky's voice took on a pleading tone. "I never should've said that to her."

Large teardrops leaked from the corners of Sophie's eyes.

"Please talk to me, kiddo."

Sophie bowed her head. Her golden ringlets hung as if deflated and tired.

Jacky cradled her hand around Sophie's thin wrist. "I didn't mean it."

Sophie glared up at her. She clenched her teeth. "Then you shouldn't have said it."

Jacky caught her breath. Sophie's wrist trembled in her hand. "What can I do to make this better?"

"Everything's already ruined." The teardrops leaked down her cheeks.

Jacky reached for a tissue and began wiping Sophie's tears. "I'm sorry kiddo. I'm so sorry."

Sophie pushed Jacky's hand away. "You destroyed everything," she screamed. "All you can say is *I'm sorry kiddo*?" She grunted and balled her hands into fists. "I hate you." She ran out of the room, up the stairs, and slammed her door shut.

Jacky stood numb in the fallout ash of her own selfish assault on their beautiful life, too guilty to argue a defense.

~ ~

As the months crawled by after that fateful day, everything blurred into one tasteless crumb after another for Jacky. The spice that once peppered life, disintegrated and left a bland film in its path. Shedding tears in her bathtub offered the only relief. They reminded her that she could still produce something other than empty promises to friends and family – empty promises that she and Sophie would eventually be okay. How could she truly promise something she didn't fully believe?

Through the maze of casseroles, cheerful greeting cards, and constant messages from friends, she clung to the false hope that somewhere underneath all the heartbreak they might find peace. Then, a cruel reminder would pop up in the form of a bill still in Drew's name or an annual doctor's appointment reminder.

Reminders poked at her from every direction. She only had to look up from her cereal bowl every morning to catch a glimpse of Drew in Sophie's face as she scrambled past her to fetch an apple before escaping the confines of the kitchen.

The kitchen had shrunk. It withered down to a dark and airless closet. Drew's death changed that once lively, seasoned room. It lacked vitality and the song of a happy family chopping broccoli and carrots together under the ambiance of track lighting and Sinatra.

Every time Jacky looked at Sophie, with her doe-like eyes, guilt hammered her, burying her deeper into the darkness. The splinters of circumstance gutted her, all because of a stupid argument over an eye appointment and freezer door.

~ ~

As time rolled on after her mother's death, Jacky insisted Sophie continue to go to counseling. Sophie followed the order, playing along for the sake of peace. She didn't want to churn the water any more than it already had been.

One night after they returned from a session, Jacky walked into the kitchen. Sophie piled ham onto wheat bread.

"Hey kiddo. Want to watch a movie tonight?"

Sophie bit into her sandwich. Jacky always assumed they could skip right back into their former relationship where laughter and piggyback rides through the house were the norm. "I can't."

Jacky smoothed her hands over her tired face. "Can I ask you something?"

Sophie teetered, gripping both her grudge and her hurt with equal strength. "Sure."

"Will you ever forgive me?"

Forgive. You forgave someone for intentional wronging. How did you forgive someone for being honest? She couldn't be mad at Jacky for being truthful. She wasn't mad, she was sad; the kind of sadness that leaks down into your gut and drowns everything, leaving it bloated and rotten. She always assumed Jacky loved her like a daughter. *She's your daughter. Not mine!* Jacky likely didn't even realize she had voiced her true feelings out loud.

So, could she forgive her? Sure. But forget? She couldn't just forget the grip of sadness.

"Please?" Strain pulled at Jacky.

Why did she beg? Exactly why did she want to break through her wall? To rid herself of guilt for not wanting to be her mother? Sophie was nothing more than an obligation to her now.

She bit into the ham sandwich, slaving to hide her emotions. "I've already forgiven you."

"You have?" Jacky cried.

Sophie wanted the conversation to end. No amount of talking would bring back her mother or the Jacky she used to trust. She would tell her therapist that she forgave Jacky, then she could move on like a normal teenager. "We're fine. Really."

Jacky moved in closer. "I love you. I hope you know that."

Redirect. Redirect. "I do." She pushed away from the counter. "I've got to get ready for tonight. Ashley and her boyfriend are picking me up in a little while. We're going to decorate the homecoming float."

Jacky brightened. "Oh. Okay. That's good. Time with friends is good." She balanced her hands on the kitchen counter. "That definitely sounds like more fun than a movie at home."

Sophie lifted the giant burden of maternal duties from Jacky's shoulders with so little ease that it terrified her. She saved her that night from having to muddle in the responsibility of someone else's problem, someone else's daughter.

A couple of hours later, Sophie pasted crumbled up tissue paper to the side of a wagon while listening to her friends carry on about senseless things like lipstick shades, dresses for homecoming, hairstyle options and whether they should rent limos or have their parents chauffeur them.

They all had parents at home who would help them decide these important teenage questions. They'd go home afterwards and laugh on the couch with their families, carefree of any weight. Maybe like she used to do with Jacky and her mother, they'd joke about the day's funny moments and plan bike rides and picnics in the park for the upcoming weekend.

How lucky. Sophie would return home to Jacky, someone who had no choice but to provide a roof and food for her. Jacky didn't choose to be a mother. Sophie was a sidekick, cute and small at first, requiring little more than an occasional tickle or visit to the corner ice-cream shop.

So she couldn't blame Jacky for being honest the day her mother died. Jacky got it right. Sophie was not her daughter, and Jacky was certainly not her mother. Jacky didn't plan on being a mother any more than Sophie planned on being an orphan.

Instead of pretending to enjoy gluing colored tissue paper to a cardboard float, Sophie just wanted to be alone in her room, escaping all of the stupid teenaged angst.

Chapter Two

Two years later…

They said adopt her. They said she's perfect and will be wonderful with the honeybees. Well, why should Brooke Hastings doubt her grandparents, Tom and Elise Cove? They never steered her down the wrong path before.

Her pepe found the dog on the side of the highway with no tags or microchip.

"The shelter will take her, but she didn't like their cage at all," Pepe said. "Maybe it's time you adopt a new dog. She's not Zippy, but she is cute."

Zippy. Her beautiful little beagle. She'd never forgive Penelope for stuffing her in the backseat of her crammed Fiat and moving her across the country with her. Brooke was more broken-hearted over losing Zippy to the state of California than about losing Penelope.

Now, a year later Brooke still teared up whenever she tripped over Zippy's bowl. She couldn't bring herself to put it away. Her grandparents urged her to adopt a new dog right away, but Brooke couldn't imagine loving another as much as she did Zippy.

Brooke stared into the stray's deep, anxious soulful eyes, unable to digest how someone could abandon her on the side of a busy highway. "Poor girl. You've had a bad romp through life so far, haven't you?"

The dog squirmed and whined. Dark tears stained her auburn fur.

Pepe bowed down to pet her. His white hair blew around in the brisk wind, adding a few extra years to him. Pepe was a handsome man who always carried a fun-loving, Santa Claus energy, complete with rosy cheeks and a white moustache and beard. He

21

cared deeply for animals, and would not let this poor little girl suffer alone. "I brought her in our house, and Ollie already tried to attack her."

Ollie, a seventeen-year-old smoky gray cat with celery-colored eyes, ruled her grandparent's house.

"I suppose she can stay with me until we can find her a forever home."

The dog shivered despite sporting a full body of red matted fur. She nuzzled her cold nose against Brooke's hand.

"I have the feeling she already found her forever home." Her nana hugged herself, already cradling that look of love every doting grandmother carried in the soft crinkles of her sparkle.

"Do you want to stay with me for a little while?" Brooke asked the dog.

She brightened and perked. She shook, and her matted fur rose from its pin curl nest, sending a whiff of stagnant pond water through the air.

"We're going to need an awful lot of shampoo to get you cleaned up." Brooke plucked one of the many leaf clippings buried in her random tufts. "That's okay because I've got plenty." Brooke scratched behind her ears and she woofed a sharp, high-pitched approval.

"This is going to be good for all of us," Pepe said, placing his hand on Nana's lower back. "Our bee yard will never be the same again."

"Our new mascot," Nana beamed. The flecks of gold in her wise eyes twinkled through the fresh moisture.

Brooke grabbed the leash and the dog stood up, wagging her crooked tail. "You need a name."

"Ruffles?" Nana asked.

Brooke shook her head. "Too obvious."

Pepe stared at her, cupping his chin with his free hand. "Red?"

Nana poked his side. "Talk about obvious, silly goof."

Suddenly, a bee buzzed past them, veering over to the sugar water near the patio's edge. It circled back around and buzzed around the dog's head before losing interest and seeking out its sugary treat.

"Bee," Brooke said. "How about if we call her Bee?"

"Bee." Nana applauded. "How wonderful."

Pepe cleared his throat. "How is that not obvious?"

The dog nudged Brooke's hands again. "It's fitting." A surge of maternal love pulsed through her. "Bee," Brooke sang out, trying out her new name.

Bee leaped and pranced in a circle.

"I like Red better," Pepe said, "but, I guess Bee will do."

"Bee, do you want a bath?" Brooke clapped her hands.

Bee's ears perked, and she yelped.

"A bath it is."

Suddenly, Bee took off toward the back door and Brooke chased after her.

What could possibly go wrong?

~ ~

Bee. Oh dear Bee.

With her exuberant charm and downright stubborn appeals, Bee turned Brooke's life upside down and inside out.

Bee, albeit the queen bee of cuteness, was a royal terror.

On her latest incident, she had chewed through the bathroom door to try and get to a friendly couple who had stopped by to purchase honey. "Just give her time," Nana said. "You were rough around the edges when you were a little one, too. She just needs you to have a little patience with her." Nana adjusted her sunhat and peeked up at the trees, pretending she didn't notice Bee attacking her lilac bushes out of her peripheral view.

As a beekeeper, Brooke should've had patience. She should've coexisted with life, undeterred by its sudden and complex challenges and open to the beauty of its wild flow. At least that's how her grandparents drifted through life.

She tried to keep calm in those first few weeks. *Even a speck of patience would be great*, she'd whisper up to the rafters in her living room. Her prayers went

23

unanswered. Bee continued to drag her through puddles, chase toads, and knock over trays of honeycomb.

"She doesn't know any better. Give her time," Nana kept saying.

Brooke gave her time alright, but not without clenching her fists and muttering an alarming amount of curse words.

"She needs exercise," Nana pointed out one day. She shoved the *Dog Bible* in front of Brooke's face. "Look. See, right here. It states so. She needs exercise. She's too intelligent and needs a release for all that pent-up energy." Her nana wiggled her hips and flexed her biceps. "A little exercise. That's it."

"Exercise? She runs around the apiary all day long, terrorizing the squirrels and bunnies."

"She needs a brisk walk, not a romp around the backyard."

She trusted her nana. After all, she managed to help raise her into a conscientious member of society. Brooke didn't smoke, do drugs or land in jail. In fact, if she ran into her nana on the street, she would buy a magazine subscription from her. She would purchase a timeshare from her without much question. Her nana was *that* trustworthy and believable.

"I'll try."

Nana tilted her sunhat and shimmied one more time before tending to her seedlings.

Armed with something productive and practical, Brooke latched onto the exercise idea, even purchasing a new collar and leash, a pouch for doggy cookies, and biodegradable poop bags.

On a beautiful early spring morning, they set out. The sun peeked up over the tall and mighty maple trees. Their branches leafed out in fresh spring greens. Birds filled the air with jovial chirps. Bee pounced along happy as anything, stopping every two seconds to piddle and kick dirt on her mess. "You're so cute, little Bee." Brooke bent over and cooed her. She inhaled a thankful breath, banking on that wise decision to let her out and enjoy the tickle of grass on her paws and the excitement of inhaling the pungent scents left behind by others before her.

She stood up on that good note, and then Bee stiffened.

In the distance, a jogger headed toward them. As he neared, Bee wagged her tail.

"Oh, you want to say hi?" Brooke steadied her grip on the leash. "Maybe he'll be nice and stop. We have to be patient as Nana would say," she whispered.

Bee leaped around in a circle, challenging Brooke's grip.

"Okay, easy does it."

The man approached and Bee growled.

He smirked, checked behind him, and headed across the street.

Bee's growl escalated into an all-out demonic assault. Brooke fought for control over her leash, but Bee pulled her along for the wild chase. The man turned over his shoulder and terror spread across his face.

"Bee, stop," Brooke yelled.

Brooke's panic forced Bee into attack mode. Where did the cute, docile dog who slept in bed with her and ate from the palm of her hand go? Bee lunged forward with all her fifty pounds of muscle, flinging slobber every which way.

She tossed Brooke around like a ragdoll, focused only on catching the man who had broken out into a sprint. He disappeared over a guard rail and into the woods.

Bee stopped, perked her ears and huffed. Snorting and hacking, she paced in front of Brooke. Then, a leaf blew by her and she chased that, chomping at the air and barking a ferocious warning.

Brooke chased Bee all the way home, hanging onto that leash for dear life. Her breathing didn't return to a healthy pace until she arrived back at her house and locked the doors.

Later that night, Nana sat on the adjacent recliner in her living room. She gazed at Bee. "What an adorable face."

"An adorable monster face," Brooke said, coddling her on the couch. Bee snored and tucked her head into Brooke's lap. "What am I supposed to do with her?"

"I'll check the *Dog Bible* for answers. Though, she's not a monster. She's just scared. Just a little more time and she'll be fine."

In the weeks following, Bee's behavior around strangers turned into a dramatic mess. Inviting visitors to the backyard apiary became an arduous task that required lots of peanut butter filled bones, baby gates, and if it were even possible, the patience of twenty beekeepers. God forbid a visitor rang her doorbell. The fangs emerged, front paws circled into a frenzy against the window, and drool splattered everywhere, creating mini lakes on Brooke's wooden planks where beautiful decorative plants once sat.

Life with Bee changed everyone's routine. Even the mailman had to readjust to accommodate the furry beast who lived in the carriage house at the end of the tree-lined driveway. He could no longer dawdle with Pepe in the garage and talk carpentry because Bee's high-pitched bark threatened anyone's eardrum within a one-mile range.

Her exercise, the very exercise that she required to shed the pent-up energy, went from an hour-long brisk walk to absolute zero.

Bee needed walks. The backyard grew smaller as her attitude grew larger.

So, Brooke experimented with a new plan. They began an early morning exercise routine. Early morning meaning before the sun had a chance to rise.

Bee behaved like a champ.

Amazing how many spider webs formed across the sidewalks at four in the morning. Brooke didn't mind because Bee loved the peace that dawn offered. Her tail wagged when she'd sniff a rose bush and her ears relaxed along with her easy stride.

Most notable, Bee walked right by Brooke's side without as much as a tug. They were two happy-go-lucky beings exploring the untouched neighborhood under the misty reflection of the different phases of the moon with the tree frogs as their most audible companion.

Brooke understood the risks of solo walks in the dark. She carried her pepper spray like a well-armed security guard, finger already on the trigger. Of course, not too much on the trigger. She'd done that once many years earlier and blinded herself. Besides, no one in her right mind would be up at that hour.

What a perfect solution.

At four in the morning, only the newspaper delivery guy challenged their serenity when he'd weave through the streets driving his beat-up Corolla, flinging newspapers on the front lawns of subscribers. Bee would hear the loud muffler from a block away and go on patrol, sniffing the air, whining, and then barking like crazy the second she'd see his car come into view.

Brooke yanked on her leash, shushed her, stood in front of her to block her view, and waited until the man drove off. She managed to calm her, further stoking her confidence that she had found a viable solution.

Well, viable for about a week.

One morning, all hell broke loose.

Brooke and Bee were walking down the dark street when Bee began to growl. Brooke dug her feet into the ground and leveraged against a tree. "What's wrong, Bee?" Brooke twisted around to get a better scan of the street. "What are you growling at?"

Bee got louder and sounded more ferocious.

Brooke tensed, bracing herself for the all-out war.

Suddenly, she heard *clack-clack-clack* and smelled a cigarette. She squinted in the darkness and jumped when she noticed a man walking up the dark sidewalk on the opposite side of the street. He wore flip-flops and nothing but a pair of shorts. He puffed away on a cigarette, mumbling nonsense. Bee launched herself on her hind legs and spun on the end of her leash, knocking Brooke down to the grass and dragging her across the sidewalk and into the street.

The man ignored them, shuffling up the street toward a block of townhomes before disappearing. Bee, the little scrapper, huffed and puffed, foaming at the mouth. Anyone in his right mind would have bolted. At least she didn't have to worry about being attacked by the man. Brooke only had to concern herself with incidentals like road burn and potential dismemberment. Bee would protect her to the end if need be.

Hours later, while checking on her bees in the apiary, she told Nana about the incident. "The guy looked like a zombie. He didn't even know we were there."

Her nana just shook her head. "I know someone who knows someone."

27

"Huh?"

"I'm just saying that I have solutions too."

"Are you hiring me a hitman?"

"Something much more efficient, dear. I've been doing my research, and it's time for a change of plans."

"You scare me when you start researching things too much."

She just laughed.

The last time Nana researched something, Brooke ended up with a pantry filled with glassware and a dumpster filled with all her plastic containers. "You're kind of scary when you start brainstorming."

"There's a woman who is known as the dog whisperer of the east coast. She trained with that man from television."

"*The* dog whisperer?"

"She's got a school very close by."

"Can you imagine me taking Bee into a school full of people and dogs?"

"She's the dog whisperer. I'm sure she's got better ideas than wandering around the dark streets at four in the morning."

Brooke lifted a hive cover to check for the honey levels. "The man didn't attack us. Bee would never allow anyone near me."

"What if he carried a gun? Then what?"

Brooke had no logical comeback.

The next morning, Brooke took one step outside in the dark and shivered. The hair on her arms stood at attention. The moon hung like a warning in the sky. The scene mirrored an amateur horror flick, the kind where werewolves hid in the bushes waiting on prey. The bushes rattled near the stairs of her carriage home. Out popped a raccoon. He just stared at her, one frightened soul to another. Bee didn't even notice. She busied herself with squatting over her petunias and peeing.

A breeze blew by and skimmed across her skin. She shivered again. A funny vibe coursed its way through her. What if that man with the stinky cigarette and noisy flip-flops still walked the dark streets; this time with a gun behind his back and a pair of handcuffs that he wouldn't hesitate to use? What if he hurt Bee with that gun, and dragged Brooke off into the woods that lined the neighborhood? No one would know. She'd die alone in the woods, and her grandparents would sit in their rocking chairs on their porch and wonder what ever happened to her, their only granddaughter.

She wouldn't put them through that.

She circled back around and into her house.

She'd rather risk second degree leash burns on her hands than be raped and murdered under an oak tree. "We will attempt a daylight walk."

Bee's ears perked.

"I'm counting on you."

A few hours later, she braved the sunrise with Bee, wearing gloves, despite the balmy morning air, and a pair of well-treaded boots in case she had to plant herself in the ground once again.

They set out on the empty street, two eager beings waiting on someone to surprise them. Three minutes into their jaunt, Bee's tail erected, ears perked, and panting began. They rounded the corner, and Brooke saw a woman and a Retriever in the grassy field a few hundred yards away. Her heart bucked and she yanked up on Bee's leash. Bee went berserk.

Brooke ended that three minute walk by pulling on Bee's leash with every last fiber of energy she could muster. She dragged her up the street back to their peaceful yard where wackos wearing flip-flops and woman walking happy dogs didn't threaten to choke her precious, over-protective furbaby.

As Bee calmed down on the wooden floor an hour later, Brooke called her nana. "I need this dog whisperer's number."

"Fantastic dear. I've got it right here."

Brooke reached for a pen. "Okay, what is it?"

"I just have the school name. It's called The Inner Circle School."

"Do you have a name for this dog whispering genius?"

"Yes, it's Jacky. Jacky Applebaum."

Chapter Three

"Hey cutie pie," Marie said to Sophie, balancing her cell on her shoulder. She tossed her dog, Zen, a puppy cookie.

"Auntie Marie, I'm glad you just called me," Sophie said. "Withdrawals began to set in."

"It's nice to be loved. Maybe you can give Jacky a lesson. She's been avoiding me, you know, dodging my phone calls and not answering my text messages. You know I don't text unless I have to."

"Hmm."

"What is she doing? She's tossing that kettlebell around in the basement, I bet, right?" Marie drew a quick breath of air. "I'm telling you, she's going to drop that thing on her foot one of these days and I'm going to stand before her with an *I told you so* grin on my face. I don't know why she doesn't go to the gym by the Giant supermarket like everyone else."

"Are you finished?" Sophie asked.

"I could go on."

"You're crazy, Auntie."

"That's not news to me, young lady."

Sophie laughed. "I hope when I get older, I turn out just like you."

"No. You don't want to. I'm lucky my ankles still hold me up when I climb out of bed in the morning, and I just discovered a white hair growing out of my nostril. Well, I didn't discover it. Auntie Hazel pointed it out."

"How is Auntie Hazel?"

31

"Oh, don't get me started on her. Did you know she used to belong to an acapella group back in her college days?"

"She may have let that slip once or twice."

"Well, suddenly she's got us going to the church on the corner of Wilbur Road on Saturday nights now to sing with a bunch of dimwits. I'm telling you, don't let friends control you like that. You stomp that foot down when you say no, so they hear you down to their crooked toes. Otherwise you're going to end up yodeling like an idiot in a crowd of tone-deaf, folk-singing fools."

"I'm tone deaf too, so I won't know the difference."

"Yeah. You are." The poor kid couldn't carry a tune if a village of small children counted on her to save their life with a song. "So what are you doing next weekend, cutie?"

"I'm going to the movies with Ashley and a few of our friends."

"I hoped you'd tell me you planned on staying home to wash your hair. But kids don't use that excuse anymore. What would you tell me if you wanted to blow me off?"

"That I was going to the movies with Ashley and some friends."

"Funny." Marie loved Sophie's sense of sarcastic wit, one of the only remarkable features Drew had possessed in Marie's humble opinion. If only she could share a laugh or two with Jacky still.

"Could I persuade you and Ashley to stay over at our place on Saturday night to babysit Zen for us instead? I promise I'll load you up with enough sugar and salty treats to make you want to sing acapella in a church hall."

"We'd love to."

"I take it Ashley doesn't get to weigh in on this decision?"

"She'll do anything I ask."

Ashley was the kind of friend every teenager wanted. She was loyal like a puppy, and never seemed bothered that she stood in Sophie's shadow. Sophie turned heads, even at fifteen years old. The girl could eat ten bags of Doritos and still wear a size two jeans.

"Okay then. That was easy."

"Where are you and Auntie Hazel going?"

"She wants to go hang out with the ghosts in Gettysburg. So I told her we'll make a trip out of it."

"*She* wants to?"

"Don't be a smartass."

"You walked into that one, Auntie."

"Can you just put Jacky on the phone? I've got to make sure she gets her butt into the school an hour earlier tomorrow."

"You overbooked her again, didn't you?"

"This client is pretty desperate."

Sophie sighed. "They all are."

They were, which helped Jacky. She needed to be needed. The clients acted as her saving grace. Well, the dogs anyway. They balanced her life with a sense of purpose. If it wasn't for them, Marie would probably be visiting her in the mental ward at Spring Grove, watching as nurses fed her meds round the clock and gave her crossword puzzles to solve. As long as Jacky kept focused on something other than her guilt, Marie would keep overbooking her and laugh her ass off when she complained about it.

"Hey, did you ever ask her about the Paris school trip?" Marie asked.

"Nah. I'm not going to go. It's not that important."

Sophie talked about that Paris school trip nonstop whenever they chatted. "It would do you some good to get away."

"It's three thousand dollars. Also, she'd need to bring me to the airport at like four in the morning. It's too much."

Marie would offer the money and the drive to the airport, but it went deeper than that. No amount of money would solve their relationships issues.

For the past two years, Jacky had put aside her own wants and focused on providing Sophie with the kind of life her mother always wanted for her; a life filled with friends and access to great education, resources and activities. Jacky gave up her bowling night, her membership to the gym and happy hour on Tuesdays with the gang from Inner Circle School to keep Sophie engaged in everything other than her mother not being alive. Sophie only saw it all as a cure for guilt.

"Jacky would love to see you go to Paris, cutie."

"I know she'd give me a handful of money and probably even get me to the airport by three in the morning. She would never say no."

"She would want this for you."

"She could use a new car. Hers barely starts in the morning. I'm not going to be selfish and put her out like that."

When Drew was alive, Sophie would throw a tantrum until she got everything she wanted. Marie suspected the poor kid didn't want to rock the boat and cause issues with Jacky. Despite Jacky's love, Sophie viewed herself as an obligation.

"Yeah, well, maybe you could earn the money then somehow. Maybe pet sit."

"Yeah. Maybe. I'll get Jacky. Hang on."

Momma J you mean? Marie would sing in a church hall for the rest of her days on Earth to hear Sophie call Jacky that again.

~ ~

Ten years ago, Jacky Applebaum and Marie opened up the Inner Circle Doggy Daycare and Training School. Jacky led the training, and Marie the doggy daycare side of the business.

They scored a huge space in a renovated industrial center, allowing them the ample room they needed to exercise and train the dogs, as well as provide top-of-the-line accommodations for any guest dogs staying on vacation with them. They secured the backend suite, which also included a large grassy area that they had fenced for doggy playtime.

Jacky escaped into the dog world. It became her temporary paradise, the kind where she could imagine running barefoot in an open field and embracing the warmth of the sunshine as it danced across her face. Those beautiful moments shared with those selfless beings protected her from the harshness of reality. The dogs challenged and entertained her, and helped her forge a path to healing.

The parents, on the other hand, drove her batty with their ignorance. They wanted perfect dogs without having to put in the work and time. She also despised when people didn't respect their appointments.

She ran a tight schedule, and when someone messed with it by showing up late, she paced.

Well, Jacky paced that day.

Brooke Hastings, desperate for solutions as Marie put it, was ten minutes late.

Jacky twisted her fingers behind her back as she opened her stride in front of the large window. Behind her, barks and excited shouts bounced off the walls as her trainers Zack and Wendy worked their magic tossing balls and redirecting energy. In front of her, the sun reflected off the chrome on a car's side window, temporarily blinding her. She snapped away and looked down at her watch. She blinked and focused on the time *again*. Ten minutes and twenty-two seconds late.

She looked to Hazel at the front desk. Her feather duster swirled around the computer screen kicking up flurries of dust. She squinted, and her wrinkles swallowed up her delicate blue eyes.

"I came in an hour earlier for this client," Jacky said, looking for more steam to keep her earlier argument with Marie boiling. Poor Hazel got stuck in the middle of them.

Jacky enjoyed spats with her best friend. As long as they debated, Jacky could trust in the authenticity of their friendship. Marie didn't sugarcoat anything for anyone. Marie had sprinkled that fake sugariness for only one week, that hell week two years ago, and Jacky choked on the aftertaste. Marie didn't do mushy well. It sat on her face like a mask, foreign and ill-fitted. She preferred Marie in her raw state, and ignited it whenever Marie softened on her too much.

Hazel glanced at the appointment book. "You have a small buffer in between clients. You should be okay."

Jacky released her fingers from their twisted rage and pushed forward to the appointment book. "If she's more than fifteen minutes late, I'm rescheduling her. This is all Marie's fault, insisting I squeeze her in."

"Yes, you're right. Marie must have called her after your fight to beg her to come in late." She rolled her eyes. "Doesn't that sound ridiculous?"

Jacky walked behind the counter, stuffing Hazel smack in the middle whether she wanted to be or not. Jacky surmised Hazel enjoyed playing the mediator. "Don't defend her."

Hazel dragged the feather duster along the edge of the display of dog tags. "She's not going to let it go." She feather-dusted Jacky's arm. "You're going to have to apologize to her first, I'm afraid."

"She yelled at me in front of that daycare client."

Marie might've had her back when it came to bitchy clients, nosy neighbors, and egotistical jerks who cut her off or rode her tail on the street, but she could whine like a two-year old if she didn't get her own way.

"You sold her favorite lamp, dear."

Jacky's right eyelid twitched. She pressed her forefinger to it. "It's a stupid lamp."

That stupid lamp with its goddess holding up a round lightbulb like the freaking Statue of Liberty tormented her the second Marie brought it in. Marie had picked it up on the side of the road in someone's trash pile. She carried it into the school like she found Baby Jesus in the manger. She spent an hour shining the charcoal-colored body with its voluptuous curves and nipples. Yes, the darn lamp even had nipples.

"You know Marie. She loves junk," Hazel said. "I don't condone her outburst. I don't. But, you know how she is."

"A half inch of dust covered it. The bulb hung on with nothing more than a string. She forgot she even had it."

"Until you sold it."

"Until I sold it." Jacky looked at her watch again, and tensed further when the minutes ticked by with no sign of her new client.

36

"Believe me, I'd love to sell some of the junk in our house," she whispered out of the corner of her twisted mouth. She dusted the computer screen again. "Maybe I could hire you?"

Jacky loved Hazel. She loved how she put up with their antics, playing along like a referee, weighing each side objectively. "I don't know how you do it."

"She's Marie." Hazel shrugged.

"Yeah." Jacky checked the appointment book. Only thirty minutes until her next client arrived. "I'm never going to have time to meet this new desperate client, go through discovery of her issues, and examine her dog."

Just then, Marie barged up to her. "Did you sell my fan, too? The little white one in the backroom?"

The little white fan. For the love of everything beautiful and practical in the world, that little white fan had no place in the Inner Circle School. What a useless piece of trash. A part of its leg was missing, so it wobbled every time she turned it on. It only worked on high speed, and if you turned the knob to any other setting, a loud grumble roared out of it. "We had a rule Marie." Jacky pointed at her. "You bring something new, we get rid of something old. You brought in the new figurine of a Yorkie, the flower pot, and that hideous painting of the sad girl."

"What else then?" Marie drove forward. "What else did you take it upon yourself to get rid of without asking first?"

Jacky hesitated. "You had two weeks. Someone had to make a move."

"What else?" Marie pressed on.

Marie would not like Jacky's answer. She turned to Hazel for help. Hazel shook her head. "I'm not getting in the middle of this one."

"What else did you toss out?" Marie grabbed Jacky's wrist.

"Your broken ukulele," Jacky whispered.

Marie flung her head back and groaned. "I wanted to repair it."

Jacky's eyelid went into overdrive, cranking out a twitch on a whole new level. "Marie not now." Jacky pushed past her, then stopped before Hazel. "If the newbie decides to show up, can you reschedule her?"

"Stop avoiding me," Marie barked.

Suddenly, the bell above the door chimed.

Jacky rushed away. "Reschedule her, please," she said to Hazel, as if Hazel earned a salary. They both relied on Hazel's good heart perhaps a bit too much.

She'd get her a gift card to Amazon soon. Very soon.

~ ~

Tucked away in the backroom, Jacky called Sophie. "Are you up for pizza tonight?"

"Tonight I'm going to Ashley's for dinner. I told you. Remember?"

Sophie did not tell her. "That's right." Jacky pressed her twitching eye. "Okay, kiddo. That's fine. Do you need a ride?"

"Nope."

Jacky waited for more, and when none came, she ended the awkwardness. "Okay, well, I'll see you no later than ten, right?"

"Right."

"Love you, kiddo."

"Yup." Sophie dragged out the letter p.

"Have fun."

"Okay." Sophie hung up.

Jacky envied Marie and Hazel. Sophie respected and adored them. Jacky overheard many of their phone conversations over the years to understand Sophie had no desire to giggle with her the way she did with Marie and Hazel. They got to see the fun, adoring, carefree side of Sophie, while Jacky suffered through the silent treatment, occasional bickers and overall gut-wrenching reality that no amount of time would ever grant her forgiveness. She couldn't blame Sophie. She didn't deserve Sophie's respect after what she'd done.

Jacky exhaled a cleansing breath. She would not give up hope. She loved that child, and would continue to search for a way to break through the protective barriers

Sophie set around herself. She rubbed her memory bead necklace, bringing it up to her lips. *Please help us Drew.*

Jacky continued to rub the memory bead when Marie pushed open the door. Her short, wiry steel hair poked up in many directions that day, as if wanting to run away to find a new home. "I've got something better than our fight to keep us entertained. Are you ready for this?"

Jacky relaxed into a laugh. One minute clawing, the next laughing. "We're nuts, aren't we?"

"I hated that stupid white fan anyway," Marie admitted, dragging her hand through the air. She smirked and her whole face contorted.

"I didn't toss out your ukulele, by the way."

Marie, with every bit of her six-foot tall stockiness, sealed her eyes shut in a moment of divinity. "Thank you." She flashed them open. "You played a good hand with that one."

Jacky eased into the familiar comfort of her best friend. "So, what's more entertaining than our bickering?"

"That new client of yours." She bobbed her head up and down, cajoling her into the beginnings of an inside joke.

"She's too late. Fifteen minutes, thirty-two seconds. It's not fair to the next client."

"You'll find *her case* quite intriguing," she said, smacking her lips together with pleasure.

By *her case*, she assumed Marie referred to a healthy set of boobs, butt, or other curvy body part. Although, Marie would never come out and say such things. Marie never talked about sexuality. She never admitted she and Hazel were a couple. Everyone just assumed. They owned a house together. Adopted Zen together. Ate turkey dinners and ham at their families' houses on holidays. Yet, they maintained separate bedrooms and bank accounts and never referred to each other as partners. Marie didn't offer insights, and Jacky didn't bother her by asking such details. She suspected her silence protected Hazel more than herself.

"Please reschedule her until next month." Jacky looked down at her phone and checked her email.

"This isn't a time to play hard to get."

Jacky stood up and got in her face. "I'm not afraid to trash the ukulele."

Marie backed up a step. "Ukulele aside, she can't wait."

"Just because a woman is beautiful doesn't mean she gets special treatment."

"How about if her dog is a beast?" Marie raised an eyebrow.

"A beast?"

"A total beast."

An excitement surged. Jacky loved tough cases. It fired up her engines. But a rule was a rule. She appointed the fifteen minute rule that day. "She showed up late."

Marie poked her shoulder. "I know how you love a good beast."

Jacky clenched her jaw. "Fine. Tell me more."

"You should see for yourself."

Jacky looked at Marie with caution.

Marie folded her hands over her chest. "I'm telling you. Her dog's a beast."

"A true one?"

"A true one."

Lately, the only training issues she dealt with were puppies peeing on carpets and dogs barking too much. "I could use a challenge." Jacky rose and walked out of the backroom.

Marie snorted and followed her out to the main room of the training facility.

Jacky spotted a brunette standing at the desk. Her cheeks dimpled as she watched Millie and Trooper, two rambunctious hounds, follow Greg, one of Jacky's trainers, in a game of *find the treat*. Her dark waves tucked and flipped as if flirting with each other, revealing a hint of auburn highlights. She wore a brown and orange striped dress that accentuated her dancer-toned body.

Jacky walked by Hazel and greeted the woman with a handshake. "Hi, I'm Jacky Applebaum. I understand you had a ten o'clock appointment?" Jacky glanced up at the large clock above the receptionist desk to mark her point.

The woman met Jacky's shake. Her blue eyes glimmered. "Yes, that's correct." She let her hand slip. "My name is Brooke, and I hope you can help me with my dog, Bee."

She sprinkled her flowery scent all over the receptionist area, numbing Jacky to any residual stress from her tardiness. Jacky looked around for *the beast*. She scanned the cars parked out front for a dog stuffed in the backseat of a car. "Where is Bee?"

"Home," Brooke said with no reservation. She looked around, smiling at the sight of lazy Mickey, the chubby Dalmatian, refusing to fetch a ball. She pulled in her lower lip when Fonzi and Tattoo, two Pomeranians, jumped through hoops that Wendy raised to her knees. "Trust me. You don't want me to bring her in here."

Marie fiddled with the case of dog tags, sporting a smug smile.

"I'm going to need to see her in order to evaluate her. Let's set up a new appointment and have you bring her in."

"I can't bring her in here."

Jacky imagined a gentle giant full of matted fur, slobbering every which way as she pounced from one shocked dog to another in search of play. "Why not?"

"There's no way. Absolutely no way."

The woman had her complete attention. "We can bring her into a private room. We have a back door."

"You don't understand." Fear laced the tiniest specs of gold in her irises. "She's a beast."

"A beast," Marie repeated in case Jacky didn't hear it the first time around.

"She is. Seriously." Panic surfaced. "It'll be irresponsible for me to walk through those front doors with her."

Marie cleared her throat. "House call," she said under her breath.

Jacky's intrigue intensified. "What kind of dog is she?"

The woman shrugged. "A feisty one, I guess?" She twirled her finger around a lock of her hair.

"Feisty," Marie said. "That's your specialty."

41

"I'm sorry," Brooke said. "I have no idea what kind she is. My grandfather found her and neither one of us could stomach the idea of putting her in a shelter to wait for adoption. So I adopted her myself. I have no idea what kind of baggage she carries. A lot, I can tell you. Poor thing wants to be happy. She just gets protective. I'm the one who's supposed to be protecting her, right? I'm just out of my realm. I need help."

"Like music to the ears," Marie muttered just loud enough for Jacky to hear her.

She did enjoy being needed. Training gave her purpose. When she helped a dog, her balance shifted, as if the help earned her points toward redemption.

Jacky picked up one of her business cards and a pen, then thumbed through her appointment book. "I can do a house call tomorrow and evaluate."

A shade of pink rose on Brooke's smooth skin. "House call? Yes. A house call is perfect."

"I've got an hour tomorrow morning at ten."

"Ten o'clock. Perfect."

"Okay. Ten o'clock on the dot, right?"

"Of course," Brooke nodded. "Ten o'clock on the dot."

Jacky wrote the appointment on a card, circling the time slot not once, but four times. "Also, can you jot down your address?" She handed her a blank piece of notepad and a pen.

She jotted it down, and placed a smiley face at the bottom. She pushed it in front of Jacky. "My house is the carriage home. You'll have to drive past the main house to get to it. I apologize because the driveway is very narrow and filled with potholes from this last winter. Just park right out front. Please don't ring the doorbell, though. I'll come out to greet you."

"Sounds like a plan. Just please don't be la–"

"She won't ring the doorbell," Marie interrupted. "She'll be waiting outside at ten o'clock sharp. So, best not be late. She gets a little antsy at that."

"Oh, I wouldn't dare do that to her again." She tapped the counter and winked at Jacky. "See you then."

In a blink, she bounced away.

The three of them watched her drift out the door and over to her silver sedan.

"Well she's a cute little thing, isn't she?" Marie elbowed Jacky. "Look at the way she's shaking her cheeks, like she's got a pendulum under that dress. I think she's moving like that to get your attention."

Jacky elbowed her back. "Every women who shakes her ass isn't a lesbian."

"She winked at you," Marie said.

"She did wink," Hazel said, nodding her head.

"You're intrigued. Admit it," Marie said.

"I am intrigued."

A self-satisfied grin took over Marie's face. "I knew it."

"Intrigued over her beasty dog, you fool. Her beasty dog."

"Uh, huh." Marie chewed on a piece of gum and blew a bubble. It smacked on her face. She peeled it off and revealed the remnants of her self-assured grin.

"I don't have time for this. I've got crazy-ass weirdo over here whose Chihuahua is afraid of the dark and Mr. Chigger over here who keeps growling at squirrels." Jacky walked away from the desk, shaking her head.

"Fine, walk away and pretend you're not blushing."

"My face is red because you're irritating me."

"Is that why you're shaking your ass now, too? You are. You and Brooke have matching pendulums." She nodded. "God strike me down if I'm lying."

Marie never lied.

~ ~

Later that afternoon, after the last training client left, Marie and Jacky picked up the yard.

Just as Marie reached down to get a ball, Jacky asked, "Can I say something to you without you getting upset?"

Marie stood tall. "Shoot." She tossed the ball to the front of the yard.

"I know you were joking around today about the shaking ass bit, but I'm not ready to joke about things like that."

"I'm sorry. I didn't meant to upset you." She frowned. "Can I ask you something without *you* getting upset?"

Since the accident, they danced around personal questions like a couple of clumsy drunks; teetering over a question, afraid to ask it, not sure if it would dig a little too deep and hurt.

Jacky nodded, not quite ready to articulate her approval of what would surely be a torture question.

"When will you be ready? I don't mean that to sound disrespectful to Drew. I just wonder how you are doing with everything. We never talk about it. So, I figure now might be a good time."

"I'm not ready to consider anyone else attractive. It's just not something that's on the top of my priority list right now. I've got Sophie to be concerned with and the business, and the house. I can't go there. Even joking about it."

"It's been two years."

"How many has it been for you?"

"This isn't about me." Marie pointed at her, like her superior.

"Why not? If we're going to have an honest conversation about relationships, maybe you could weigh in on it a little too. I mean you never talk to me about your life."

"You're heading over to an edge that's dangerous." Marie waved her off and collected a pile of poo. "I promised Hazel privacy, and I won't break it. Please don't ask me to."

The warning stopped Jacky. "Okay. Fair enough."

"Besides, I'm okay. I'm happy. Any silence I keep is out of respect for someone else, not out of a lonely suffering." Marie tore off her gloves. "But, you. I worry about you. That's why I'm asking. If you'd rather not discuss, we can go back to picking up poo on opposite ends of the yard."

Jacky glanced down at the grass. Many arguments piled up in her mind, ones that haunted her each night. How could she possibly explain herself when she didn't understand either? "It's not easy."

"Talk to me."

Jacky settled in for an honest confession. "I've been empty since Drew died, and I'm afraid to fill it with anything."

"Because you want to keep hiding in the guilt."

She sought out refuge in the horizon folding beyond the trees. "I'm afraid if I don't, then I'll lose sight of her loss."

"You worry about losing sight of Drew?"

"I promise her every day that I won't let her go."

"Moving on doesn't mean letting go."

"It does to me." She bent over at her knees, weighted by the drain. "You want me to move on. I see it in your face and can hear it in the way you breathe sometimes. Like, you're just dying to shake me out of a funk. Two years seems like a long time, but it's not. It's two years she hasn't lived." She couldn't package away the love of her life in search for joy after just two years. No. That would take her a lifetime.

"You've honored her legacy. No one will think you're a terrible person if you lived your life now."

"I'm not concerned about what others think. This is what I think."

Marie slipped her gloves back on. "Fair enough." She sighed and lifted a nearby shovel. "Let's get back to work."

Jacky gladly obliged.

~ ~

Later that evening when Sophie arrived home with just two minutes to spare before her curfew, Rosy jumped off the couch and curled up around her legs. She bent down and kissed the top of her soft fur. "Hi baby girl. Did you miss me?"

Rosy whined and dropped to the ground, begging for a belly rub. Sophie dropped her pocketbook and kneeled on the wooden planked floor next to her. She looked up to find Jacky sitting on the sofa smiling at her. Her blonde hair, freshened up with new highlights, hung in loose waves at her shoulders. She looked relaxed and at peace.

"How was dinner at Ashley's?"

"Fine," Sophie said, looking at Rosy again.

"Did Ms. Kate fix you pizza?"

Sophie shrugged. "We ate out."

Jacky folded one of her knees under her. "Any place good?"

Sophie defaulted to Rosy for distraction. She ached to be able to plop down on the couch next to Jacky and fill her in on every last detail like old times. But, those times died. Instead of telling her about the amazing art sculptures she just saw in Inner Harbor, she settled on part of the truth. "Just a burger place that Ashley's family likes."

Jacky sat up straighter. "I have to meet up with a new client tomorrow morning. Do you want to go shopping for spring clothes after that? I figure we can hit the new Buckle store at the mall, then grab some burgers?"

Sophie missed their shopping sprees and the ice-cream sundaes they shared after each one. *She's your daughter. Not mine!* "I have to work on my class project."

"Take a small two hour break."

"Can't."

Disappointment – a clever disguise for guilt – spilled on Jacky's face. Sophie escaped it by pressing her face into Rosy's fur.

"Okay, kiddo. So what's your school project on?"

Sophie didn't have a clue, and Ashley was no help. They were supposed to come up with ideas over the art sculptures, but Ashley got sidetracked by Gabe, their friend Missy's brother. "Still deciding."

Jacky gathered her magazines and stood up. "Okay, well, let me know if you want any help."

"Okay." Sophie peeked up from Rosy long enough to watch Jacky walk down the hallway looking worn and defeated. Her pajama bottoms dragged on the ground. She had gotten thin over the last few years, too thin. Sometimes she looked pale too, despite the freckles on her face. Sophie took a deep breath, releasing the tension.

She pitied Jacky.

That kind of pity could hurt Sophie, though. She needed to stay strong and independent.

She dragged herself to her feet and walked up the stairs. When she arrived at her bedroom, she closed the door to seal into a privacy she'd grown to accept as necessary. She opened up her drawer to the table she and Jacky had painted together one summer a long time ago, way before the shit hit the fan. Inside the cover of a Taylor Swift CD jacket, sat the letter. As she did anytime she wanted to get back to reality, she read it and let it sink in.

That letter reminded her why she needed to stay mad at Jacky.

Chapter Four

On a bright Sunday morning, Jacky pulled up to the tall, two-story Cape Cod house with a full wrap-around porch. A hand-painted sign stood prominently in the front lawn, *Local Honey for Sale*. A two car garage hugged the side of the house, its door open and revealing a four-wheeler, a driving mower, and an assembly of rakes, pitch forks, and shovels hanging on its walls.

A homeowner's dream.

She veered past the home and down the pebbled driveway toward the carriage house. Jacky braced for the bumpy ride, gripping her steering wheel and gritting her teeth over every divot.

Once she cleared a bunch of tall trees, she got a better view of the fancifully cut wooden trim and scrolled brackets adorning the carriage house. Jacky marveled at the steeply pitched roof and decoratively carved gable trim. A wooden, picket fence surrounded the grounds.

As she approached, she noticed yellow and orange wooden boxes stacked up in rows way beyond the picturesque house. She lowered her window, and heard the faint song of birds echoing behind the frantic barks of what could only be *the beast*.

Jacky parked her car in front of the house. The barking grew more hysterical. She glanced to the front bay window and saw the fluffy, red-haired dog freaking out in classic over-protection behavior.

Poor girl.

She spotted the pronged collar and cringed. Jacky climbed out of her car irritated, bracing for what could end up turning into a wave of resistance from a defensive doggy mom.

49

The woman, Brooke, emerged from the front door sporting a look of relief, looking very much like she just climbed out of a train wreck and caught sight of a first responder sent in to save the day.

Okay, there may be hope for Bee after all.

~ ~

Brooke stepped out onto her front stoop and drew a deep breath, attempting to water down some of her nervous energy. Bee growled ferociously in the front window, wild-eyed and crazed, steaming up the glass with her stressed breath. Brooke's heart raced, but she pressed toward the trainer regardless. Bee's growl deepened as Brooke passed by the window.

Jacky shook her head and bit her lower lip, obviously frustrated with the scene.

Brooke strolled up to Jacky, attempting to be cool and collected. "Good morning."

Jacky walked toward the side of her house, turning over her shoulder. "Let's meet over here, before she hurts herself."

Brooke walked past her mulberry bushes and toward Jacky, kicking herself for setting up the appointment. Four o'clock walks seemed like a much better idea than putting any of them through the ordeal.

She met up with her under the Dogwood trees by the fence. Bee's bark intensified. "I'm so embarrassed. I'm the worst doggy mom in the world."

Instantly, Jacky's face softened. An empathetic whisper circled the blue of her eyes as she eased her posture, tucking her hands into the front pockets of her cargo pants. "I've seen worse."

"Well, I guess that's pretty good then. Well, I don't mean it's good that there are others who are horrible at being a doggy parent. That's not what I meant." She stopped and took a breath. "Sorry, I'm rambling."

"I'm not judging you."

Brooke saddled onto Jacky's kindness. The woman's light and wild hair flew every which way in the morning breeze.

"I admire you for adopting her," she continued. "Let's focus on that smart action."

Awesome. Yes. Okay. Let's focus on that. "I adopted her and saved her from, well, gosh, I hope not death. To even consider that some shelter might've put her down for being left alone, well, I won't even go there." Brooke exhaled. "My major concern is that I let this go on a little too long. I hope I didn't destroy her chance at a normal life. Have I?" She braced for the honest feedback.

Bee's enduring barks splintered through the cool, crisp morning air.

"You didn't ruin her. In my opinion, no dog can be ruined, only healed." Jacky turned toward the house. "She's barking like that because she loves her mom and will do anything to protect her." Her lower lip trembled in the cool breeze. "Obviously, it's good to know she's got your back."

"Hmm. Maybe if I lived in the middle of a crime-infested city."

Jacky's lips curved up. "She just needs some direction."

"Direction. Okay." Brooke seized that recommendation. "We're all yours, if you can help."

"Don't worry." Jacky looked back to the front window where Bee stood on patrol, panting and pacing. "With some work, she'll be just fine."

"If you can help revive peace to my neighborhood, and of course to Bee, I'll toss in a lifetime supply of honey for you."

Jacky kicked around the rocks at her feet, and glanced up at her. "My daughter and I love honey, maybe just about as much as we love dogs."

"How many dogs do you have? Like ten?"

Jacky laughed. "Just one. Her name's Rosy and she rules the house."

"I bet she's perfect."

Jacky laughed again, tilting her head back and exposing her long, sleek neck. "Rosy is nearly as perfect as they come, except when someone opens a jar of peanut butter and doesn't offer her any."

"Entitled, huh?" Brooke cocked her head, sounding a wee bit too flirty.

"Yeah." Jacky stretched her ear toward the house. "Hey, someone gave up."

Brooke listened. *Amazing.* "She normally fights it for an hour when someone is in her domain. It's gotten to a point where we can't conduct tours of the apiary without one of us staying in the house with her behind a closed window shade."

"Is she good with your children?"

"My children?"

"Sorry, I just assumed when you said one of us."

"I'm terrible training my dog, imagine a child?" Brooke laughed. "I was talking about my grandparents. They live in that giant spectacle of a house in front."

"It's beautiful."

"It's too big. I mean look at the height of it. My grandfather still climbs double ladders to clean the gutters. My grandmother stands at the bottom of the ladder and cringes every time." Brooke tapped her hand to her chest. "But, it keeps him young." Brooke stopped talking. She needed to stop rambling. Jacky's polite interest would last only so long.

Jacky glanced at the house. "It's like something out of a Norman Rockwell painting."

"My grandfather was born and raised in it."

Jacky now shifted her gaze to the hives. "What are those boxes?"

"Those are hives for honeybees. I manage over one hundred and fifty of them."

"Ah. It's a honeybee haven." Jacky dipped her head. "Hence the name Bee."

"Yes, indeed."

"How is she with the bees?"

"Remarkably undeterred. She knows they're part of the family. Put a squirrel or fox back there though and she'll chase it away much like she wanted to chase you away a second ago." Brooke laughed.

Jacky grew serious and stood taller. "We need to address that issue."

The heavy reality of her failure with Bee pressed against her. "Yeah. I wish I could manage her as easily as the bees."

"I can help you."

Brooke crossed her arms over her chest. "You mean you can help *her*?"

"No," Jacky said with a chuckle. "I meant you." She lingered on a wry grin.

Brooke blushed. "Are you sure you're up for this challenge? You can walk away now. We'll pretend we never had this conversation."

"I've seen it all."

"Don't be so sure. She's something else. I've seen her rip balls apart with one shake of the head. She growls at bunny rabbits. Bunny rabbits! And don't get me started with the mailman. I used to walk her before the birds woke up. I can't walk her in the light of day. She'd either rip my arm out of its socket or we'd find a bunch of houses going up for sale. I don't know what you're going to do." She caught her breath. "I'm very curious."

"Oh, don't worry." A smirk streaked across her face. "We'll get her walking in the light of day again."

"How can you be so sure?"

"Let's just do it." Jacky walked toward the back of the house.

"Right now?" Brooke followed, tripping over her panic.

"We need to calm your energy first. She'll pick up on it, and get nervous too."

Brooke knew that as a beekeeper she needed to stay calm. The bees could smell nervous energy, and would sting to protect against it. "I'm afraid of a walk in the park with my dog, yet I can stand amongst tens of thousands of bees without concern. How silly, right? Logic says I should be able to tap into that same energy. But, fighting with a fifty pound ball of fur is entirely different."

"Well, you understand your bees," Jacky pointed out. "You know why they act as they do. I'm assuming, they're predictable?"

"For the most part."

"With Bee, you're in new territory, unsure of her random patterns. She senses this, and reacts accordingly."

"She freaks out. I'm afraid she'll bite someone."

"I understand." Jacky spun around once they got to the back patio. "But you don't want to lock her away, because doing that will only reinforce her overprotective and aggressive instincts."

"How do we start?"

"Just imagine you are with your bees. Place yourself in that mindset. You're a leader when you're around them, right?"

"More like a peaceful observer."

"You intimately understand when your energy is calm and assertive, right?"

"Of course."

"When you're in that zone, fear doesn't come into play because you're in control and understand how they work. The same will be true with Bee once you understand why she's acting out, and how you can help her overcome that."

"You make it sound so easy. Like step one, step two, and step three. Just do this, and that will happen. Put corner A with corner B and you'll get a new corner C."

Jacky laughed. "Why don't you put a leash on her and bring her out to meet me?"

"Now?"

"Take a deep breath and go get her."

Brooke marched to the back of the house, giddy with hope this could actually work.

Once inside, Bee circled around her, sniffing. Brooke reached up for the leash. "Want to go for a walk?"

Bee leaped and whined, then sat waiting for Brooke to fasten the leash.

Brooke bent down and met her gaze. "She seems nice, so be a good girl, and keep those teeth to yourself. Do you understand?"

Bee fixated on her, squirming.

Brooke stood, took a deep breath, and headed for the door. As soon as she opened it, Bee fled through it. Brooke dropped the leash to save herself from falling against the concrete patio. "Bee, no jumping," she yelled out, mortified.

Jacky turned her back to Bee. Of course, her little devil, with all those cute curls, didn't understand and jumped up on Jacky's back. Jacky, with her stoic posture, kept looking straight ahead toward the apiary, ignoring Bee's tantrum.

Finally, Bee surrendered. She ran over to the honeybees' sugar water and helped herself, already bored with this newcomer.

"I'll be damned." Brooke watched with awe as her charming Bee acted like a normal, run-of-the-mill dog.

"How about that walk?"

"Yes, how about it?" Brooke tapped her legs and called Bee over to her. Bee ran past Jacky and straight to her.

"Is that the only collar you have for her?" Jacky gawked at the pronged collar.

"It's the only one that allows me to control her."

Jacky's jaw tensed. "Aversion collars like this cause pain and can do a lot of damage both physically and psychologically."

"The person at Dog's World insisted it was a humane device. He said it mimics the mother's gentle teeth."

"That's a myth. It's a negative reinforcement tool. So, when Bee is out for a walk and sees another dog or person, then experiences tension from the prongs when she lunges, a negative association is formed. Whenever she sees a dog or other person after this, she remembers this tension and ties it to the dog or person, further increasing the chances of escalating her aggressive behavior."

Brooke sank back on her heels. "I had no idea."

"Don't feel badly. I can teach you how to reinforce good behavior without using tension as a motivator."

Tears stung Brooke's eyes. How could she not have realized this herself?

Jacky softened. "I've got a harness that will adjust to her size." She slid a backpack off her shoulders and a moment later, unveiled it. "This will allow for control and safety." She bent down and petted Bee's chest, then removed the pronged collar and slipped on the harness.

Bee stared at Jacky with love.

"You're amazing with her. She never lets anyone but me or my grandparents next to her like this."

"I've been accused of being part dog," she said as serious as one would state her date of birth.

"Well I certainly wouldn't argue."

Jacky stood up and laughed, grabbing hold of the leash. "Let's take a nice easy stroll down the street. Our goal is to reinforce good behavior."

Brooke gulped. "You don't understand. She really does turn into a beast around other dogs and people, and they're out right now."

"We won't act irresponsibly. I promise." She held up two fingers for a scout's honor. "We're going to praise her like crazy on this short walk." She lowered her fingers. "Come on, let me teach you."

Brooke nodded, then followed them as they proceeded around the side of the house. A squirrel ran past the tree line, and Bee's ears shot up.

"Bee," Jacky called out in a commanding tone.

Bee looked at Jacky.

"Good girl." Jacky's voice animated high, then she offered Bee a small treat.

"It's about redirecting her attention on us instead of the point of fixation. The moment she looks at me, I'm going to reward her. Soon, she'll relate looking at me or you with something positive."

They continued down the driveway, past the garage, and eventually out into the front yard where reality waited to be explored.

"My daughter would love this yard," Jacky said, drawing a noticeable breath. "She used to do a lot of gardening before... well, before all her activities took over."

Brooke drew long breaths, too, trying to keep herself calm. "Bring her by for a tour," she managed in between one of her inhalations.

"I might suggest that to her." Jacky breathed in more of the fresh morning air.

A calmness emanated from her.

"How old is your daughter?" Brooke asked, hoping the small talk could redirect her own nervous energy.

"Fifteen going on thirty." Jacky led them toward the street.

"Weren't we all at that age?" Brooke's heart began to beat faster as she released a nervous chuckle. "I can't believe we're doing this."

Jacky checked both sides of the street. A couple with a yellow lab mix walked away from them on the other side. "Bee," Jacky called out in her commanding tone.

Bee perked her ears and tilted toward Jacky.

"Good girl!" Jacky tossed a treat in her mouth, and Bee swallowed it whole.

Bee looked at the couple with the dog again.

"Bee!"

Bee looked at Jacky again, earning herself more praise.

They volleyed these steps back and forth a few more rounds until Bee looked ahead with an air of ambivalence.

God, I hope you stick around, Ms. Applebaum, you wonderful dog charmer you.

"We're ready to take this up a notch." Jacky opened up her stride, leading them forward with confidence. "Bee is a quick learner, not to mention a good girl. She wants to please, which is an excellent sign that everything is going to be okay with her."

Brooke's heart relaxed. "How can I ever thank you?"

"You already did by walking out of your front door at ten a.m. sharp as promised."

Brooke caught Jacky's glow. *How charming.* "That's all I had to do?"

"I don't demand much. It's the simple things that go a long way."

Punctual clients were obviously her simple pleasure and treat of choice, that much Brooke guessed from her tense face the day before. "I'm sorry I showed up late for my appointment at the school."

Jacky held up a biscuit, jokingly.

"Funny," Brooke nudged her arm, and Jacky broke out into a chuckle. *Oh, she's adorable.*

Brooke liked this woman's energy. She also admired her intelligence and capability. Thanks to her, for the first time ever, she and Bee were able to ease into a comfortable stride in the light of day.

~ ~

Sophie heard the front door close while in the kitchen spreading peanut butter on her bread. Jacky walked into the kitchen. "Oh, hey, kiddo."

"Hey."

Jacky plopped down on the stool and placed a bottle of raw, unprocessed honey down on the counter.

Sophie reached for it. "This is the good stuff."

"It should be. It came straight from the honeycomb."

Sophie turned the bottle over to check for herself. No back label, which probably meant authentic. "Where did you get this?"

"My newest client runs a bee apiary down on Rocky Gorge Ave. She manages over a hundred hives, and she offered us a tour whenever we want."

Jacky crawled her gaze around her face, waiting on a reply.

Wouldn't you be happier if you just walked away from having to raise someone else's daughter?

"That's a lot of honeybees."

"How cool would that be to experience being around so many?"

"Hmm." Sophie focused back on her peanut butter and bread. With each swipe of the knife, she imagined herself in a bee suit with hundreds of bees sitting on her shoulders and arms, a dream of hers since she read *The Secret Life of Bees*. She read about how the wings of honeybees created a breeze and tickled the face.

Jacky watched her spread peanut butter across the bread. She couldn't take it. "Want one?"

"Sure," Jacky whispered. "I'd love one."

Sophie took out two more pieces of bread from the loaf and spread a glob of peanut butter across them. She sliced it in half and put it on a plate for Jacky.

"Here you go." Sophie slid it in front of her, then walked away, leaving her alone in their big kitchen. "I've got to get back to my project."

"Of course, kiddo," Jacky's voice echoed behind her.

Sophie bit into her sandwich as she walked down the dim hallway toward the staircase. Once inside her bedroom, she plucked up one of her gardening books from her shelf and began to thumb through it. She read through a paragraph about how the rinds of a watermelon break down and create sustainable fuel for flowering plants. The author talked about his experience adding coffee grounds into the composter, and how they smelled earthy when mixed with the other raw elements.

She tossed the book down, bored. She craved hands-on research, the kind where she kneeled on the ground and got her hands dirty with something real, touchable, breathable.

She could start a garden again that year. Garden soil, vegetable waste, huge tomato plants didn't compare to what she suddenly wanted to experience. Bees. They beat composting. Jacky seemed interested enough too. So, she wouldn't be bugging her by asking her to take her. Maybe they'd get more honey out of the deal, too. The subject needed attention. Honeybees were dying, after all.

She climbed to her feet, stuck her head out the door and yelled, "Can we really take a tour?"

The chair screeched across the ceramic tiles in the kitchen. "You bet," Jacky rang out.

~ ~

Jacky first met Sophie when Drew had invited her to play tennis, something Jacky had never played before in her life. Of course, wanting to impress Drew, she purchased a very expensive tennis racket, and took a few private lessons in the days leading up to their date at the Catonsville Tennis Club courts. She arrived to find a cute little springy child wearing a pink sundress with little polka dots and her hair in two ponytails. Her center part resembled the perfect lines down the tennis court. The girl giggled and tossed balls at her very beautiful mother who wore white shorts and a black tank top. She styled her hair in a low ponytail and sported a pink visor. She beamed as she caught one of the balls the little girl tossed her.

"I couldn't find a babysitter, so I decided she could be our ball girl." Drew jogged past her and tossed the ball into a bucket near the gated entrance to the court.

"Yeah, I'm going to be a ball girl." She bent down and leaped up in the air. "My name is Sophie. Who are you?"

In those early moments, Sophie never stopped talking. Her breaths connected to each word, and she had an endless supply of air to grab hold of. She absolutely exhausted Jacky by the end of their thirty-minute tennis match, and owed some of that to Drew's lack of tennis skills. Jacky assumed Drew knew the game, but it turned out she had never picked up a racquet before that morning. Turned out Drew loved new experiences, and decided she wanted to experience the rush of chasing balls around the court.

From that first day, Jacky fell in love with Sophie's inquisitive side. In those first few years, Sophie taught Jacky about the world through the sheer nature of her incessant need to question everything and anything.

Jacky missed that side of Sophie, and would do just about anything to get her back.

After finishing the peanut butter sandwich that Sophie whipped up for her, she poured herself a glass of lemon water and drew a bubble bath. She stepped inside the soothing bubbles. She lay back against the bath pillow, and swirls of lavender steam curled up around her, offering her the rest she needed.

An apiary tour could be just what they needed. Sophie would like Brooke. The woman had an intriguing quality to her that would put Sophie at ease, instantly. She was refreshing and, admittedly, very cute. *In a friendly way, of course.*

Chapter Five

Several years back, Brooke's nana spiked a fever of one hundred and five degrees Fahrenheit. She lay in a hospital bed suffering through a severe kidney infection. Brooke and her grandfather spent every minute they could with her, both fending off the demons of fear as their minds ventured to that place where death barged into their hearts and toyed with them. On the third day of receiving intravenous meds, her nana finally became lucid and called Brooke to her side. "How are my bees?"

"They're fine," Brooke said, smoothing her nana's white hair back from her forehead.

"I miss them terribly."

"Of course you do."

"Bring them to me."

Brooke peeked up at her pepe and shrugged.

He looked away, misty.

"Nana you know I can't bring your bees here."

"Yes you can, dear." She closed her tired eyes. "Bring them to my imagination," she whispered. "Please, I miss them."

Brooke bowed her head not sure what to do.

Her pepe moved up to their side. He cradled Brooke with one arm and ran his worn fingers through his wife's snow-colored hair with the other. "It's early morning and the first sunbeam has awoken you," her Pepe whispered. He moved in close to her face. "You're the first to witness the start of the day."

She glowed. "Ah, yes."

Her pepe nodded to Brooke, urging her to join in. Brooke set her hand on her nana's warm forehead, brushing her hair back. She closed her eyes and traveled back to her childhood, back to those bedtime stories Nana would whisper in her ear about bees and butterflies.

Your antennae are kissing the first wisp of morning air, and a wave of blissful tranquility passes through you, she began, crafting a new story of her own for her Nana.

You arrive at the foot of the hive, taking your first brave step. You're calm and alert.

You step down onto a second landing, sliding deeper into a state of complete joy.

Now you take another bold step down onto the wooden frame of the hive box. Your heart warms with gratitude for the new day.

Then you take a final step onto the soft blades of grass. You're alive and renewed.

You've graduated to a field bee. There is so much to celebrate and explore.

You look around and take in the full beauty of the early morning sunshine. It sparkles on the dew dripping from each blade of grass. You flutter and perch on the vibrant spring green leaf of a strong and noble sunflower. The earth tastes of green grass and succulent honeysuckle. You raise your body and breathe in the freshness. It whets your appetite and spikes an earnest desire to bring back a full load of life-sustaining nutrients for the beloved Queen and the rest of your beautiful hive family.

Guided by the dance of those who foraged before, you lift up and trust in the power of flight. You fly up and away on a journey. You glide over blades of grass that dance in the breeze. You look over your right wing and spot others bursting with gratitude for another new day. With wings fluttering, their yellow markings mirror the beauty of the sun. You travel across the pond near a big oak tree, soaking up the bright blue sky's reflection in each ripple. A great black bird with large wings and a regal head passes by you, singing a song, headed in the same direction as you, toward a spot where appetites come bursting to life. You know the sweet spot. Your sisters have waggle-danced its location for you. You know its exact position from the hive and the sun, and have no doubts. You are on your way to a place where life dances on the petals of pretty flowers and where the nectar runs wild.

Colors of violet, pink and yellow come into view beyond the pond's edge. You fly fast, all the way to the luscious petals of a purple Aster. Your heart is happy as you take in the light and airy flower with its pop of color and magnificent yellow pollen. Before your very eyes, you see the runway pattern, guiding you to land right in the exact spot where tender nutrients wait to be harvested. Its mouth-watering aroma plays a heartfelt tune on your senses, bathing you in a delightful sense of harmony. Your journey across the field and over the pond has been all worth it, as the figure eight dance of your sisters had promised.

You look forward to returning. You'll let the others know all about your incredible venture. They too will want to join in your travels the next day, accompanying you to this field of ecstasy where earth presents its most remarkable fruits. You will return and dance for the sake of sharing your new knowledge, hiding not one smidgeon of your story because that's how we bees work. You will share it and let others indulge on a petal next to you. One for all, all for one.

You fly back with a full belly and light heart, comforted that you are exactly where you are supposed to be. You fly past the big, black bird and he once again sings his song. You pass over the pond with its reflective ripples and joy tickles your heart. You spot the strong sunflower swaying in the air and connect to its strength. It lends you her nectar and it lands softly on your tongue where it is swept inside of you. Finally, you step upon the ledge of your beloved hive. You are safe and filled with nutritious sustenance. You settle into the evening for a well-deserved rest that will revive your spirit and send healing energy throughout the hive. You have lived an ultimate day, blessed by insights and beauty few are privy to experience. You are sleeping soundly now, one restful heartbeat after another lulls you into a deep slumber. You have lived a day of purpose, and tomorrow is even brighter.

Brooke kissed her nana's forehead. Her nana's gentle breaths tickled her neck.

She exchanged a knowing look with her pepe, one that told her they'd all be okay, eventually.

Within three days, her nana woke up and her fever had descended to a manageable one hundred degrees. She sat up in her bed and ate scrambled eggs, begging for another bee tale.

"Your story healed me," her nana said in between sips. "You always ask me what I want for my birthday. Well now you know. I want more stories. I can picture myself sitting outside at sunrise and listening to them."

Her nana always supported and marveled over her. Since that day, in between running her bee apiary and nursery, Brooke wrote and narrated short five to ten minute visualization stories for her nana. She'd see her outside with a steaming mug of tea, earbuds in her ear, sunhat pulled down low over her forehead, waking up to her stories of bees, flowers, mountains, rain, sunshine, anything nature had to offer that could be related back to the human experience.

She even decided, at her nana's insistence, to educate herself. She earned her transformation meditation certificate in a home study program. If she wanted to soothe, energize and heal, she'd have to learn how to effectively write and record those meditation sessions. Nana encouraged her even further by paying for the certification program. Brooke folded into the encouragement, as she always did. Her nana lifted her up and took away the sting of abandonment she felt when her parents up and left the state. The result left her thankful and able to forgive and move onward, shedding fears and insecurities brought on by her ego and opening her up to the understanding that life was dynamic and free-flowing. Life worked itself out. Her parents ended up in New York. She ended up right where her heart was happiest, in the apiary and on the path to help herself and those around her heal.

When Penelope came into her life, she recorded several for her. Of course, hers were more sensual in nature. Brooke handed her a flash-drive of them so she could load them into her iTunes. Penelope never did. She never once mentioned one single thing about those stories Brooke labored over for her, and for her only.

"That's okay," Nana said. "I love your stories. And, you know what else?"

"Tell me."

"A lot of people love them." A sneaky grin bloomed.

64

"You didn't." Brooke's blood rushed from her face, leaving her naked and vulnerable. "You shared them?"

"They're good, Brooke."

"But I'm not a professional. I just wanted to learn how to make them special for you."

"Others could use them, too," Nana said, rubbing Brooke's arm. "You remember when Sally's granddaughter got appendicitis?"

Brooke nodded. She remembered alright because she and her nana were about to take off for Ocean City when Sally called. Brooke missed out on her first sailing lesson as a result.

"I let her listen to the one about the butterfly in the field of lavender. It relaxed her, despite the roadway of staples the doctors had put in her poor stomach."

"Who else?"

"Well, you know I've got a lot of sick friends. When you reach my age that happens. Honestly, Brooke they love them. They fall asleep to them each night. They share them at the nursing home where Pepe's uncle lives. They trade them like candy."

Perfect strangers enjoyed the stories that revealed parts of her soul that, at times, even took Brooke by surprise. Yet Penelope, the woman who claimed to be in love with her, couldn't bring herself to stick an earbud in her ear and have a listen.

Back then, Brooke couldn't swallow the hurt from Penelope's rejection.

None of that mattered anymore. She no longer feared being alone. She enjoyed depending on herself for a change, and even her stories took on a new vibe. She just finished recording one about the open road that morning. Just as she uploaded it to iTunes for her nana, her cell rang.

It was Jacky Applebaum, and seeing her name light up on her screen sent a series of flutters through her tummy. She had been a very bad student. She had yet to lift the leash off the kitchen hook as she had promised Jacky she would.

She took the call anyway. "Okay, so I did not take Bee on a walk this morning."

"Hmm."

"The reason isn't because I caved on my homework. I have a very good reason."

"Let me guess. She wanted to sleep in?"

Brooke relaxed into the warm embrace of the woman's good sense of humor. "Would you believe me if I told you she could be lazy?"

"Not a chance. So, it's a good thing I'm not calling about that."

"To what do I owe the pleasure, then?"

"My daughter has a school project, and when she saw the honey she got excited. Were you serious about the apiary tour for her?"

A flurry of trills danced in her chest. "Absolutely. I love showing off my bees."

~ ~

When Sophie arrived home from debate practice on Monday, she found Jacky hanging upside down on her Hang-up machine.

"I called the beekeeper," she said.

Sophie's heart twirled. "And?"

"We're on for Saturday."

Her upside down face freaked Sophie out. "Cool."

She escaped before Jacky flipped right side up.

She went upstairs to her bedroom and closed the door. Then, like every other time she sensed letting her guard down, she headed over to her Taylor Swift CD. She read the letter that she wrote herself two years prior and waited for the cold, hard facts to hit her.

After five reads, she gave up and picked up her book, *Bee Time: Lessons from the Hive,* instead. She spent the rest of the night reading it.

The next morning, Sophie gathered her books and headed downstairs for a quick trip to the cupboard for a granola bar and package of crackers. That day she would present her project idea to Mr. Benks, her science teacher and advisor. She would focus her research on colony collapse and ways the general public could help save honeybees. Hopefully, on Saturday when they toured the apiary, she'd get some concrete ideas straight from the beekeeper.

Mr. Benks would be stoked to know she would be conducting hands-on research with a real beekeeper and live honeybees.

As Sophie headed out of the kitchen, she ran into Jacky. She was wearing checkered pajamas.

"Hey kiddo. Want a lift?"

"I'll just take the bus." She hurried toward the front door, and when she did, her books tumbled down around her feet. She kneeled and began shoveling them into her book bag.

"Geez, you've got to be lugging around at least fifty pounds of books." Jacky leaned over the kitchen counter so much so that her boobs threatened to dangle right out of the corners of her checkered flannels.

Sophie glanced back at her books. "The bag I've got is just fine."

"That can't be good for your neck and shoulders. I'm going to get you one with wheels."

A glow blanketed Jacky's cheeks, like she had been pumping weights in the basement or running on the treadmill no one had used for two years.

"I don't want one on wheels. Thank you anyway." She shoveled the last two books in her bag, then started gathering the pens that had scattered.

Jacky rounded the kitchen island. "You sure you don't want a lift?"

"I'm good." Sophie knew if she didn't get her butt down the street, she'd miss the bus. If she missed the bus, she'd be late for her meeting with Mr. Benks. If late for that, then she'd likely get a drop in her grade. She weighed her choices as she wrestled to loop the book bag over her shoulder.

"I'll be home late today. I'm going to Ashley's for dinner." She rushed toward the front door, and halfway to it, her zipper broke. Suddenly, all her books and pens crashed to the floor again.

"Let me grab you a tote bag," Jacky said, rushing past her toward the staircase. "You can use that for now until we get you something sturdier." She ran away up the stairs and out of sight. Her feet pounded against the floorboards, sending creaks and crackling noises through the silence.

Just outside the door, she heard the familiar sound of the bus screech to a stop at the end of her street. Jacky would be stuck driving her. She probably had clients lined up and would run late.

Moments later, Jacky reemerged downstairs with an oversized laptop case on wheels and dressed in one of her light blue training shirts and tan cargo pants. "This belonged to your mom. She'd want you to have it."

Sophie cautiously examined the black case with all its useful pockets and zippers, fearing she'd somehow ruffle her mother's peaceful rest in heaven if she dared to grasp the handle and take charge of it.

Jacky wheeled it toward Sophie. "Go on. It's not doing anyone any good hiding in that big closet." Jacky bent over and unzipped the middle compartment. "Look, it has room for your lunch tote and a change of clothes for your PE class."

It was a beautiful replacement. It would certainly support more books than her current bag. She wouldn't have to leave her books in her locker overnight. She could take them home and reference them instead of relying on Ashley to look something up in hers.

Jacky was right. Her mother would want her to have it. Her mother would not want her breaking her back each day. Her mother would approve. She'd nod her head the way she used to whenever Sophie choose a wise snack over junk food or offered her favorite toys to needy kids.

Besides, to become independent and get a scholarship, she'd have to read a lot more books than she had been. That would require some heavy lifting.

By accepting the case, she'd free Jacky to eventually live the rest of her life the way a single woman should, without a kid attached. What would she do when Sophie finally grew up and moved out? Would she still be offering Sophie beautiful laptop cases and pretending she loved being in her mother role? What choice did she have but to be nice? Dump the orphan and all her wife's belongings onto someone else and scream *fuck off, she's not my daughter,* as she sped away from the curb?

Jacky was a good person. That reality saddened Sophie the most. How could a good person like Jacky not want her? Something fundamental had to be wrong on Sophie's end. She had to work on herself to fix things. She had to keep her life as clutter-free from emotional and physical attachment as possible.

She'd never be a burden.

So, as much as it pained her to step on her mother's grave by taking over her personal items, Sophie grabbed the handle of the laptop case and wheeled it closer to her dilapidated book bag with its stupid broken zipper. She needed the proper tools to succeed.

Sophie kneeled. "I'll just be a minute," she whispered, as if in a church filled with people praying for her mother's soul while they trampled on her former physical self by taking over her possessions.

Jacky kneeled beside her. "Let me help you."

Together they moved her into a new paradigm where tiny bits of a once hardened wall weakened under the touch of what Sophie could only describe as sincerity.

As Jacky drove her to school that morning, Sophie stared out at the sunshine sprinkling its colorful golden rays over the leaves. New flowers sprouted up from freshly-tilled soil beds. The air smelled like cucumbers, and the promise of longer days floated high above the still chilly early spring mornings.

Springtime used to excite her.

For the past two springs, though, she couldn't have cared less about any of that. Springtime, fresh air, flowers, none of it mattered.

"What do you want to listen to?" Jacky asked, turning the knob to the tuner.

"Whatever. I'm not picky." Sophie hoped to glide through the ride without wreaking any more havoc on the day. She knew Jacky had to have clients lined up for the eight o'clock opening at the school. Already the clock flashed seven ten. It would take her at least twenty minutes to drive her to school, and another twenty to get to the Inner Circle. That only left her with ten minutes to spare.

Jacky continued to search for a song on the radio. They passed by the neighborhood park where the three of them would spend most of their weekends swinging, sliding, and pushing each other around on the merry-go-round. Sophie leaned her forehead against the window and looked up at the canopy of oak trees circling the park. She used to love watching them come to life. Back then, she didn't have to masquerade around trite things. She didn't have to force herself to eat dinner with Ashley's family most every night of the week to avoid having to sit across from Jacky and listen in pain as she attempted small talk to rekindle what they once had.

As Jacky finally settled on a James Taylor oldie, Sophie thought about her dream of honeybees the night before. She imagined herself covered in them, and fell asleep to their collective hum. Their buzz filled her with an energy that lifted her enough to see that, despite the remnants of their tattered lives, some beauty still echoed from the far reaches of the world and landed on her heart like a hug.

She took another glance at the young leaves popping up on the trees. She loved when nature woke back up.

"What's putting that smile on your face?" Jacky asked, turning the corner into the school lot.

"Just thinking about a funny cat video I saw on YouTube this morning."

As they drove past the line of busses in the school parking lot, Sophie spotted Ashley talking to Brian, her latest crush. If Jacky saw her too, she'd surely invite her over for dinner or something uncomfortable. "You can drop me right here."

"There's a spot right up front. Don't be silly."

"No." Sophie gripped the door handle. "Right here is good."

"There's a line of cars behind us. I can't just stop here."

Jacky maneuvered ahead and parked right in front of where Ashley and Brian huddled. Sophie pulled the handle and jumped out. "Thanks for the ride. I'll see you later on."

"Your bag!"

Sophie doubled back the two steps, and reached for the back door handle.

"Is that Ashley?" Jacky yelled out.

Ashley spun and faced them. Her face turned red.

70

Brian tipped his head and snarled up his lip in his usual stupid fashion, something Ashley found sexy and Sophie found just plain creepy.

"My God, I haven't seen you in ages," Jacky said, leaning forward.

"Oh, hey Mrs. Applebaum." Ashley remained rooted near her boy crush.

Good. Stay.

"How's your mom? I haven't seen her in ages, either."

"She's good. She's getting along just fine now since her divorce."

Sophie groaned. The girl talked too much. She had no filter. This would cost her at least another five minutes.

"Divorce?" Jacky's face contorted.

Ashley puffed up her cheeks and scanned the busy scene of students rushing past to get to their homerooms on time. She finally looked at Sophie.

Sophie warned her with a flick.

"I've got to go," Ashley said, bowing away from Brian and his snarled lip and from Jacky and her twisted face.

"Okay," Jacky yelled after her. "Come by for dinner one night. We'll make homemade pizza like old times."

Old times were old times because they no longer existed. No matter how hard they tried, they would never be able to go back to those old times and shine them up in this second version of life.

Sophie grabbed her laptop case from the backseat and yanked it out.

"You didn't tell me her parents got divorced."

"I didn't think it mattered." Sophie pulled up on the case's handle and wheeled off toward the school's entrance, shouting over her shoulder, "Thanks for the ride."

Chapter Six

Jacky spent the week working overtime with the clients she had previously scheduled for that Saturday's training sessions. Nothing would keep her from driving Sophie to her tour.

Sophie would adore Brooke, and of course Bee and all her crazed perplexities. Already impregnated with the premature cravings of creating a shared memory, Jacky survived the late nights of catering to her demanding clientele.

Sophie needed a good experience. Their relationship strained to the point of breakage. One more pull on that rope could fray it into an unrecognizable fiber, the offspring of which could dismantle the core integrity of their future. They needed a break from the everyday stressed melody that echoed its constant reminder of their dread.

Sophie needed to get away from her bedroom and start exploring life again like she used to do. Under her current constraints, she wilted. She either spent her time with Ashley, went to cheerleading practice, or closed herself in her bedroom alone.

Sophie loved adventure. She had dreams of climbing Mount Everest one day, of parasailing, and of skydiving. The promise of heart-jolting activities used to drive her to get out of bed and wake up the house in an energetic attempt to rouse everyone from the warmth of their blankets. She needed that fire to start again. She needed a moment that would supply her with a new sound, a bold flavor, an intense arousal to the senses to get her off the current trajectory and onto a new one not littered with frayed ends.

Brooke offered to show her such a time. The woman may have been afraid of walking her dog, but underneath that coating of fear lived someone who grabbed onto the esoteric force of nature. She walked like a breeze, smooth and flowing. She smelled like a spring day and emitted an aura of mystery and connectedness. Her spirit reminded Jacky an awful lot of Sophie two years prior when she shined with the promise of delight at every breath.

If nothing else, she hoped to have something new to talk about with Sophie. Preferably not a bee sting, of course.

They arrived at the apiary on Saturday morning, with five minutes to spare. The trees began to sprout green buds, drizzling the early morning with a delight that brought a sense of joy to the already exciting time ahead.

Bee began her barking tirade from the bay window. "She's not going to be happy when I tell her that window is off limits from now on."

"Who's not going to be happy? The dog or the beekeeper?" Sophie asked.

"I suppose both," Jacky said on a nod, then climbed out of the car and breathed in the ripened warmth and sunshine of the day.

~ ~

Brooke emerged from the backyard door and circled around the side. Jacky and her daughter walked toward her. The young girl wore her hair pinned back in a tight bun at her nape and dressed in long yoga pants, her socks already pulled up over them. She looked around, squinting and cupping a hand over her eyes. Jacky on the other hand, wore cargo shorts and a short-sleeved t-shirt. Her blonde hair splayed out in fun directions, dancing with the morning breeze.

As they neared, Brooke caught a whiff of Jacky's citrus scent. The honeybees would certainly like it as much as she did.

They welcomed each other with a smile, meanwhile Bee barked frantically in the background.

Brooke offered her hand to the girl. "I'm Brooke." She scanned her tucked yoga pants. "I see you've done your homework."

The girl's face beamed. "I'm Sophie, and yes, I prepared." Her cheeks turned rosy and shined in the morning sunlight. "This place is so pretty." Sophie twirled toward the trees. "Are those cicadas I hear?"

"Oh yeah. They've just started to sing all day long."

"I love cicadas." Her hazelnut-colored eyes twinkled. "I can't wait for their next invasion."

"You're the only person besides my grandfather who I've ever heard say that."

"I would've loved to have seen them during their last invasion."

The girl had a sing-song chime to her voice, like hearing the beauty when one's finger slid across the edge of a flute glass.

"Did they really sound super loud back in two thousand three?"

"Oh, you're aging me," Brooke teased. "Yes, I do remember that year. You couldn't walk outside without getting pummeled. I couldn't hear much of anything else aside from their high frequency pitch, but I didn't mind at all. I actually missed them once they all died off for the season."

"Only another five years to go until they come back." Sophie placed her hands on her small hips, looking ready to tackle whatever the day tossed at her. "I was too young to remember, but my mother told me I used to play with them. I'd line them up on the sidewalk and pretend I was a nurse tending to them." She shrugged. "My mother adored cicadas too." Sophie's voice trailed off.

"She doesn't anymore?" Brooke asked, winking at Jacky.

Sophie just kept exploring, ignoring her question.

Jacky pulled in her lower lip. "Um, so," Jacky started. "Sophie is really excited to learn about bees. As I mentioned on the phone when I called, she's doing a school project on them. Your honey is what piqued her interest."

She sounded so business-like.

Sophie rolled her eyes.

Jacky flinched when she saw the eye roll.

Brooke's curiosity rose.

Silence gripped the air, strangling the life out of it.

Okay, then. Time to segue. "Tell me Sophie, have you ever been around hundreds of thousands of them before?"

"Never." She bloomed to life. "But, I've always wanted to."

"Well today's your lucky day."

"I've read a lot so far, but I can't wait to see for myself." She bent down and fidgeted with her sock and yoga pants. "When did you first experience bees?"

Brooke enjoyed her inquisitive nature. "My grandparents probably carried me out here the day I was born." She laughed. "For as long as I can remember I've been around them. I've been a curious worker bee since the day I took my first steps, I'm sure."

"Can we see them?"

"Of course."

Jacky rubbed the back of her neck, and red blotches rose on her face.

Where did my fearless trainer go?

"They're very active today," Brooke continued. "I went down to the hives earlier to clean up around them. We've got these runaway vines that take over the backyard. The bees love them. They're full of nectar. They cling to everything in their path, including the hives. So, a little snip here and there and some redirection keeps everyone happy." Brooke placed her hand on Jacky's arm. "Did you bring any long pants with you?"

"I should've done my own homework, too." She twisted her mouth and looked to Sophie.

Sophie snapped away from Jacky and focused on the cicada buzzing trees.

An unease separated them, and Brooke wanted to know why.

"I can hook you up," Brooke said, monitoring the growing tension between the mother and daughter.

Sophie already began walking down the path to the apiary.

"We're going to suit up in that green house by the gazebo," Brooke called after her, then she turned back to Jacky. "So, yes? Hook you up?"

Jacky laughed. "As fun as that sounds, I'll just take Bee for a walk while you show Sophie around the hives. I'll catch the next tour."

Brooke angled her head, hanging on the edge of curiosity. *Does she fear the bees?*

"I love how you let the weeds grow back here," Sophie called out over her shoulder. "The wildflowers are so beautiful." She breathed in the air in a dramatic pause. "Oh look, a bee is dancing on this blue flower." Sophie braced on her tiptoes to get a closer look. "I read somewhere how a honeybee visits 50 to 100 flowers during a collection trip." Her words spun out in front of her like a ball of yarn, flowing and artful. "Is it true? Do they do that?"

"They do," Brooke said, releasing the prying question from her mind and focusing back on the girl. "And did you know that the average worker bee produces about one-twelfth a teaspoon of honey in her lifetime?"

"That's so cool." Sophie breathed in again. She leaned over another patch of flowers. "I also read that as soon as a bee approaches a flower, it changes it to a positive charge."

Oh, this is going to be fun.

Brooke turned back to Jacky. "The leash is hanging on the back of the door, which is unlocked. And her new harness is hanging up by the leash."

Jacky nodded, gazing at Sophie with a bittersweet smile.

Hello! Anyone home? "New harness," Brooke said.

Jacky snapped back to the present. "Okay have fun."

Right. Okay then.

Brooke backed away and walked toward Sophie, dusting off the desire to keep poking and prodding.

~ ~

Sophie had read at least five books on beekeeping before stepping foot in the apiary. All those words she'd read never could've prepared her for the rush of being in the company of thousands of honeybees.

She stood in front of the hive boxes with a ball of excitement in the pit of her stomach, waiting on Brooke to lift the cover to one of them. Brooke used a metal hive tool to inch it up.

"Each stack of these boxes contain about forty-thousand bees." Brooke opened the cover and tapped it so the bees fell down into the vertical trays inside.

Sophie counted ten trays.

"Most of these top trays will be half full of bees because a lot of them are in the lower boxes filling those honeycombs until they can cap them. The queen is typically much lower in the boxes too, along with her court."

Bees began to swarm around Sophie's head, tickling her senses as they investigated. A few landed on her netted hat and watched her. "What do you mean court?"

"Oh, the court is something to see. Dedicated bees surround her, matching her pace, doting on her, cleaning her, treating her like the royalty that she is." Brooke pointed to the half-filled honeycombs. "They've got a lot of work to do, yet. The field bees are out foraging right now and will come back before dark. The worker bees will then deposit their nectar in these combs."

Sophie leaned in closer to the box. "It looks like there are more bees on the middle trays. Can I see one of those?"

Brooke moved slowly. "Absolutely." She placed the tray back in and dug out one of the middle ones.

"Wow, that's a lot of bees on one small area." Sophie's heart zoomed.

"Want to hold it?"

"Really?"

Brooke handed it to her. "Just be careful as you place your fingers on the edges. Go slowly and they'll move out of your way."

Sophie did as instructed, fingering the edge of the hive so she didn't squish a bee. The tray weighed more than she imagined.

She eased into the peace, enjoying the buzz and letting nothing else tamper with the moment. For the first time in a very long two years, she stepped into a new arena, one filled with lovable creatures, as gentle as puppies, and at her feet, purple, pink and red flowers growing in tandem with the wild grasses.

She leaned in closer to the tray. The bees created a breeze that passed through her netted hat. It kissed her cheeks, filling her with love as she observed their peaceful world.

Sophie's breath flowed, dissolving all traces of negative energy and taking her on a journey where every muscle relaxed, every nerve retreated.

She inhaled, taking on the full pleasure of the buzzing. Despite the hundreds of bees moving around her fingers and arms, she knew with certainty they wouldn't harm her. She also knew that as long as she continued to remain in awe of their magnificent presence, they would welcome her into their domain. She read that, and now understood.

Sophie enjoyed every tiny flutter.

She met Brooke's sparkling eyes.

"I have no fear."

"No reason to. It's one of the most peaceful places on the planet."

The sun shone its pristine rays on the honeycomb tray, highlighting the subtle golden hue on the backs of the busy bees who were working with intense focus. She embraced the magical moment, existing in perfect harmony with the bees. She slipped into their domain, a space full of charm, and surrendered to the wonders of their friendship.

Brooke tapped her shoulder and pointed at larvae in some of the cells.

"Incredible," Sophie whispered.

They continued to marvel at the honeybees for the next hour. Brooke showed her new trays with more larvae, nursing bees, and capped honeycomb.

She buzzed along with them. In such a short amount of time, they welcomed her in and trusted her, revealing their hidden doorway into their home. She handed Brooke back a tray.

She eased it into the hive box, then sealed the lid.

"I had no idea," Sophie whispered as they both stared at a few foragers returning, bustling their way in through the hive's bottom. Overcome with gratitude, tears spilled down her cheeks.

"What you just experienced is called bee time, that special moment when nothing else in the world matters but the beauty of the present moment."

Sophie's heart swelled with a love she didn't quite know how to explain. Their wholesome and pure hearts blanketed her in a peace she'd never want to live without now that she'd experienced it.

Brooke led her from the bee hives back up the trail to where ordinary life continued to play out, a life that dulled by comparison.

~ ~

Jacky sat on Brooke's patio, feeding Bee water from the hose. Bee lapped it up and splattered it all over the place. Suddenly, Jacky heard Brooke and Sophie in the greenhouse. Sophie had wanted her space that day, that much she hinted. Solo time with Brooke at the hives paid off. Because Sophie's giggle drifted up the hill, curling in the air like a feather, wispy and joyful.

Jacky relaxed back and enjoyed the sound of her happiness. It had been so long since she heard her laugh.

Bee pulled on the leash and whined.

"Alright." Jacky stood. "You win. Let's go see them."

Bee trotted alongside Jacky's wide stride, wagging her tail.

When Bee arrived at the entrance to the greenhouse, she ignored Sophie and ran over to Brooke, nudging between her knees for a good pat. Sophie stayed calm and focused on folding the bee outfit in her hands.

"How is she not jumping all over you, Sophie?" Brooke asked.

"Probably because I'm not afraid." Sophie shook off the compliment. She wiped the sweat from her forehead with her shirt sleeve, then squatted down to pet Bee. "Hey pretty girl."

Dogs adored Sophie.

"So, it turns out Sophie knows more about bees than me." Brooke kissed the top of Bee's head. When she looked up, she brushed a piece of curly hair away from her flushed face. Her whole being lit up, stealing the breath right out of Jacky's chest.

In the time-lapsed moments that followed, a discernable exchange occurred between them; one that blurred everything and pulled at every nook and cranny of her being. Then poof, the moment disappeared as mysteriously as it swept in.

In her peripheral, she caught Sophie's stare.

Jacky fought for focus, and when it returned she noticed that Sophie had already cued out, fanning herself and untying her bun. Her long, thick, healthy golden hair hung in perfect tendrils down her back.

Returning to the conversation, Jacky said. "So, Sophie being a bee whiz doesn't surprise me. She's a smart kid."

"Yep. Just like my mother," she stated.

"Oh, that is so sweet." Brooke projected an innocent sigh. "Your mother sure is smart. She's tamed the inner beast in Bee in no time."

"Oh, she's talking about her mother Drew," Jacky admitted, steadying to break into her painful admission.

Brooke tilted her head.

"Drew passed away two years ago," Jacky explained.

Brooke cupped her hands around her face and peered up at her with shock. "I'm so sorry."

An uncomfortable mist filled the space between them.

Jacky nodded her customary thank you.

Brooke dropped her hands and exposed her tears and quivering chin. "That's just terrible. I can't imagine how difficult it must be for you both."

And just like it did every time she told someone new about Drew, the dreaded void of words now permeated the air, sucking the life right out of it. Jacky still didn't know how to traverse the terrain even though she'd spent more than enough time on it. Drew always navigated those circumstances better, pulling them out of awkward conversations with her wit and grace. Jacky lacked such dignified characteristics. She didn't need that ability with dogs. They didn't ask questions.

"She would've loved this place," Sophie said, looking around at the colors popping to life. "She loved gardens and flowers and green trees."

A lump formed in Jacky's throat. She gritted her teeth to stave off the trickle of emotions.

Brooke hugged herself, furrowing her eyebrows as though in pain herself. "I'm so sorry."

Sophie fidgeted with the strings to the netted hat.

Eager to change the vibe, Jacky clapped her hands. "So, how was it?" Her question rolled out with a desperate force.

"Well," Sophie said with a joyful ring. "I felt alive, just like all of the books said I would." She lifted her gaze to Brooke. "I did my due diligence by reading Mark Winston's book *Bee Time: Lessons from the Hive* as soon as Jacky told me about your apiary."

"Maybe you're a beekeeper in the making." Brooke exhaled and eased her arms down to her sides. She stepped forward, opening up the perfect pathway for the sun to shine its brilliance on her chocolate-colored curls. They beamed, creating a halo effect around her head. "You know. I could always use an extra set of hands around here, if you're interested."

"Me?" Sophie's jaw dropped.

"Saturdays get busy with people stopping by to purchase honey, pollen, and our garden veggies. I could use the muscle power, too. When the honey starts to cap off on the trays, they get heavy. It's a two person job at that point. Then, there's also the hydroponic gardening."

Sophie twisted her mouth. "Saturdays are my cheerleading day. Practice sits smack dab in the center."

"I used to cheerlead too." Brooke circled around to her side. "So, I understand."

"I really want to say yes," Sophie said with the maturity of a seasoned professional in high demand.

"Well, if life ever tosses you a free moment, consider the apiary door open." Brooke turned to Jacky and pointed to her folded bee suit. "Next time, we're stuffing you into one of these, too."

Jacky laughed, enjoying the lift into lighter, filtered air.

"Who's getting stuffed into what?" An older man with hair as white as snow and skin as wrinkled as fine leather folded in on them in the greenhouse. "Did she put you into this hot one?" He asked Sophie, taking the folded suit from her arms.

Sophie giggled like she used to do as a little girl being twirled around on her favorite merry-go-round. "Ms. Brooke said it was the best one."

He shifted his stocky chest to Brooke. "Oh, did she now?"

"Oh, don't listen to him." Brooke punched his upper arm.

The old man faced Jacky. "I'm Tom, by the way. Brooke's grandfather." He turned and opened his arm to an older lady with even whiter hair and a gingerly vibe walking in from the path. "And this is Elise, my wife."

Elise carried herself with the same breeziness as Brooke. She dipped her head, extending her hand to Jacky.

"I'm Jacky and this is my daughter, Sophie."

"Hi," Sophie waved without moving forward. She fingered through her tangled hair. "I love your apiary."

Jacky hadn't seen this social prowess in Sophie for the longest time.

Elise bent down to pet Bee, peering up over her flowery frames at Sophie. "I saw you down at the hives. What did you think?"

"Amazing. The bees created wind and it blew on my cheeks." Sophie animated just as she used to as a little girl when she'd jump waves with Jacky on the Eastern Shore.

"Did you get to see one of the queens?"

"No, we looked for her in some of the top hives, but no luck," Brooke said, cutting into the conversation. "Pepe we'll need to add our pollen collector trays soon."

"First order of business after lunch is we have to get to Mr. Pesticide's yard, then we can do the collector trays. Some of Gary's bees have swarmed in his tree."

"Fantastic," Brooke whispered, facetiously.

Elise moved toward them. "The man used to spray pesticides around like tap water. Hence his nickname. Then, Brooke had a talk with him and convinced him otherwise." She scrunched up her face to mark her disapproval of Mr. Pesticide's former ludicrous ways. "Obviously Gary isn't managing his hives again. It's not the first time he let his hives get too large."

"I've told him a thousand times how to control a swarm," Tom said. "He doesn't listen. And of all yards to swarm, the bees had to pick Mr. Pesticide's?"

"I'm going to talk to Gary," Elise said. "You always talk too much golf when you're together. He probably isn't hearing what you're saying to him." Elise shook her head.

They tossed their opinions around like a couple of kids razzing on each other at the playground. They probably argued over silly, normal things like losing the remote control to the couch cushions and forgetting to lock the doors at night. They were adorable.

Jacky waved Sophie over to her. "We should get out of their way, so they can go tend to this swarm."

"I'd love to see a swarm," Sophie said.

Jacky would too. In fact, she'd love to hang out with these people all afternoon if she could. She loved their down-to-earth, nonjudgmental attitudes. They could probably enjoy a lively debate, then offer hot cocoa a moment later. But, they had serious work to do, and Jacky didn't want to push.

"We've taken up enough of their time for today," Jacky said. She walked toward the entrance of the greenhouse. "We'll let you get to work."

Brooke reached out for Sophie's arm as she passed her by. "I promise there will be more swarms if you come to work for me."

"Especially if we don't get over to Gary's and educate him," Elise said with a straight face.

Brooke smirked at her grandmother, then turned her attention back to Sophie. "So think about it, okay?"

"Okay."

They exchanged smiles.

Meanwhile, Bee sat like a perfect dog. Too perfect, in fact. Her training would be over before they could blink. "Hey," Jacky stopped short of the entrance door. "Let's set up another training. This time you will be walking her."

"Me?" Brooke's face flushed.

"How about Monday morning at eight o'clock?"

"Really?" Panic spread across her pink face. "Am I ready?"

"I don't know. Are you?" Jacky asked with unintended tease.

Brooke tucked a piece of hair behind her ear and offered her a blink. "I suppose I might be."

Brooke's innocence aroused a curious spark in Jacky. "Then Monday morning it is," she said with unreserved playfulness.

Brooke winked. "See you then."

Jacky's heart galloped, firing back to life the rapid flutters that long ago used to power a passionate breath in her movements; flutters she didn't deserve.

Even after she and Sophie buckled into their respective places in the car and watched as Brooke disappeared behind the back of her house, she still buzzed. Even her skin tickled as the light breeze blew in through the window, covering her in the romantic scent of a heartfelt high.

Sophie sat smiling and staring up at the budding trees. "I've made up my mind." Happiness sprang from her core, filling the front seat with air that helped Jacky return to reality.

"Oh?"

"I'm going to quit cheerleading and become a beekeeper."

Infused with visions of bees, warm gooey honey, happy-go-lucky laughs from Sophie and more sights of Brooke's innocent blinks, Jacky relaxed into the idea with a shrug. "No argument from me. Whatever you want, kiddo."

Chapter Seven

Mr. Pesticide, so appropriately nicknamed by Pepe, was a jerk who moved into the neighborhood the summer before. He would spray his lawn and plants with pesticides. Pepe attempted to educate him on the damaging effects of the chemicals on the honeybee population, but the man refused to listen to a word he had to say because Pepe mistakenly pulled up on his lawn with his Tacoma creating instant mud holes. Mr. Pesticide kicked Brooke and Pepe off his property as Pepe yelled out his window, begging him to stop using chemicals in his yard. Well, being yelled at didn't sit right with Mr. Pesticide, you see, because that very day, he pulled out his container of toxins and doused his front lawn with it.

They couldn't have that happen. Their bees foraged in his yard. Honeybees typically foraged in a five mile radius from a hive. So, from the time Brooke walked and talked, she sat privy to those conversations with new neighbors as Pepe educated them on why they shouldn't use the chemicals.

Pesticides and weed control sprays were horrible substances that wreaked havoc on the environment, bees, and humans. They should be banned, yet every major retailer in the country displayed the toxic chemicals on their shelves. At the very least each container should have labeled a warning that those chemicals could kill honeybees. Without honeybees, they'd have no fruit, vegetables, or pretty flowers. They'd die. Yet, no one seemed alarmed by that.

Not only did every neighbor get a free supply of honey for their beneficial contribution to honeybees, but they also got to enjoy toxin-free honey.

On the second day that Mr. Pesticide pulled out his poisonous container and ventured out to his front lawn wearing a mask, Pepe begged Brooke to help.

Brooke had arrived, carrying a plate of cookies up their front walk. Mrs. Pesticide rocked in her chair on the porch. "Do you have a few minutes to chat?"

"About what dear?"

"About mine and my grandparent's honeybees." Brooke inched her way up the first step. "My grandfather asked me to come by and bring you cookies because he feels badly about how he and Mr. Pest–" Brooke coughed, "and your husband got off on the wrong foot. You know men, especially the old grouchy kind like my Pepe. They have no clue how to be civil at times."

The lady chuckled, covering her mouth. Her eyelids creased and cast a shadow over her delicate icy blue eyes. "My husband is the worst," she whispered.

A moment later, Mr. Pesticide had sprung out of his front door as if flames lapped up against his back. "Get off my walk." He pointed to the street. "Go on now."

"Absolutely not," Mrs. Pesticide said, springing up from her rocking chair. "She is my guest, and she will sit next to me." She had motioned for Brooke to sit in the empty chair beside her.

Brooke climbed the steps and halted in front of him. "Cookie? They just came out of the oven."

He eyed them and growled, folding his arms across his chest and taking a strong lean position against the porch railing. "What is this about?"

"I wanted to ask a favor."

"Now, why would we do you a favor?"

"Because I'm asking nicely." Brooke looked to the lady who nodded her approval.

"Go on now, sweetheart. What is your favor?" she asked.

"Our honeybees are dying. The pesticides you're spraying are killing them."

"Oh this is rubbish." He tossed his hands in the air.

"Shush, you old grouch," his wife said. "Listen to what she has to say."

Brooke continued. "If honeybees eat nectar from a chemically treated plant, they bring those toxins back to the hive and can infect the other bees with disease and produce chemically treated honey. The bees from our hives help pollinate your garden and flowers. Our neighbors, many innocent children, eat the honey. The bees are wonderful workers, and they need our help to continue their good work. Will you stop using the chemicals in exchange for honey that is free of toxins and straight from our hives?" Brooke exhaled the residual emotions loitering in her chest.

"I've told you," his wife said, pointing at him. "You're going to poison us with those chemicals." She turned to Brooke. "He tells me he needs to spray the roots to keep the bugs from eating his precious tomato plants."

"If I don't, they're going to rot." His voice grew loud.

The wife looked to Brooke again. "He loves those tomatoes more than he loves me, I think. He spends all day talking to them, shining up the leaves, watering them, feeding them, pruning them, and when harvest time comes, he's like a kid in a field of strawberries. He loves his tomatoes."

"I can't stand the taste of store-bought ones," he said, wagging his head. "They're bruised and knotty, and they taste like cardboard."

"There are organic ways to garden," Brooke said. "I'm happy to share some ideas with you."

His jaw hung. He looked to his wife, then at the plate of cookies.

"Do you want one?" Brooke offered him the plate again.

He contemplated the move toward them with a clench to his droopy jaw. "I suppose one couldn't hurt." He reached for one and bit into it. He sealed his eyes closed, savoring it. "So bugs won't get at my tomatoes if I do this organic thing you're talking about?"

"That's right, and you won't be poisoning yourself or my bees."

He bit into the cookie again. Crumbs dropped to his feet. "Have we destroyed your hives?"

His wife scooted up in her chair. "We?"

He cleared his throat. "Fine, I. Have I destroyed your hives?"

"We've got one hundred and fifty of them that are still thriving. So, it's not too late to help them."

"I'm not doing this for that old man of yours. You hear me?" He arched his wiry eyebrow. "I'm doing this for my tomatoes and the bees, and them alone. And only because I've got the biggest, juiciest tomatoes this side of Howard County. I've never seen juicer ones. I don't want to screw that up."

"With healthy bees, you'll have healthy crops. I promise. You can thank the bees for your tomatoes being as juicy as they are already."

"Well." The man had turned out to the yard and stretched out his arms. "Thank you bees."

That conversation happened a little over half a year ago, and despite Brooke spending a few afternoons with him teaching him about organic gardening, Pepe and Mr. Pesticide still hadn't spoken. When Pepe would drive by, Mr. Pesticide would chuck him the bird.

~ ~

When Brooke returned home after tending to the swarm in Mr. Pesticide's yard that afternoon, she strolled out to the patio and relaxed with some lemonade. Since Penelope left her, she enjoyed those quiet expanses of time when she could sit alone for half an hour. She didn't have to worry about ruining Penelope's afternoon by forcing her to do something as simple as enjoying the quiet. She didn't have to answer to anyone, and that freedom thrilled her.

Did she miss the idea of having someone to cuddle up with, cook with, or dance with? She wished she had that. Penelope never cuddled, cooked or danced. The television blared or they went to a mall. She wanted Brooke to change into someone who enjoyed loud television shows and crowded malls.

Brooke was a romantic at heart. She wanted the cuddling, cooking, and dancing. Penelope couldn't provide those things. Neither could any of the women she dated. They turned from bad to worse, always turning out to be narcissistic, petty, or just plain dull.

As she sipped her lemonade, she tossed Bee a ball. She fetched it, leaping and returning it with slobber. When Bee grew tired of that, she began digging around the bushes to uncover bones she had buried.

Brooke leaned back in the lounger and closed her eyes. A moment later, her cell rang. "Hi Brooke! It's me Sophie. I've been looking over my project notes from this morning's visit. Can I ask you a question about bee colony collapse?"

"Of course. What's on your mind?"

"I want to include information on how pesticides affect the health of a hive. I looked it up online, but I'd rather talk with you about it."

"That's a question that could be better answered by my grandparents. They go around to different bee organizations and talk about just that. Maybe you can come by the apiary next Saturday to chat with them?"

"Can I start working for you then, too, and climb back into the bee suit?"

"So, you're interested?"

"The bees were so cool. They're so gentle, and all they want to do is thrive. I want to help them thrive."

A wave of motherly pride for her bees caught her off balance in a delightful way. "What about cheerleading?"

"I don't really care for cheerleading, to be honest. The only reason I joined the squad was to help my friend Ashley overcome her shyness with the other members. She's more outgoing than me now. Besides, I'm ready for something new."

"Well, then, I'm so excited for you. You're going to love it! We're going to have so much fun."

"What time do you want me there?"

"I'm not like your mother, Jacky. You can show up whenever you please."

"Oh, she's going to want a time."

"You tell her we're on bee time. That means we work hard when we are called to duty and we rest with gusto."

"Yeah, that's not going to fly with her," she laughed. "I need a time."

"If it'll settle her, tell her ten in the morning until four in the afternoon."

"Okay, bye!"

Brooke eased her phone down, then released a happy squeak.

The teacher in her awoke. She couldn't wait to introduce the girl to the wonder and magic of bees, and their incredible life lessons.

Chapter Eight

Monday morning had started out as any other for Marie and Hazel. They sat across from each other in their breakfast nook eating steel-cut oats with honey and sipping Earl Grey tea. Marie chomped into a mouthful of oats. Honey pooled around the edges of her spoon and dripped. As she caught it, Hazel asked her, "Am I getting dark circles under my eyes."

Marie couldn't lie. Hazel knew that. "You do look more tired than usual."

"So that's a yes," she asked with a high pitch.

"Yes. I do see dark circles. But–"

"But?" Hazel stood up and punched her thighs, before darting off down the hallway in hysterics.

"Oh for goodness sakes, Hazel," she yelled after her.

Marie allowed little leeway on lying. She omitted the truth only if no viable solution existed that would help the situation. In the case of Hazel's dark circles, some simple frozen metal spoons on the eyes first thing in the morning would do the trick. That or more sleep. They were in their mid-fifties, after all. Heck, for weeks, she had spent an extra hour awake, rubbing her tired eyes to get through crocheting a blanket for their lead trainer's new baby. So what if she had dark circles? Big freaking whoop dee do.

Marie stomped down the hallway to their office to defend her case. She always did. Hazel knew that too.

She found Hazel's face buried in her hands, tears leaking through her tense fingers.

"Why ask me if you don't want an honest answer?"

"Maybe sometimes I just want to hear something compassionate come out of your mouth." Her voice muffled under the pressure of her stressed fingers. "Sometimes I just wish you'd be more empathetic and sensitive."

Marie stood staring at her, at a loss for what to do. "You know I'm crazy about you, even with dark circles. Who cares about them?" She inched into the office. "Look at me. Look at these dark spots on my face." She pointed to her cheeks. "If I cared enough about getting rid of them, I would. There's always a solution, even for your dark circles."

"You're digging yourself deeper." Hazel stood up and wiped her red cheeks. "I'm jumping in the shower, then let's just go to the school. I'm done discussing this."

And just like that, she disappeared back into the hallway and into the bathroom, leaving Marie to gasp at the unjustified attitude.

"Would you rather have me lie to you?" She yelled.

"Sometimes, yes!"

Marie walked backed into the breakfast nook and cleaned up their dishes, fully expecting Hazel to emerge, showered and dressed in her freshly laundered tan uniform. Then, she'd open up her arms to Marie, her typical move after an emotional outburst. Marie would then fold into them, and Hazel would tap her back, soothing her and letting her know she appreciated her honesty after all.

Well, Hazel never offered her that. Instead, Hazel drove to the school on silent mode, not once turning to blanket Marie with her usual look of gratitude and love.

When they arrived in front of the school, Hazel panicked, "I don't have the keys to the school."

"Why aren't they with your car keys?" Marie shouted, equally panicked about the time.

"It happens," she said as smooth as powerful liquor.

"Where are they?"

"I don't remember." Hazel smoothed her fingers over the steering wheel.

Marie stared at her, frowning. "How do you not remember something like this?"

"Hell, Marie." Her shoulders tensed. "Stop yelling at me."

"Well, how am I supposed to get into the school?"

She looked at her with a slow, cool gaze. "You can always call Jacky."

"And tell her what?"

She shifted the car in drive. "The truth ought to do." Her words dropped from her mouth without any hesitation, as if she'd been waiting for just the right moment to launch her distaste of constructive feedback.

"You're punishing me for telling you the truth this morning?"

Hazel inched the car forward. "I don't have to listen to this."

Marie's heart beat heavily, wanting to shake sense into Hazel. "Well, neither do I." Marie climbed out of the car. "I'll call Jacky." Marie slammed the car door right before Hazel sped off.

Marie watched as Hazel peeled away and halted to a screech at the stop sign. Then, she zoomed past the eyesore of a convenience store on the next block and turned onto the interstate ramp.

Marie stood on the street staring at the sidewalk sign in front of the convenience store. Even without her glasses, she could read the special on cigarettes and Pepsi. Suddenly Marie craved a cigarette. She would fume her anger away in a well-deserved nicotine high.

~ ~

Halfway through gulping a glass of milk, Marie called Jacky in a panic. "I'm locked out of the school."

Marie always freaked when things didn't go according to plan. Everything had to be aligned or Marie's face blotched and she dashed around swinging her arms as if that would solve everything.

"How did you lose them?"

"I don't want to talk about that right now," she seethed. "I just need you to open it up for me."

"Of all days."

"Tell me about it," Marie scoffed.

"I'll be there as soon as I can."

She hung up and called Brooke to apologize.

"I can't believe I'm calling to tell you this," Jacky said, "but I'm running late."

"I run on a different clock than you, dear."

Her warm honey voice soothed Jacky. "I hate being late."

"It's just a second hand on a clock. It means nothing," Brooke said. Bee barked in the background. "Though, don't be too long. The electric guys are up in the wires today, and Bee's not happy."

"Tell Bee it's all my friend Marie's fault. She forgot her key to the school, and she's freaking out. So, rather than have her drive the thirty minutes back to her house angry, I think it's safer if I just drop by and open it up for her."

"Do you want me to be brave and just jump in my car with Bee to meet you there? You have a private room, right?"

God the woman had a soft tone that could melt ice cubes.

"To go out on a limb like that, you must be afraid of how she'll react to the electric guys."

She giggled, and it tickled Jacky's ear.

"The scene isn't exactly playing out in my mind like a Hallmark movie," Brooke said.

"A man poised up in a lift with electrical wires dangling around him is what I call a fantastic training opportunity. I'm sure you wouldn't want to miss that." Jacky's light-hearted tone sounded foreign to her own ears, like she was trying on a new flirty personality and would soon be discovered as an impersonator.

"I don't like missing out on opportunities," Brooke played back.

Suddenly, Jacky envisioned Drew sneaking in on this phone conversation, poking around it with her finger to fully digest the heightened inflections from both women. Guilt began its rise through her. She changed her tone to something more appropriate between trainer and client. "Can I pick up a coffee for you on the way?"

"You're not late enough, now you want to toss a coffee run into the equation too? Who's going out on a limb?"

"You're turning me into a rebel. What can I say?" *I'm flirting. Stop flirting.*

"Rebels are cool. Coffee is also pretty cool. Bring both, and maybe you'll get a freshly baked scone if you're lucky."

"Mm scones." A moan way too seductive for platonic conversation trailed. "I'll run some traffic lights just for that." *You sound like an idiot. Stop speaking.*

"I prefer my rebels in one piece."

"Then one piece I shall remain," Jacky said, ignoring her inner voice.

"You're silly."

"You're even sillier."

She never flirted. She'd never stepped foot outside the friendly zone with anyone since Drew.

A flirt didn't make her evil.

Or did it?

Cashiers flashed evocative glances at total strangers, and bartenders, let's not even go there on the playful exchanges with people who walked in off the street. At least she knew Brooke. A little. Didn't that count for something?

I'm evil. Pure evil.

Brooke snapped her fingers. "Lock. Coffee. My house."

"You're snapping at me?"

She snapped again. "Time is ticking."

Not fast enough. She wanted to be leaning against the hood of her car, waiting on Brooke to walk out of her front door and take her breath away again. "By the way, I'm ringing the doorbell today."

Brooke gasped. "You are not."

"Oh I am." She hung up on a wink that Brooke wasn't privy to, and one that sent her spiraling in both joy and an underlying guilt.

~ ~

Jacky pulled up in front of the Inner Circle School to a very disturbing sight of Marie pacing the sidewalk and smoking a cigarette.

She climbed out of her car. "You said you quit."

"Well, this is what happens when Hazel angers me. She lost our keys." Her voice cracked on her exhalation.

"Hazel will not be pleased to know you're smoking again." Jacky waved away the cloud of smelly smoke.

"Right now I don't care." She drew on the cigarette and its head turned an angry red. "I've got a bunch of daycare doggies who will be showing up any minute, and she forgets to bring the keys with her. Then, she acts like she can't remember where the big ass, gaudy keychain is. How does one lose a Bull Mastiff keychain with a pink rubber ball? I mean, what did she do? Drop them down a storm drain and forget they fell out of her hands?"

Jacky scanned the sidewalk. "Where is she?"

"She's at home." She glanced at her cell. "No text, either, to tell me she's found them." She crushed out her cigarette against the sidewalk. "Let me in, please, before I have a nervous breakdown."

Jacky turned her key in the lock. "You've got to see your doctor about getting on some hormones. This whole healthy, natural approach to menopause isn't working." She pushed open the door.

"What the hell do you know about hormones?" she snapped, then high-tailed to the front desk.

Once inside, Jacky glanced at the empty training floor, then to Marie who perched herself on a stool behind the front desk. Her angled, thick black reading glasses slipped down the bridge of her nose, exposing an arched eyebrow. "I'm sorry," she said, lifting to meet Jacky's gaze. "My God, I'll end up on the sidewalk with a flat pillow if I don't fix this rage." She tore off her glasses and tossed them on the desk. "Poor Hazel. I treated her terribly. She's probably flipping over furniture and crying."

"I'm thinking an expensive dinner is necessary."

"Speaking of dinner." Marie eased backwards on the stool. "Your daughter and Ashley sure ate us out of the house last night when we returned from our trip to Gettysburg. They eat like a couple of truck drivers. We ran out of burgers. They each ate two."

She never ate like that with Jacky. The familiar ball of jealousy lodged itself in her throat. "Well, you wanted to go on a trip. You've got to pay up. Apparently they take payment with burgers. You'll be wiser for it next time."

"Okay, I'll ignore your sarcasm for now. But hey," she said, pointing her glasses at her. "Sophie told us about the beekeeper."

Jacky's heart pounded. "What did she say?"

"That you set up another private house call this morning."

"Her dog is nowhere near ready to confront our open training floor."

Marie ogled her flushed face.

She managed a swallow. She hadn't struggled to draw a breath like that since the days she used to pace her living room floor waiting on a first date to arrive. The clammy hands, the scratchy throat, the inability to draw even breaths into her dry mouth.

"You were captivated, weren't you?"

"Sophie was captivated." Jacky marched over to a red ball laying in the middle of the training floor and picked it up. She massaged its supple surface, securing her into an undeniable moment of weakness where everything she viewed and touched reminded her of Brooke's soft allure.

"You're full of baloney."

"I'm telling you, Sophie's the one who's captivated. She's even giving up cheerleading to become a beekeeper." Jacky tossed the ball into the bin, missing it altogether.

"You blotched up, didn't you?"

"Did Sophie say that?" If Sophie had noticed, then Brooke must have too. A resurgence of prickly heat rose on her cheeks, supplying her with too much buzz. She didn't deserve the buzz. "It was hot outside. Of course I blotched."

"It's April, dear. Don't blame this on the heat."

"Drop it please. Nothing is happening with Brooke. I told you already, I'm not there, yet."

"Yeah, I know. The guilt. I get it. But, you've got to let go of it before it chokes the living shit out of you. It will. Believe me. I'm only going to say this once, and we're going to drop it." She paused, then, "I've seen it with Hazel firsthand. Her husband's been dead for twenty years, and she's still afraid to show her kids she's moved on, as if she's done some evil thing by living the rest of her life. You think her husband would've cared about how his kids viewed him? That asshole still has his grimy little paws in her life, and consequently mine too. Guilt affects everyone."

Jacky's jaw dropped.

Marie bowed her head and examined a spreadsheet.

Jacky respected Marie's desire for privacy by keeping quiet. She picked up the red ball again and tossed it in the bin, and in a blink the strong undercurrent of a giddy rush charged in when she realized she'd be seeing Brooke in less than half an hour.

"Do you know anything about this charge from New Way Supplies for eighty-three dollars?" Marie asked.

Jacky poked around the bin looking for deflated balls on a mission to renounce the sudden and inexplicable sensual cravings that were hijacking her better senses. "Not a clue."

"A training harness ring a bell?"

Jacky straightened up. "That would be for Bee." She wanted to surprise Brooke with it, but she had already purchased one herself.

Marie took off her glasses. She opened her mouth, then paused, squeezing a plastic water bottle in her hand.

Jacky's cell vibrated. She glanced down and received a message from Brooke. "You'd be proud of me. I not only managed to not burn our scones, but I also braved the front porch, electricity men and all, and managed to help Bee not whip herself into a frenzy. My girl is an angel. Either that or you are the angel for teaching her some manners. I'm going to owe you big time for this, aren't I? Hugs."

Drenched in tantalizing emotions, Jacky braced against Marie's wry grin.

"Your face just turned blotchy."

They stood face to face waging each other to swing or withdraw.

"I'm being ridiculous, I know." Jacky pressed her lips together and lowered her eyebrows. "I'm completely out of my element here."

Marie nodded in agreement.

"My heart won't stop racing. I don't like being out of control."

Marie gulped down a mouthful of water. She walked over to Jacky and placed a hand on her upper arm. "You've got choices. You can choose not to continue as Bee's trainer."

"Bee needs me. She's headstrong and capable of taking the lead and dragging a person around like a ragdoll, defenseless against her strength. She has the power to take off like a misfired bullet and seize hold of an unintended target, rendering it helpless and tagging it as a victim to her power."

"She's got some power, for sure." Marie's voice changed to a more serious tone, and a gentle understanding blanketed the creases near her eyes.

"That kind of power is dangerous and shouldn't be left to wander to those who have no business tangling up in it."

"Of course not."

"Power like that needs to be nudged away from the direct line of fire so it doesn't gather the strength to turn into something too explosive. I, as the trainer, should know how to do this, surely as I know how to tie my shoes and how to place food on my tongue. Yet, I stand before you, an innocent to this battle, and tell you that I don't have a clue how to defend against such a beast. That makes me feel guilty as hell, too. How can one remain calm and assertive when faced with such a firestorm?"

"Go on. Monologues can be quite helpful."

"She needs to be redirected. She can't be allowed to pull that leash in whatever direction she desires because the results are never good when that happens. Someone always ends up tripping and falling, smacking into the unforgiving concrete. No amount of scrapes, cuts and bruises are worth that risk for just a romp through the wild and unexplored forests that encircle the tried and true grounds. I can't afford to screw anything else up in life when I still have so much to make right."

"Stop using that adorable beast as a moral indicator in your inner search for peace."

Jacky stood up tall and gathered her nerves. "I hate this."

"I love it." Marie pushed her toward the door. "Now go out there, do what you're born to do, and have fun."

"I'll make copies of my set of keys and bring them by later on."

"Don't bother. Hazel will find them. These kinds of misunderstandings are temporary with her."

"Misunderstandings?"

"Just go." Marie waved her off.

~ ~

Jacky landed in the front seat of her car breathless and flushed. She drove straight to Brooke's gulping for air, remembering her promise to bring coffee only after she passed the electric truck and pulled into the long driveway.

She drove past the grandparent's house and up to Brooke's adorable carriage home.

Suddenly, Brooke appeared on the front porch with a crazed Bee leaping and barking and twisting into a mess. Brooke's delicate silhouette warmed the brisk morning with its penetrable glow, showering refreshing droplets of nourishing dew upon Jacky's erratic heart.

An intoxicating rush assaulted Jacky's usual sense of control. The flush rising on her face overpowered her, taking her prisoner into a tall and churning wave. She

climbed out of her car and strode over to the duo, attempting to outrun the force of the rush and save herself from drowning in its tumultuous push and pull on her senses.

Bee lunged forward, and slobber sprayed every which way.

What a beautiful sight. "I see I'm still needed here."

Brooke struggled with the leash until finally she just let go of it and let Bee have her way with Jacky's leg. "She's looking for the coffee."

Jacky corrected Bee by waving her finger and reclaiming the leader vibe. Bee halted to a sit position. Jacky glanced down at Bee's expectant eyes and couldn't help but laugh. "You have no idea how to be a beast, and we both know it."

Bee leaped to all fours and moved in for cuddles and kisses.

With Bee's head in her hands, Jacky looked up at Brooke. "She's not going to find any coffee here. I drove right past the coffee shop without notice. I worried about being late."

"Well, that's great because now I have a little wiggle room for the next time I'm running behind." Suddenly Brooke's cell rang. She fished for it in her front pocket. "Oh please. I swear. These people are crazy." She shook her head and put the phone back in her pocket.

"Honey crazed loonies?"

Brooke's cell rang again. She sighed. "I'm sorry. Let me shut this off." She fumbled with a button.

"Another swarm emergency?"

Brooke laughed. "You could say that. Of course this one doesn't involve honeybees, just an over-zealous person trying to set up a date."

She wondered what type appealed to her. Tall, short? Dark or blonde hair? Athletic or book nerd? "Hmm. Is he handsome at least?"

Brooke met Jacky's stare. "I've only seen a picture from the online dating site. *She's* handsome in a feminine way, sure, but not my type."

A woman.

She dated women!

Okay, calm the fuck down.

Her phone buzzed a new voicemail.

"She's an eager one," Jacky said.

"It would seem." Brooke placed her phone in her back pocket. "Where were we?"

Jacky eyed Bee. "We were about to embark on a great opportunity."

Brooke clasped her hands behind her back and swung side to side. "Sounds so intriguing when you say it like that."

Jacky grazed the full length of Brooke's long legs, seductively entombed in a pair of leggings that complimented her toned curves, then landed back on her playful stare. "Well it should. What's opportunity without intrigue?" Her voice sounded too eager. She needed to chill out before her heart leaped out of her chest and exposed her for who she really was in that moment – a deprived woman suddenly yearning for human touch.

Marie, in all her stocky and robust build, would be doing leaps and clicking her heels together in joy if she could peek inside her mind and see the carnival of thoughts.

"Well don't keep me waiting then. I may not survive the suspense." Brooke brought her hands to her chest and looked up at the canopy of trees, feigning the agony of uncertainty.

"Your momma is silly," she whispered to Bee.

Brooke kept her head lifted to the trees. In the morning sunlight, her face looked more freckled. She had a beautiful smile, friendly, warm and genuine, and it brought out the faint laugh lines lining her jaw. Those lines, lucky as they were, sat front row to the things that brought this curious woman happiness, escorting her through life's magical moments.

Brooke lowered her gaze to Jacky.

Embarrassed at being caught staring, Jacky tore away. She settled on Bee's well-behaved mug, instead. She could feel Brooke's eyes upon her, and that sent her body into a clumsy spiral. In those few moments, an intense rush of giddiness and pleasure swam in her. Jacky widened her grin as the seconds passed between words.

Jacky liked Brooke. She liked being in her presence. She had a calm, yet stoic vibe that comforted her.

"Shall we get started?" Brooke asked.

Jacky stood, attempting to calm her heart and act more like a credible trainer than a lovesick puppy with too many endorphins flooding her system.

~ ~

On Tuesday morning, Jacky awoke to a body full of flutters. She stretched and turned over on her side, remembering her seductive dream as if she just walked out its door. She buried her head, willing herself to climb back into that slumber where everything touched her with tender, intoxicating strokes.

She grasped a handful of the pink, velour blanket and snuggled up to it, imagining Brooke in her arms. Brooke's delicate pink lips and infectious twinkling eyes played out in Jacky's mind, arousing a flush that burned from deep inside.

In her dream Brooke kept gazing at her with those bold caramel-colored windows to her soul, daring her to come closer and abandon her inhibitions. Her pull capsized Jacky's ill attempt at staying a safe distance. Jacky broke free of all restraints, opening herself up to the free-falling thrill of the moment.

They danced under a starlit sky to the slow and steady rhythm of a romantic waltz, cheeks brushing and emotions flowing. In her arms, Jacky found solace and entered into Brooke's enticing sanctuary where nothing else mattered but the caress of another's skin against her own as they shared a small pocket of unadulterated air.

Mesmerized, and with millions of stars as their witnesses, Jacky met Brooke's breath and together they became one. Arm in arm, they swept across the earthen pathway, indulging in every flower's scent and every cricket's chirp, satisfied only by the other's presence and thrill of knowing they'd yet to even enjoy the rush of brushing against the other's lips.

Jacky moaned under her blankets, tormented by the reality that faced her outside the haven of her dream. She could never feel that alive in real life ever again. How could one be granted that kind of grace twice in a lifetime?

Chapter Nine

Free time didn't exist when you owned a small business. When Jacky first quit her job as an assistant director in the human resources department of Park Square Credit Union and began her entrepreneurial adventure at the Inner Circle School and Daycare, she envisioned long stretches of hours just for her and her family.

She planned to wake up without an alarm clock, go for a run, cook a gourmet breakfast, schedule a few appointments, take a nap, schedule a few more afternoon appointments, and be home to cook a healthy dinner. Then, she and her family would sit around the table and discuss life while they shared laughs. She'd end the evening with a good book and retire by ten o'clock. Life would be like a vacation, doing what she wanted when she wanted, answering to no one but herself.

Yeah right.

A day off would've been a gift, let alone several free hours.

Bills came in. They needed to be paid. If a client called and needed help, she couldn't refuse. They'd call another dog trainer if she couldn't get them in. So, when clients called, she booked them when they wanted, where they wanted.

Saturdays to a dog trainer were like Monday through Fridays to a bank teller. People were off work and expected her to be free. They came to her with problems like excessive barking, pacing the yard, digging holes, lunging at strangers, snapping at children, you name it.

When Sophie told her about starting at Brooke's apiary on Saturday and how she'd need to drop her off by ten and pick her up by four, Jacky cleared her morning and late afternoon schedule to be available. She would forfeit new clients if it meant half a chance at bonding with Sophie over those twenty minute rides to the apiary.

When she dropped her off that morning, Sophie leaped out of the car in a flash. "Tell Brooke I said hello."

Sophie waved and dashed. She walked halfway up the driveway before even Bee realized she should've been barking.

The rest of the day dragged, despite having a mix of challenges from aggressive dogs. Typically she loved such days, but she couldn't get her mind past the idea that in a few short hours, she'd see Brooke again.

At four o'clock sharp, she arrived to pick up Sophie.

She spotted Elise balancing a tray of glasses and walking toward the greenhouse. Bee, of course, guarded the front window. Jacky pointed her finger at her as she passed by, and she stopped barking. *Good girl.*

Jacky waved to the group as she approached. Sophie and Brooke were removing their netted helmets and Tom wrestled with pulling a leg out of his jumper. He wore a sweatband and patted his shiny, bald head with it.

As Elise brushed past him, heading for the workbench that housed a stray hive box, he stumbled over his jumper and bumped into her. She saved the drinks. "Honest to goodness, Tom."

He shrugged. "It's these new sneakers you bought me. They don't fit right."

"Well you should have come with me to buy them yourself."

Brooke cleared her throat, and they stopped squabbling.

"I figured you might need some water," Elise said.

Sophie took one and emptied it in a long gulp.

"Good lord child," Elise said. "You're dehydrated."

Sophie's whole face lit up.

What a gift.

"How was your first official day," Tom asked her, taking a glass for himself and pouring it over his head.

Elise shot him a look.

"What? I'm hot."

Elise scowled and turned to Jacky. "Men!"

108

Tom eased himself down on a nearby bench. "So, it's always customary on a first day to invite the new employee out to eat at Sprago's." Tom looked at Sophie. "Do you know Sprago's?"

Sophie shook her head no.

"It's this cute Italian restaurant." Elise leaned forward and whispered, "They've got the best baked ziti ever." She looked at Jacky. "Would an early dinner work for you both?"

"It sure would," Sophie asserted.

"I guess it will," Jacky said, then shared a private smile with Brooke.

~ ~

An hour later, they sat at a round table with a white starched tablecloth and a single red carnation in a vase in the center. The waiter had placed a basket of bread in the center of the table, then began pouring water into everyone's glass. Sophie reached for the warm buns, then turned to Elise and offered her the basket first. "Bun?"

Elise's eyes gleamed. "Oh my! Aren't you a polite one?" She reached for a golden bun and handed the basket back to Sophie. "You're next, then pass it to your mother. Mr. Hastings can wait."

The couple reminded Jacky of how she and Drew would fight about ordinary things like spilled water and eating too fast. She used to walk out of the room when Drew would chew potato chips because she couldn't stand the ferocious crunching. When Drew would snore after drinking too much wine, Jacky would contemplate the vulgarity in pinching her nose to wake her up. Those little things meant so much to her now that she couldn't complain about them anymore. One day, Elise would contemplate the necessity of all those times she wanted to pinch Tom's nose or toss his potato chips down the drain and she'd probably land herself in a sorrowful cry over the railing of her porch.

Life was cruel like that.

Jacky gazed at the red carnation and fell silent on its petals as she listened to Sophie ask the patient couple a gazillion questions about bee colony collapse. Whenever they'd answer, she'd sit up tall, getting right up in their faces, and absorb their words like a brittle blade of grass needing rain. Their animated answers provided Sophie with the kind of moisture that grew fields of tall, healthy flowers and forests of trees. Each word acted as nourishment, bringing Sophie back to the sort of life Jacky only remembered pre-accident days.

Tom and Elise fed a part of her soul that had been decaying from lack of nutrition, a nutrition she refused from Jacky time and again.

When Brooke jumped into their conversation on Russian versus Italian bees, Sophie's entire being lifted. Even the wispy hair around her face bounced.

"The Italian bees are little piggy poos," Elise explained. "They eat all their honey during the winter and forget they're supposed to keep a surplus to get them through to spring."

"That's adorable," Sophie said.

"Those Russians, they are the best housekeepers," Elise continued. "They're immaculate, which helps against disease."

Tom buttered another bun. "They're amazing little creatures."

Sophie also took another bun, and chomped into it without butter. "I love working with bees. I'm going to help save them. You watch."

Her daughter transformed, blossoming into a new bold, vibrant version of herself.

Jacky relaxed against the comfort of Sophie's beautiful attitude for the remainder of the delicious dinner with all its tangy tomato and garlic flavors. They ate homemade pasta, stuffed mushrooms with spinach and ricotta cheese, and sipped red wine as they indulged on grapes for dessert. Drunk on the tasty food and lively conversation, Jacky gazed at the group and enjoyed the comfortable pull on her heart.

Later, when they returned to Brooke's home and belted into the front seat of her car, Jacky let out a relieved sigh. "We needed that, don't you think?"

Sophie stared out the passenger window and offered her usual response, an ambivalent shrug.

Jacky would've dug further had Elise, Tom and Brooke not been waiting for them to back out of the driveway so they could wave goodbye. Biting her tongue, she turned the key.

The engine wouldn't turn over.

She tried again.

It sputtered and refused to catch.

"Did you leave the lights on?" Sophie asked with a trace of genuine concern.

Jacky fiddled with the lights. "No. It's not the battery."

Sophie scratched her forehead as though embarrassed of Jacky in front of her new friends.

Jacky opened her window. "Bad news. The car is dead."

Brooke leaped forward. "Oh no." She looked to the star-filled sky, pausing. A moment later, she glanced back at Jacky. "Do you want a lift home and just deal with this in the morning when it's light outside."

Sophie already broke out of the door before Jacky could suggest calling a cab.

~ ~

When Brooke pulled up into Jacky and Sophie's driveway, the home appeared just as she imagined – quaint, subtle and understated. The Cape Code style home sat tucked into a suburban cul-de-sac. The mailbox replicated the bluebell siding and brown trim of the house. A golden light illuminated the front living room, and Brooke spotted a cute dog, likely a cocker spaniel and retriever mix, in the front window.

"That's Rosy," Jacky said, fingering the door handle.

Brooke gazed in the window and glimpsed a blue and tan plaid couch, draping the home in a country, cozy look. Rosy's head bounced side to side, blocking Brooke from seeing into the house any further. "She's a cutie."

"You should come in and meet her," Sophie scooted up in her seat.

"I've got delicious green tea, if you're interested?" Jacky offered.

"I've never met a green tea I didn't like."

111

Sophie opened her door and leaped out. "Green tea it is."

She and Jacky followed suit.

As Brooke took her first step into their home, the smell of pumpkin spice danced on the edge of the warm lighting, wrapping her in a sense of home and hearth. Brooke admired her decorating taste and talent. Whenever she attempted to decorate her house to look like one of those IKEA showcases with the practical, yet sophisticated vibe, she always ended up mismatching the wall hangings with the furniture and lamps. A room filled with second-hand clutter resulted.

Rosy curled up around her feet, tossing herself on the floor and exposing her wavy-haired belly. Brooke lowered to her knees and rubbed her. "My God, I'm in love." Rosy squirmed and snorted like a baby pig, soaking up every stroke Brooke offered.

"Looks like she is too." Sophie giggled, taking her jean jacket off and tossing it on the recliner.

"Well, while you and Rosy get to know each other, I'm going to get the tea brewing." Jacky walked toward the kitchen. "Make yourself at home."

"I'll make the tea," Sophie said. "You two can sit and chat."

Jacky stopped short, eyeing Sophie with a cautious twist.

"Seriously, go, sit and talk. I'll make the tea." Sophie waved Jacky toward Brooke and Rosy.

Jacky surrendered. "I'll just be a moment," she said to Brooke. "I have to go use the little girl's room."

Brooke nodded and returned her attention back to Rosy.

Alone in their living room, Brooke glanced around trying to decide, aside from the lighting and good furniture, what else bathed the room in that homey feeling. She couldn't put her finger on it. Was it the pumpkin? The burnt orange and sienna blue area rug? The great big floor plant? Or maybe all the happy family pictures covering most every flat surface in the room? A beautiful portrait of a blonde woman staring out across a field with mountains in the backdrop warmed up the space above the Ben Franklin style fireplace. The woman's face glowed in peace, the kind one only feels when everything balanced out in life. Brooke surmised her to be Jacky's wife, and she also guessed from her glow that they had a beautiful marriage.

Jacky entered again, swiping her hands together as if cold despite the warmth of the room. She motioned for Brooke to join her on the couch. "Don't worry, Rosy will follow. She won't let you get away with just a one minute rub."

Brooke cradled Rosy's cute face between her hands and touched noses. "I'll pet you all night long. Don't you worry." Brooke realized how wrong that just sounded. "Well, I mean for at least the next few minutes while I sip tea with your mum."

Jacky sat down and rubbed her eyes.

"You're tired." Brooke walked over to the couch. "Of course, my God, you've been working all day and then we dragged you out to dinner. You must be exhausted."

Jacky eased back against the couch. "I'm just relaxed, not tired." She stifled the early warning of a yawn.

Brooke selected a spot on the couch, a comfortable distance from Jacky. "I'll drink my tea and be on my way so you can get some sleep."

An awkward stillness drifted between them as they jockeyed for a comfortable position. Jacky landed her gaze on her. "I had a wonderful time at dinner."

"Me too." Brooke hugged herself, securing her light spring sweater across her chest.

"Sophie did too," Jacky whispered, looking over her shoulder toward the kitchen.

She watched as Sophie opened the lid to a bottle of honey, then dipped a spoon into it. She stirred the honey into teacups with a smile on her face.

"She's a delightful girl."

Jacky turned back to face Brooke. "She likes you, a lot."

"Sophie strikes me as the type who likes everyone. A lot." Brooke stretched out the words.

"This job is just what she needs."

"She enjoys the bees. Actually she adores them. I could sense instant love between them."

"It's the first time she's taken an interest in something new since her mother passed."

Brooke hugged herself tighter. "If she lets them, the bees will teach her a lot about life."

"I hope so because I can't break through to her." Jacky twisted her mouth and avoided Brooke's stare.

Brooke saw a scared woman unsure about her ability to nurture and mold the curious and naïve daughter who depended on her.

"She's going to be alright," Brooke reassured in a whisper.

"I hope so," Jacky murmured back as Sophie entered the room carrying two steaming mugs on a tray.

"Where's yours?" Brooke asked.

She placed the tray down on the wooden coffee table. "I've got ideas and feelings to put down on paper from today's time with the bees." She swiped her hands on her jeans. "No time for tea. You two enjoy." She swept toward the staircase. "I'll see you next weekend!"

They watched her jolt up the stairs, and Rosy clumsily following.

A moment later, they sat in silence.

"You know, we used to get along so well." Jacky's lips cradled the edge of her mug. "She'd fill the dining room with her voice, sometimes never letting me or Drew sneak a word in. She had so much energy, always animated and full of stories. She'd have fascinating ones, and when she'd talk her eyes would get big and bright. She'd speak with her hands and forget to eat dinner. I'd have to tap her plate to remind her to scoop a mouthful of mashed potatoes in between her sentences."

She paused for a brief moment, and Brooke saw the bittersweet longing the loss created.

Jacky collected herself and continued. "She always talked so candidly. She even told us about her first kiss with a guy named Billy. She beamed with pride because he was the hottest guy in school." Jacky laughed at the memory. "He surprised Sophie one day by walking up to her and asking her if she wanted to go on a walk. They

114

kissed on a park bench near a smelly pond. She couldn't picture his face after that without remembering that smell."

Brooke giggled.

"I miss those times."

"She'll come around, if you keep supporting her as you do."

"I just want to get back to our talks and laughter. I'm just not sure how."

"If she hangs around the bees long enough, maybe they'll rub off on her. They're excellent communicators. The masters of dialogue and constructive debate."

Jacky beamed. "Oh really?"

Ah, she blooms. "Yup. They're intense communicators."

"How so?"

"They excel at exchanging information. No secrets. No lies."

"Oh come on. No one can be that angelic."

"They're truly selfless. Everything they do, they do for the hive. They trust each other completely. Trust is all they know. They have no idea how to withhold information from each other. That's what keeps them alive and healthy, that intimate trust, honesty, and connectivity. Without it, they'd die."

"Die from a lie?"

"Their entire survival depends on their ability to discern and dispel information in a timely, and more importantly, accurate means."

"How exactly do they do this?"

"They dance."

Jacky's eyes twinkled. "Fascinating."

"They dance, sometimes competitively, to get their point across." Brooke tapped her fingers along the edge of the couch. "The more vibrations and intensity in the dance, the more the hive pays attention to them over another bee trying to communicate her field reports."

"A whole different world." Jacky sipped the tea. Her lips trembled around the rim of the mug.

Why did her lips tremble?

Was she uncomfortable to have a woman sitting on her living room couch? Brooke massaged the soft, plaid cloth. She imagined the blonde woman in the picture curled up next to Jacky each night to watch the evening news and play Scrabble, a roaring fire crackling in the background.

Was she questioning the early birth of their potential friendship? How did one know the customary time to form new friendships and get on with life after losing one's soulmate?

Brooke looked around the space some more. Picture after picture of Jacky and the beautiful blonde with piercing green eyes warmed the room. The pictures ranged from wedding portraits to tennis matches, to pool scenes, to ones of the three of them posing with Rosy in front of wooden bridges and waterfalls.

Brooke tiptoed over the idea of asking her about Drew. She wanted to know how she died. Was it tragic? A disease? Did Jacky spend the last two years crying herself to sleep? Did she suffer alone? Did she have someone to talk with about her feelings?

Okay possibly too creepy and forward.

Under the pressure of the questions parading in her mind, she let an innocuous one loose. "You loved your wife a lot, didn't you?"

Jacky looked at a picture of them in front of a sign that read Charlie's Seafood Shack. They wore bright yellow raingear and pointed at each other. *What a beautiful family.*

"I sure did. I mean, I still do. So much." A taint of ache shadowed her face.

"I can tell. Just the way you stare at the pictures tells me you adored her."

"I truly did."

"That's so beautiful and rare." Brooke lifted her mug to sip. The scent of mango green tea drifted in as she inhaled. She wondered if someone would ever love her the way this woman loved her wife. "Tell me about her." Brooke pulled her feet in under her. "Tell me something fun and quirky."

Jacky's face lightened. "Oh she had plenty of quirky habits. I could go on for hours."

Seeing the happy upturn to her cheeks, Brooke urged her to keep the momentum. "Choose one."

Jacky picked up a coaster and twirled it. She leaned her head back and stared up at the ceiling as she talked. "She had this habit of breaking into hysterical laughter at something that happened months before, and the more she tried to explain her laughter, the more she couldn't stop."

Jacky lowered her head. "She'd turn this bright shade of fire engine red." She chuckled, bringing her hand up to under her chin. "A few times I'd worry she'd never pull through the fits of laughter. Then, she'd come to an amazing stop, like someone pulled the cork on it and it ran out. A few cackles would release like an engine sputtering. Then, she'd try to explain the laughter again, and she'd fire into another laughing rage." She laughed and placed her hands in her lap, still fingering the coaster between her fingers. "She was a nut."

"Tell me another."

Jacky lingered on her gaze, sending a warm rush through Brooke.

"She used to do this thing every night before bed where she'd tuck herself into the sheets out of fear that something would come up and grab her in the middle of the night. It was adorable. And of course, I got to shine as a result because I'd let her fall asleep first. She could relax, which opened up some wiggle room between the sheets."

"Wiggle room." Brooke glanced down at her tea, suddenly overcome with a sense of shyness. "That's good. Wiggle room is always a good thing."

She could feel Jacky's gaze and the heat rise on her face.

Jacky tossed the coaster at Brooke's folded legs.

Brooke picked up the coaster and dragged her finger around its smooth edge, enjoying the friendly tease.

They sat in comfortable quietness for a few moments longer, then Jacky offered more. "Drew loved attention. She knew how to embrace it."

"How so?"

Jacky's face softened into a reflective stretch. "She would've loved the attention her car accident brought her with all the people flooding into that funeral home to pay

117

their respects. She would've taken it all in, watching as people shared stories about her in those intimate corners of the parlor where tissue boxes hid."

Car accident.

Brooke inhaled, bracing for a serious talk.

"She would've ripped a few of the eulogies apart, though." She shrugged and bowed her head, clenching her jaw. Her hand trembled as she lifted her mug to her lips again, but they trembled too much. Without taking a sip, she placed it back down again. "Have you ever had anyone close to you die in a tragic accident?"

"No," Brooke whispered, suddenly feeling inadequate to be the sounding board for such an important and personal conversation. She felt like an intruder eavesdropping, as if she'd happened upon two people at the water cooler and she had nowhere else to go except the spot she occupied. The most devastating life event she experienced was when her parents moved to New York City in her freshman year of college.

"I can't imagine what you went through."

"Death is one of life's most known facts. Yet, it's hard to accept. Even now, over two years later, I have a hard time swallowing it."

"I'm glad you and Sophie had each other through it all."

"Hmm." Jacky looked away toward the front window. "We had a lot of support from friends. We ate more casseroles in the first month than most people eat in eighty years." She laughed to herself. "And the cards. My God, every day a dozen or so of them would arrive. Then one day," she paused, "they just stopped. All of it stopped, the casseroles, the cards, the check-in calls and emails from friends just stopped. Everyone got back to normal life."

The room closed in on them, growing too warm.

Brooke didn't know what to say, so she just waited to listen.

"That nudge back to reality hurt me the most. I had to carry on, buy groceries, cook meals, go back to work, drive Sophie to school, take out the garbage, and clean the shower. All those simple, mundane tasks take on a sharp, biting edge in the wake of death."

"I would imagine they do." Brooke cautioned on her inhale, afraid to disturb Jacky's flow.

Jacky shook her head. "I'm sorry. I don't know why I'm saying all of this to you."

Brooke leaned in a little. "It's okay. Sometimes it's easier to talk with someone outside the big picture."

She looked up at her. "You're easy to talk with."

Sometimes shedding pain onto someone unbiased and unrooted simplified telling the truth.

"I'm glad you feel comfortable enough to talk with me about it."

Jacky reflected on the yellow raincoat picture again. Her chin quivered and her cheeks clenched.

"I used to sit on the park bench and get angry when I saw people walking their dogs or pushing their baby strollers. I used to think they were the lucky ones who escaped. They didn't dread leaving that park and heading home to an empty house. They weren't thinking that they had to cook one less potato and chicken leg than usual now that their loved one died. They didn't have to worry about opening up the mailbox each day and finding a statement from a credit card with their deceased loved one's name on it. They didn't have to worry about settling the affairs and masquerading as a parent to a child who didn't want them around anymore than they wanted that dreadful death to slip into their lives and destroy it."

Brooke cupped her hand around Jacky's wrist.

Jacky continued with little pause. "They didn't have to look at Facebook and see an old post pop up with their loved one's picture in it, and contemplate turning off that Facebook account for good. But if they did, they'd worry they'd never have access to the delightful surprise of seeing them captured in a happy moment in time. They still got to worry about things like whether they should cook out on the grill or say fuck it and go eat at McDonald's."

Jacky bit her lip. "When I'd see people jogging on a ninety degree day in the park at the height of sunlight, I wanted to scream at them, *hey you, just splurge and eat an ice-cream cone for God's sakes. Go and eat a cheeseburger and stop fretting about the two pounds you gained last week. Who cares? You're going to die one day anyway. Enjoy yourself. Don't aim for obese, but, lighten up. It's an ice-cream cone, not a deadly disease."*

Brooke placed her mug down. She studied the pain etched on Jacky's forehead as she unloaded feelings she'd probably kept hidden even from herself all that time.

"I can't imagine how hard it must have been to lose her." Brooke shifted her weight forward.

Jacky blew out a sharp breath. "I've never experienced anything more difficult." She pointed her eyes at Brooke. "I have moments where I get angry with her for dying on me. How silly is that, right?"

"I'm pretty sure it's a normal reaction."

"We were supposed to have a long life together. We had so many plans. We were going to take cooking lessons in Italy, learn to sail, and travel to South America and hire a guide to take us through the Amazon jungle. There were so many things that we wanted to do and now we can't."

She swallowed hard. "She broke my heart when she died."

Tears began to roll down her cheek as the sadness pooled. "I'm sorry to be getting so emotional like this." She shook her head. "I'm so sorry." Jacky swiped the tears as they fell, flinging them from her face.

Brooke cupped her hand around Jacky's wrist again, taking on her pain. "Don't say you're sorry. Don't ever say you're sorry about loving your wife as much as you do."

Jacky stared at Brooke's hand around her arm. A trace of something peaceful rested on the softness of her cheeks. Finally, she looked back up at her. "Thank you for saying that."

Brooke squeezed her wrist for reassurance, and Jacky's face relaxed even more.

Brooke let her hand slip from Jacky's wrist. They sat in comfortable quiet, sipping their tea.

"Uno?" Jacky asked, breaking the silence after a while.

"Uno?"

Jacky bent forward and grabbed the game Uno from the bottom shelf of her coffee table. "Want to play?" She held the card game box up to her face and offered a cheeky smile.

Grateful for the refreshing segue, she reached for the box. "I haven't played this game in forever."

Jacky opened the box, and they happily dove into the lighthearted journey of matching colors and numbers. Brooke enjoyed watching Jacky relax. Her eyes took on an even lighter shade of blue when she smiled.

They played a full round, and Brooke won. Of course, she delighted in her victory over Jacky with a few fist pumps and a quick jump to her feet to break into a happy dance.

Jacky eased back, folding her arms over her chest. "What would you be like at a casino?"

Brooke laughed and plopped back onto the couch, breathless. "A total fool, that's what."

Their eyes met, and they hung onto a gaze. Brooke tucked her knees underneath her.

"Can I tell you a secret?" Jacky whispered.

Brooke nodded.

An earnest playfulness spread across her face. "You irritated me when I first met you."

"Oh really?" Brooke swung her legs out from underneath her. "Tell me how you really feel."

"Well, hold on." Jacky played with a sardonic grin. "You didn't let me finish."

"You don't have to. I already know you are the queen of timely quirkiness."

"Well, you were very late."

"Ten minutes." Brooke stood her ground on a tease.

"Fifteen minutes, thirty-two seconds."

"You are so rigid." Brooke nudged her.

"I have a bit of a thing about time."

"A bit?"

"Something I may need to work on," Jacky took a deep, restorative breath.

"May?"

Jacky sat up and bumped Brooke's shoulder. "Okay, more like definitely."

Brooke picked up her mug and sipped some more. "Spend some time with the bees and you'll learn to look at time in a totally different way."

Finally, Jacky indulged in a long sip of her tea too. "How so?"

"I can't explain. You'll have to have that experience for yourself."

"I may just do that, then."

Oh, please do. "Good. I may just enjoy that."

"May?" Jacky's warmth pulled at her.

"Okay, I definitely will enjoy that."

They exchanged a look that gripped Brooke's heart.

"So," Jacky began, "in the spirit of keeping things balanced, you now have to tell me something about yourself so when you walk out of here tonight I don't feel like I'm tipping over. I need balance. I need a quirky habit here."

Brooke loved the shift to humor. It suited Jacky, for sure. "Okay." She searched her brain for something quirky and interesting. Jacky already knew she loved bees, lived in her grandparent's carriage house, and had dark curly, crazy hair. What more could she say?

"Tell me about this clingy date you were trying to ditch the other day."

"Janet?"

Jacky dipped her head. "Janet. Yes. Tell me about Janet. Not your style?"

"I have no idea if she is. I haven't met her yet. I can tell by her profile that she's looking for a soulmate."

"A profile?" Jacky twisted into a crooked smile. "So she's looking for her soulmate on an online dating site?"

"Yeah."

"Like she's shopping on EBay?"

Brooke rolled her eyes. "Exactly."

"Kind of takes the romance out of it."

"I haven't had much luck with it."

Laughter filled Jacky's spirit. "The dating scene. No thank you."

"The dating scene," Brooke repeated. "The land filled of crazies and the desperate ones looking in all the wrong places for all the wrong people. At least that's how it feels. I just want dinners at fancy restaurants, the ones where they serve balls of sorbet in between dinner courses to clear the palette, followed by a night of dancing at some dark and sexy nightclub."

"Of course." Jacky played out a serious expression.

"Wine and dine, and then say goodbye."

"So why the apprehension of getting serious?" Jacky asked.

"Oh, going right for the personal jugular!" Brooke playfully kicked Jacky's leg and Jacky grabbed it.

"Tell me and you might get your foot back."

"Well, alright then." Brooke cocked her head to the side. How should she answer that question without looking like a loser for having a girlfriend walk out on her? "I'm taking a nice long break from relationships. I was stuck in one for quite a while with someone who changed over time and withdrew."

"Withdrew?"

"Yes, withdrew."

"You make it sound like a bank transaction where she walked up to the teller window and demanded her cups, plates and furniture, leaving a zero balance before she skipped town and deposited herself in someone else's life."

"You have quite a way with words, don't you?"

"I do," Jacky said, straight-faced.

Brooke laughed from somewhere deep inside.

"Seriously, so did she hurt you?"

"She had the opposite effect on me when she left. She freed me. The weight of the world crumbled off my shoulders and I could finally move with a suppleness I didn't know existed. I breathed without struggle. I woke up with hope in my heart. I kind of like that feeling right now."

Jacky studied her. "So why date?"

"Wine and dine."

"Yes, wine and dine." Jacky released her foot. "I relinquish control."

Brooke bowed her head. "Why thank you ma lady."

They broke out into a series of hiccupped giggles.

In a matter of moments, the solemnness dissipated from the room, allowing the warmth of their budding friendship to ease in and take over.

~ ~

Sophie sat on her bed, hearing giggles from Jacky and Brooke in the living room downstairs.

It had been a long time since she heard Jacky giggle.

Sophie picked up a picture of her mother on her bedside table. She had only then, in that moment – an entire ten hours after waking – thought of her mom. Guilt stabbed at her.

For the first time since her death, Sophie did what she said she'd never do, she traveled through the whole day without once pausing to consider her mother.

She clutched the memory bead around her neck. "I'm sorry Mom. I didn't mean it." She buried her head in her hands, willing a good cry.

No tears came.

Sophie searched her mind for a clear picture of her mother, but no matter how hard she squeezed her eyes shut, she couldn't see her mother's face. She couldn't remember what her mother looked like. She opened her eyes and stared at the picture of her swinging a bat at Cold State Park. She searched the laughter on her face for signs of her mother, the mother she remembered as her confidant, her lucky charm, and her co-joker when it came to messing with Jacky's Type A personality. Together they could be a menace, always trailing one step behind Jacky to tinker with a pillow she had just fluffed or to toss one of Rosy's toys on the floor after she just tidied up the living room.

Sophie couldn't picture her face anymore. She couldn't smell her fruity shampoo. She couldn't hear the high-pitched laugh she'd create when she or Jacky tickled her belly. She couldn't remember what her latest hairstyle looked like. Was it wavy or straight? Was it highlighted or lowlighted with a chestnut hue?

Oh my God! You're gone.

She imagined her mother standing in a bed of clouds, waiting to hear from her, and then falling to her knees and choking on the fog when she never checked in that day.

Sophie rolled over on her side. How could she forget her mother for the entire day?

She lay on her bed, massaging the memory bead – all she had left of her mother in the physical state. She stretched and picked up the picture of her mother and Jacky sharing a pile of crabs on Fourth of July. She traced her finger down her mother's cheek. "I should've checked in today."

Sophie continued to massage the memory bead around her neck. "I wish you were still here. I wish we could snuggle up under our favorite blanket on the couch, the velvet one with white swirls, not that green one you tried to get me to like so much, and watch that Cosmos show. The other day, they talked about universes the size of pinheads on every surface of the Earth. With so many universes, you've got to be in one of them. Maybe this bead is a universe and you're living there."

She undid the necklace and stared at the wisps of white mixed with the sea green glass bead, a touch the artist had derived from her mother's Irish green eyes. Her mother would've admired the handiwork. Ironically, with her wispiness incased in glass, she looked freer than when alive. Her mother always searched for something greater in life. She looked shackled when she'd stare at the television or sit down to a family dinner. She needed plans. She always needed something bigger and better.

In the bead, she danced along the imaginary breezes of a multi-dimensional world. She could shift from one happy movement to another. She could twirl and thrive in her beautiful shiny new world.

Sophie spun the bead. In that world her mother could take many trips and never tire of the same sights twice. The skies would be brighter blue than here on Earth. The clouds would be fluffier, too, and turn every color of the rainbow.

Inside the protective sphere, angels watched over her as she dared to wander and discover its hidden treasures, the beautiful prisms of its inner core; the tiniest of creatures who, too, traveled around in search of awe and enlightenment; the lightness of the air that when breathed in eradicated all disease instantly; and the softness of the gel-like substance that cradled each and every step and height soared.

In that world, her mother reemerged to dance with those who came before her. New friendships, the kind that never faltered, grew and swept her over in a sugary haze of giddiness where she could indulge in treats that swelled beyond the indulgences of Earth. She'd never want for anything because in that world she could have anything she craved. She'd fly around in a halo of pure happiness. The only tears shed were ones produced by the selfless actions of others, filling her being with the ultimate sense of pride and satisfaction. She'd never be lonely in such a magical place.

Sophie returned the picture to her nightstand, reassured, for at least the moment, that maybe, just maybe her mother found joy and just went on a small trip in her new world, soon to return to her heart.

She heard Jacky and Brooke laughing over something again. She missed Jacky's laugh. She used to laugh all the time, and back then, Sophie believed those laughs to be true.

She exhaled and looked up to the ceiling, feeling the pressure of the guilt return. They had both gotten on with their lives that day without her mother. They had laughed, had their breaths taken away, scored new friendships, and even survived despite the fact her mother was still dead and not coming back to share in days like that.

First hanging with honeybees, next getting married and having kids without her there to meet them. Her mother would never get to hear the fascinating things she learned about how bees communicate through dance or how they spend the day foraging and travel back to the hive by nighttime to rest in anticipation of working another day. Her mother would never know the delicious treat of eating honey right off the comb, or how pollen tasted fresh out of the dehydrator.

Did moving on mean she'd forget her mother?

She still couldn't remember the fine details of her mother's face.

She couldn't feel her presence.

A lonely chill filled the room, like someone drilled a hole in the side of the house and let out all the air.

She was alone.

She lay staring at the ceiling, summoning her mother to return to her room and wrap her in the gentleness that always marked the end of each day.

She focused on her breathing, imagining with each inhale, her mother's spirit coming closer, diluting the loneliness that Jacky's laughter created.

When that didn't work, she opened the drawer, the one where she hid her Taylor Swift CD and letter, and closed it a moment later when Jacky laughed again.

She missed her conversations with Jacky as much as with her mother. She wished she could return to the girl before everything happened, the girl who believed Jacky loved her as a daughter. How she wished she could be that innocent girl again, clueless to the cruel reality that no one could be fully trusted. She lived on her own in a big, scary, solitary world.

Sophie kissed her memory bead and hung it back around her neck, praying the temporary comfort of having a part of her mother so close to her heart would last her through the night.

Chapter Ten

Jacky and her mechanic had come to get her car by nine in the morning. The mechanic was a young guy, Brooke guessed early twenties, dressed in overalls and covered in grime. He froze at the sight of Bee's foaming mouth in the front window.

"She's alright," Brooke reassured. "Her trainer is here."

"That's not my doing." Jacky shook her head. "She's not supposed to be in that window," she said to the mechanic.

Brooke couldn't bring herself to block Bee from the window. As long as no one appeared in her viewpoint, which typically no one did because of how far the carriage house sat back from the road, Bee acted calm and collected. She sat there all day long and perked her ears as she watched nature unfold before her. That perch allowed her to witness bunnies playing, squirrels working to gather food, and birds flying high. It offered her access to a rich life. Blocking her from it would shut her out from the joy of everything beautiful and natural in the world.

"There has to be a better way." Brooke folded her arms.

Jacky arched her eyebrow at Brooke, then handed the frightened mechanic the keys. "Just ignore the barks," she said to him. "She's fine."

While they both dipped their heads under the hood and tinkered, Brooke stood in front of the window and pointed a warning every time Bee barked. Of course, she continued to yap.

Even if she wanted to remove Bee from the front window, she'd be unable. When Bee turned into a beast, she quadrupled in strength. Brooke would need the muscle power of ten men to pull her away from her fixation.

For twenty long minutes, she fidgeted under the strain of her dog parenting nightmare, then finally, the engine turned over.

Jacky closed in on her as the mechanic picked up his scattered wrenches and tools. "You've been a very bad student."

Brooke fluttered her eyelashes. "I have. With good cause."

Jacky inched a step closer. "And what would that cause be?"

"She's happy on the perch, for the most part."

Jacky tapped the tip of Brooke's nose. "Lessons are far from over."

Brooke looked up into Jacky's playful eyes. "I'm okay with that."

"Good." She drew an audible breath. "That's very good."

Her breath tickled Brooke's nose. "Yes," Brooke whispered. "That is indeed very good."

"I'll call you later to set up another session."

"Okay," she managed to murmur.

~ ~

Brooke's head still spun as she suited up and walked down to the apiary. She turned her cell phone's ringer up to full volume, then placed it on a dry log.

She walked up to a hive box and removed the lid, peeking inside for an up close and personal look at the progress. She noticed the wax oozing over the top of some of the trays. She removed the wax-filled ones and set them aside, tapping the bees from them so they'd land safely in the other trays that would need attention.

She held up one of the honeycombs and observed her bees. "I flirted with a woman today," she said. "Yes. A real live, in-the-flesh woman, not a virtual date. I found her by natural foraging means. And yes, before you wonder, a true flirt. I even cocked my head the way people do in the movies."

A bee buzzed around her head. It perched itself on the rim of her hat and watched as she flipped over the tray. "I like her. Perhaps too much for my own good."

Standing under the apiary's tallest tree, she closed her eyes and took in the melodic hum of the honeybees' wings. Bee stood by her side. "I enjoy myself when she's around. It's like she's interested in what I have to say. That's new for me."

Bee sniffed her feet, and a bee buzzed around her head. She eyed it, remaining calm and allowing it to inspect her.

Brooke walked over to a second hive, easing open the lid. She removed one of the lighter trays and admired the bees as they worked. Then, her phone rang. She jumped toward the log, then stopped.

No, she warned herself. *Absolutely not. You're not going to get in over your head like this. If it's Jacky, then let it be Jacky. She can leave a message just like every other person who calls my phone. She's just like everyone else, except not an apiary customer or a date. She's your trainer.*

Her heart raced when the pinging continued. Every ounce of her being wanted Jacky to be on the other end of that ping. She inspected the tray again, watching as the bees scurried about doing their work, like good focused members of a well-oiled machine. She focused in on a few bees tending to larvae. "The way she looks at me with those deep and gripping eyes," she said to them, "and the softness of her hands when she grabbed my ankle, oh well let's just say, she intoxicated me. And, gosh, she always smells so good."

The bees remained dutiful, listening as they worked.

"I'm doing it again. I'm talking to you." They continued to work without judgment. "She's not exactly relationship material, at the moment. She's still in love with her wife. To get involved in any other way than friends would be irresponsible on my part. She'd wake up one day and realize she moved too quickly, and that no one would ever compare to her beautiful Drew. Then, I'd end up hurt for sure. I get her circumstance. I do. It's just that I really like her."

Brooke continued collecting wax-laden trays. "You know what? One last word and I'm done talking." She raised up a tray and spoke to a herd of bees in the far corner. "A part of her might be interested in me too. But guilt blocks her. I can tell. I

131

will never tell anyone else what I'm about to say." Brooke paused and leaned in to whisper, "She liked flirting with me too. I think she liked it a lot."

~ ~

The following Saturday, Sophie arrived at the apiary excited to get started on another day of beekeeping and gardening. Elise called her over to the back patio while Brooke got Bee situated with a toy and water.

"I've got a little something for you," she said, sneaking a flash-drive into Sophie's jacket pocket. "It should help with your research."

"What is it?"

"You'll see." Elise's eyes shined.

Brooke came up behind them, and Elise swiped her hands together. "Okay, time for me to go shopping while you two get working."

Joy sprinkled in the air.

"Ready Sophie?"

"Can't wait," Sophie said, catching the edge of a wink from Elise as they turned toward the nursery greenhouse.

They spent the morning exploring the various flowers and plants in the greenhouse. Curiosity filled Sophie. She asked burning question after question with barely a breath in between. Sophie couldn't contain the excitement. Instead of waiting for answers to her questions, she hopped right into telling Brooke about the school project.

"I want to save the bees, and I want everyone else in my class to as well. Most of my friends have no clue the bees are in trouble or how that affects them. I told one kid that without them we won't have all the colorful fruits and veggies that are in the grocery stores. He laughed and said he hated fruits and veggies anyway." She pruned a browned leaf off a bell pepper plant, and used the back of her hand to brush away some loose strands of hair from her face. "I could create a bookmark and list five ideas people can do to save the bees."

"I'd love to help you with that."

Sophie beamed, then continued her garden work.

At one point, Brooke stopped clipping. "You're going to make a fine beekeeper."

~ ~

Once they finished up their work in the greenhouse, they took a break and sipped some lemonade.

Brooke sat on the wide, flat rock near the hummingbird feeder. She patted the spot next to her. "Have a seat."

Sophie sat on command, taking a sip of her drink. She looked out over the field of green, contemplating the world's troubles. "Will the honeybees eventually die out?"

Brooke pulled her knees up to her chest, hugging them. "If we continue to be careless."

"You're not careless, are you?"

"On some level, we're all to blame."

"I don't understand."

"Well, we go to the grocery store and buy apples, lettuce, almonds, and don't contemplate how they grew to be so delicious and beautiful. We just pick them up, buy them, and eat them because that's what we've always done."

"Let me play devil's advocate."

Brooke giggled. "Okay. Let's hear your argument."

"Well, we do need to eat."

"We do. But, for every pesticide-ridden apple I purchase, I'm supporting the decline of bees."

"So, unless you're rich, you can't support saving the bees?"

"I'm not saying that. It's the little things that add up to bigger things. So, if you can't afford organic produce, maybe you can afford a package of wildflower seeds to plant in your yard or a flowerbox on your window."

Sophie considered her rebuttal with a tilt to her chin, absorbing her idea.

"We do what we can and with as much heart as we can. Honeybees are the glue that binds all of us together. They are what's known as a keystone species."

"A keystone species?"

"Yes. It means they have a much larger role in the grand ecosystem than most any other species. Without them, major disturbances would take place. The ripple effect would spread far and wide. The entire system as we know it would destabilize without their presence."

Sophie stared at a hummingbird feeding, sobering over that terror.

In Sophie's world, her mother had been the keystone species. Her mother had stood at the center of her life. Things worked when she took the helm. She kept order where there could've been chaos. She casted light in the dark tunnel of life's mysterious twists and turns. When she died, that light dimmed and everything went dark. Everything died along with her. One thing at a time shriveled – her friendships, her desires to continue school activities, her fun, her laughter, and her hunger for exploring beyond her once happy family home. The ripple effect had cast wide and was just recently slowing down.

"What would happen if the bees died? I mean would we die too?"

"If bees died out, the world would not look, sound, taste, or feel the same. Plants wouldn't be pollinated, at least naturally, and that would result in fewer seeds produced. With fewer seeds produced, fewer plants would bloom the following season. Now, if fewer plants are grown, then the species that rely on those plants for survival would be effected. They'd have less food, and thus begin to die off. Think about all the life out here. The birds, frogs, lizards, insects, squirrels, and raccoons would be in a fight to survive. They'd do what they had to do to get food, even the unthinkable. Those who feed off each other would also lose their food supply. The birds who eat the insects would suffer from the death of the insects. The ripple would continue to spread outward across the entire system all because one major species, the honeybees, disappeared. They are that powerful. They are that necessary. Will we die? Who's to say? If we do live, it'll be in a world without color, variety, and the deliciousness we're used to. That's for sure."

"It's by our need to eat, that we're killing them." Sophie stated. "We're the ones spraying crops and destroying their natural habitat."

"We do tend to mess things up in this world."

"There's a lot of us to feed, though." The helpless reality saddened her.

"More than ever. Of course to feed the population takes a lot of work, and a lot of land."

"The same land the honeybees rely on to eat," Sophie said with a heavy heart. "Your grandfather told me a little about this at Sprago's."

"Farmers get it wrong when they use one-hundred percent of their land to grow those fruits and veggies for us."

"Well, they probably don't want to waste any land because it's expensive."

"They've been educated wrong. They fear they'll waste land if they don't plant on it. It's not true."

"Your grandfather said the same thing."

Sophie enjoyed having intelligent conversations for a change. Ashley only wanted to talk about boys lately. This talk reminded her of the way she and Jacky used to hash out ideas over ice cream sundaes.

"According to Lora Morandin, a woman who conducted a study on wild bees foraging on canola, if farmers left thirty percent of their land uncultivated, they'd have better pollination by the wild honeybees. We'd have more food for us and leave more of a healthy variety of wild flowers for the honeybees. It would be a win-win."

"Then, why aren't they doing it?"

"Because just like anyone else, we get stuck out of fear. They know what they have to do to yield what they need to profit. But, they don't want to gamble on an idea that they've never experienced. They don't trust the new system will work."

"The government should step in and force them if it helps keep honeybees alive."

Brooke sighed. "Yeah, I don't know about that. People aren't fond of governments stepping in to enforce new ways of doing things."

135

"Then they should reward people who do apply these techniques. You know like Jacky does with dogs. She rewards them for good behavior."

"You're full of great ideas."

"I should be president one day," Sophie joked. "I'll be the first beekeeper president."

"You really should be."

Sophie didn't want to get off track. "In your opinion, why are the honeybees dying?"

"Aside from over managing lands, there's also the problem of pesticides. They're toxic to bees. Sometimes bees will die after they've landed on a recently treated flower. Other times the impact is delayed. They return home and either die, or infect the young, immature bees in the hive. Some pesticides target the brain of bees and this turns it into a slow learner and forgetful bee. Many times they can't remember floral scents, and that spells disaster for them."

Anger curled its way up through Sophie's blood. "That's insane."

"They use pesticides to protect the seeds, and when the seed grows, it spreads through the entire plant."

"So the pollen and nectar have it too?"

Brooke nodded.

"Then the bees eat it," Sophie said with even more heaviness.

Brooke nodded. "If only farmers would put aside some land for them. Then the bees would eat off the wild habitat and thus be less exposed." Brooke paused, drawing a dramatic breath. "If people planted more gardens with bee-friendly plants, then bees would have more to forage on, and less pesticides to deal with."

Sophie wanted to go home and plant a bunch of flowers. "What if you don't have room for a garden? You know, like people who live in cities?"

"That's easy. They can plant wildflowers in hanging planters on their windows."

Sophie sipped more of her lemonade, contemplating all the information.

By the time Jacky picked her up and they all said their goodbyes, Sophie had a stream of ideas running wild in her mind. She didn't even consider the consequences of saying yes to Jacky when she asked her if she wanted to get pizza and watch a movie. On autopilot to anything around her, Sophie agreed.

As she sat next to a smiling Jacky on the couch later that evening, watching *Eat, Pray, Love*, she cultivated more ideas. She would urge people to write to their local council and political representatives to tell them they needed to save the bees. They needed to stop the use of pesticides in public spaces, plant more bee-friendly plants, and open up space for wildflowers along public roadways. So much could be done. She couldn't wait to get started.

As she snuggled up under a blanket with Rosy, her heart fluttered for the first time in a while. She fell more in love with nature every time she entered into Brooke's yard. She stepped inside of something bigger than herself. She became a necessary part to a larger cause. A sense of happiness flowed in her.

Something finally excited her.

Chapter Eleven

On Sunday morning, Marie called Jacky to invite her and Sophie out to lunch.

"Let's meet at Flavors of India," Marie suggested.

Jacky's mouth watered dreaming about their Chicken Tikka Masala. "Come on, you know that Sophie hates the taste of Indian food." Jacky sighed. "Damn I wish I could say yes."

"I'm not in the mood to eat out anyway," Sophie said from behind her.

Jacky swiveled around. "Weren't you on the deck, reading?"

Sophie's mouth trembled the way it did whenever someone hurt her. "I was." She grabbed her water bottle on the counter and shot out of the room.

"I'll call you back," she said to Marie, then ran after Sophie.

She arrived at her bedroom door just as Sophie began to close it. "Hey kiddo, you know I didn't mean that the way it sounded."

"It's okay. I get it. You like Indian food. I don't." She spoke like a poised executive, straight-faced with no emotions. "I like junk food. You don't."

"I'm so sorry." Jacky stared into her innocent eyes. "You're right. I do like Indian food. In fact, I've got a serious weakness to it. So, if I sounded disappointed, I guess I was." Jacky stopped talking when she saw Sophie's jaw drop. "I'm terrible at this communication thing. I'm sorry I keep upsetting you."

"It's alright." Sophie crossed her arms over her chest. "If only we could communicate more like bees, we'd have no need to worry if we're upsetting each other. I guess we'd have to learn how to dance to do that, though."

"Dance?"

"Yup. It's one of the ways they communicate."

"If only I knew how to dance."

"Yeah." Sophie sighed. "If only." She started to close her door.

"Seriously." Jacky pushed the door back open. "I can have Indian food any other day. I don't need to eat Chicken Tikka Masala right now. Auntie Marie will survive without it too." Jacky paused, waiting on Sophie to agree.

"Go get Indian. You only live once. So why not?"

"It's not as much fun if you're not there too."

"I'll be fine. I want ice-cream anyway, and we've got a freezer full of it." Sophie arched her eyebrow and tried to close the door again.

Jacky stopped it with her arm. "Then how about dinner? Let's eat dinner together."

She opened up the door slightly wider. "Maybe," she whispered.

~ ~

Marie and Hazel spotted Jacky's silver SUV next to the lamppost at the far end of the parking lot. In a few minutes they'd be sinking their teeth into yummy rotis and basmati rice.

"Why does she park a mile away from the restaurant?" Marie asked. "It's not like she's driving a BMW or Lexus. Even if someone bumped her door, no one would be able to tell. She buffs the damn car like it's a freaking diamond on display in a jewelry store. She cares more about her car than her own life at times. The stupid thing barely runs." Marie pulled into the spot next to hers. "Oh geez, and look at how she parks the damn car sideways. I'm going to lay into her right now."

"Don't. You'll hurt her feelings," Hazel said, wrapping her hand around Marie's wrist. "Not everything demands a lecture. Let her park her car sideways if it brings some joy to her heart."

Hazel protected feelings like she guarded the future of mankind. Marie could be walking around with a piece of spaghetti stuck to her cheek and Hazel would never tell her for fear she'd hurt her.

"It's so wrong."

"Zip it." Hazel opened up her door.

"Fine." Marie fastened her mouth shut for the sake of a good meal in the making, one she didn't want a heap of metal on wheels to ruin.

As they approached her, Marie caught sight of a newly relaxed version of her friend, replacing her usual defeat. "You look amazing." Marie studied her smoother looking skin and brighter eyes. "What happened?"

"I woke up on the right side of the bed, I suppose."

Jacky took the lead to the restaurant, and Marie and Hazel fell in line behind her. "Is it me or is something different about her today?" Marie whispered.

Hazel nodded.

Marie watched her friend stride across the parking lot with a bounce to her step. That kind of pep could take a lady places, and if she surmised correctly, a certain beekeeper planted that in her.

~ ~

Jacky entered the restaurant and was unable to stop her cheeks from their upward pull. Since her night of Uno with Brooke, she couldn't wipe her from her mind.

Even when she ordered the buffet for lunch, she couldn't stop smiling. Marie watched her, causing Jacky to break out into a goofy grin.

The three of them walked up to the buffet station and gathered their plates, silverware, and napkins. As Marie spooned lentils onto her plate, she barged into Jacky's business. "I bet the ten dollar bill in my wallet that your smile is coming from something other than this Indian buffet."

"Can we get through the buffet line before you start?" Jacky slapped Marie's hand and the lentil spoon fell into the pile of roti.

Marie paused in dramatic fashion, so the entire buffet line could listen to their hushed conversation and speculate on the critical nature of their dialogue. "I can't take you anywhere. You're like a two-year old."

141

Hazel snuck up between them, her plate already overflowing with vegetables and creamed spinach. "Why are you whispering and hitting each other?"

"Because Jacky's hiding something from us." Marie piled creamed spinach on top of her rice.

"Whatever's on her mind is none of our business." Hazel pinched Marie's side, grabbed a roti and headed back to their table.

Jacky finished filling her plate and headed back to the table, too. A part of her wanted to talk about things. Her emotions festered and grew too big on their own. Maybe by puncturing their incubator, they'd stop feeding off her vulnerability and fade away.

"Okay, listen," Jacky set her plate down and faced the curious stares from her friends. "Let's just say Brooke and I are on the verge of forming a friendship and leave it at that."

They collected her words and shared secret opinions with each other on their side of the booth. They didn't speak, only stared at each other, exchanging eye rolls and curled up lips as a prelude to what would eventually come out of their mouths. They often spoke in a silent language, crafting entire conversations and working out problems without ever opening their mouths.

Their food grew colder with their attempt to tighten their lips.

Finally, Jacky dug her spoon into her curried chickpeas, gathering up a scoop of rice on the way to her mouth.

"A friendship," Marie finally said. "Sure why not."

Jacky chewed, contemplating her next move. Just like in a chess game, she needed to be strategic. Say too much and she'd never hear the end of it. Say too little, and Marie would dig until she bled. "She's got a nice smile."

Marie slapped the table. "Ah ha!"

Hazel elbowed Marie. "Take it down a notch."

"This is why I don't talk to you. You turn everything into a big, goofy deal. In your mind you probably equate a nice smile to *I want to rent a U-Haul and move her in.*"

142

"Well, your comment does beg the question," Marie said. "I mean, a smile is a big thing for you."

It was a big thing. The last time she told Marie she liked a woman's smile, she ended up renting that U-Haul and moving Drew in. "What can I say? I'm a sucker for a beautiful smile."

"There are worse things you could be." Marie gulped some water.

Jacky picked at her chicken. "I feel guilty."

"You're not a robot," Marie hissed. "Good God woman, you're entitled to enjoy a smile."

Hazel cupped her chin in her hand. "She does have a beautiful smile."

Marie's jaw dropped, and her eyebrows furrowed.

Jacky picked up her spoon and shoveled a pile of rice into her mouth, avoiding the obvious jealousy. They didn't have to announce their love for each other. Times like that, one only had to look at them to understand they shared more than the disguise of friendship.

Marie shoved half a roti between her lips. Hazel flinched and stabbed her spinach with her fork.

The two of them attacked their food like they were slaying dragons with dull butter knives.

Jacky washed down her food with a mouthful of water. If Marie could bait her with questions, why couldn't Jacky return the same? "What just happened?"

"Nothing," Marie snapped. "Mind your own business."

There went her damn hormones again.

Hazel faulted in managing a grin. It landed on her face like a twisted heap of metal, poking out here and there in haphazard directions.

Poor Hazel.

~ ~

143

When Jacky returned home after lunch, she found Sophie on the couch, knees propped up by a pillow, head resting back, eyes closed, earbuds plugged into her tiny, perfect ears. She tiptoed past her and into the kitchen where she put a turkey sub with provolone cheese in the fridge for Sophie.

She gazed out through the serving counter and into the living room. She'd never seen Sophie look more relaxed. The bees must have been having quite a positive effect on her, as Brooke said they might.

Jacky bowed her head. She picked up the pile of new mail that had arrived and flipped through it, tossing the junk mail into one heap and the bills into another. Drew's name still appeared on the cell phone bill. She picked it up and stared at her name. Seeing it on the envelope kept Drew closer to her, but she knew one day she'd need to cancel her cell phone and put the name into her own.

She may as well suffer through a second death.

She shuddered. She'd never take that bold step.

She tossed it on top of the bill paying pile.

Another month won't harm anything.

She walked back out to the living room and past Sophie.

"Oh, hey." She rose up into a seated position, her knees still propped up in front of her.

"I got you a sandwich in case the ice-cream didn't fill you."

"Thanks."

"What are you listening to?"

She shrugged. "Research."

"On?"

"Bees."

Their one word discussion tore at Jacky. "Anything worthwhile?"

"Yeah. A lot." Sophie pulled the pillow out from under her knees and stood up. "You can listen to it if you want." She offered her earbuds and iPad. "I've got it set to play again."

Jacky eyed the iPad, reluctant to accept. She'd rather have an interesting conversation with Sophie instead of being shoved into a corner to listen alone. But, Sophie did extend a branch, albeit a small twiggy one. Jacky reached out. "Sure. I'll listen."

Sophie circled around Jacky and called Rosy. "Come on girl. Let's go for a walk."

"I can go too," Jacky said.

"Nah. You'll enjoy listening more."

In other words, Sophie didn't want anything to do with her. Again. "Alright, then. Have fun and be safe." *I won't force myself on you.*

Sophie secured Rosy's leash and opened the front door, leaving Jacky frustrated.

She looked around the room and saw a pile of dirty dishes on the coffee table. Sophie's sloppiness irked Jacky. *Just like her mother.* She acted like fairy goddesses flew in through the vents when she left a room and swept up the mess with their magic brooms.

She wouldn't nitpick though. She swallowed the bitter taste that crawled up her throat and picked up the mess. She brought the dirty dishes into the kitchen and began washing them before they got any stickier. Then her phone rang.

It was Brooke. Her heart thumped.

"Sophie forgot her pocketbook here," Brooke said.

"Did she?" How did Sophie not notice?

"I can swing by and drop it off tomorrow if you'd like. I'll be in your area."

Sophie would never wait a day if she knew. "It's a beautiful day, and I'm just hanging around my house washing dishes. A drive will do me good." She hated the way her voice sounded too excited.

"I'm heading out, so I'll just leave it with my grandparents if that's okay?"

Jacky's heart took a nosedive. "Of course. Yes. No problem."

Jacky hung up, and stared at the pile of sudsy dishes. Maybe if she left that second, she'd run into her.

Like a desperate fool, she left the rest of the dishes soaking in the sink, jotted a quick note to Sophie to let her know she'd be right back. Then, she dashed out of the door to get the pocketbook, hoping she'd pluck it right from Brooke's fingers.

~ ~

Elise handed Jacky the pocketbook. "You just missed her. She's heading out to the Eastern Shore for a date with some rich one, I suspect. She owns a boat." Elise smirked and fanned her face with the back of her hand.

Jacky gulped back the harsh taste on her tongue. "Ah, a date."

Elise scanned her face with a grin. "I wish she'd smarten up and date someone more like you."

Jacky's face burned hot. "Me? Oh no. I'm not ready for that. I'm still trying to…"

She wrapped her hand around Jacky's wrist. "I know, dear. You don't need to explain. A grandmother can wish, though, can't she?"

Jacky blushed even deeper. "I should get going. Sophie's waiting."

"Of course, dear." She dropped her hand from her wrist. "Enjoy your afternoon with her."

Jacky walked down the path to her car, climbed in and drove away, fighting off a jealous twitch. Who was this rich woman, and did Brooke like her? Was Brooke already laughing and smiling at her from the front seat of her car, likely a cute little cherry red Porsche. Would they kiss? Would they sit under the setting sun, clinking champagne flutes and staring into each other's eyes?

She groaned, and pressed harder against the accelerator. She didn't need this distraction. Brooke was a single woman free to date and charm others.

She sure did know how to charm.

Jacky heaved a sigh and clicked on the radio. Michael Jackson's *Billy Jean* played. She blasted the music and sang along with him, drowning out the repetitive thumping on her heart that told her she dove in over her head, and needed to climb out of the rising waters before the tide rolled in and swept her clear off her feet.

~ ~

When she returned, Sophie was back in her room. So, Jacky lay on the couch with her knees propped under a pillow. Then, she saw Brooke's smiling face in her mind and the silhouette of a beautiful woman romancing her on the deck of an elaborate boat out in the middle of a moonlit harbor.

To wipe that terrible sight from her mind, she placed the earbuds in her ears and pressed the play button.

Soon, light piano music filtered in, and rising in the tiny cross sections of those little earbud wires came Brooke's soothing whispers instructing her to take deep soulful breaths.

Brooke's voice crooned, sending warm ripples of peace through her. Her words, short, eloquent and willowy, brushed against the rough parts of her, softening and smoothing them over. She spoke to her as if leading her by the hand and introducing her to a whole new fabric of the universe where plants grew brighter greens and flowers bloomed the color of sunshine and rainbows. They skipped along the edge of a meadow where wildflowers grew around the knotty roots of Redbud trees. They dipped in to quench their thirsty need for rest.

They sat on the edge of a rock, soothed by the scent of sunlight and apples.

Bees are the most selfless creatures on the planet, she whispered. *They put the health and safety of their hive above their own life. They're not marred by the selfish ways of the ego because they don't have one.*

Gentle music pulsed in the background, transporting Jacky to breathtaking scenery where they glided through the dewy morning, lavishing on one delicious flower after another. The land, with its wild and flavorful treasures, sat ready for them. They spent the time enjoying the aroma of pollen dust and returning to the center of their world on the hush of the gentle wind.

Their priority is to the colony, and bees will sacrifice themselves without hesitation if they perceive a threat, she continued. *They understand the virtue and*

147

value in honest communication. It's at the heart of community. They are exceptional communicators and use vibrations and pheromones to share complex ideas and messages. Bees are not capable of telling a lie. They're creatures to admire and respect. Our very existence depends on our ability to do just that.

Brooke spoke about the intricate communication channels of bees, lulling Jacky into the peaceful retreat of her lullaby. Eventually, Brooke eased Jacky back to reality on a melodic, energizing countdown that took her from the center of that garden oasis to the safety and comfort of her living room.

She ended on a breathy gesture, wishing her peace and an abundance of honest, loving energy.

Jacky removed the earbuds and stared up at the swirled, plaster ceiling, relaxed for a change.

She needed more stories.

She jumped off the couch and headed down to Sophie's room. She knocked.

"Come in."

Jacky poked her head through the door. "Hey, kiddo. Do you have any more of those stories?"

"Yeah," she beamed. "A whole bunch."

Chapter Twelve

As the weeks rolled by, Jacky's affinity toward Brooke grew. She fell asleep each night to her guided meditations, imagining her whispering them into her ear.

Sophie admired Brooke, too, viewing her as a role model. Sophie began talking with Jacky about her and how she was helping her finalize her school project. Mr. Benks even wants to become a beekeeper, too," she said as Jacky pulled into Brooke's driveway one Saturday morning.

Brooke and Bee were walking in the side yard near a patch of willow trees. Bee went berserk, of course, and tore right out of Brooke's hands, dashing toward the car like an attack dog. Foam and craze sprang up and sprayed everywhere, as her knobby legs and eager spirit catapulted toward them.

"She's wasting her money on the training, huh?" Sophie asked, forehead to the window.

Jacky still hadn't taken a dime from her, despite Brooke insisting. She kept telling her they'd square up together after Bee graduated. Of course, they'd starve and find themselves on the streets living in cardboard boxes if every client turned out like her.

"Let me get out first." Jacky opened her door, and Bee recognized her instantly. She bent to the ground offering her a wag instead of a mouthful of teeth.

Brooke's hands remained cupped over her mouth, her eyes wide, and her face pink and flustered.

Despite being adorable, Jacky had to say something about Brooke's ill attempt to train Bee. "It's really important that you follow the techniques we talked about.

We don't want her to hurt herself or someone else, you know?" Jacky asked gently before bending low to pet behind Bee's ears just the way she liked.

Brooke dropped her hands. "You're right. I haven't been giving it my all."

They shared a gaze, then Sophie's voice sailed in from the front seat. "Is it safe to come out, yet?"

"Is it?" Brooke asked Jacky.

Jacky reassured Brooke with a smile.

"The coast is clear," Brooke sang out.

Sophie appeared slowly, offering Bee the back of her hand to sniff.

"So you two have a lot of work to get to, I'm sure," Jacky said. "I don't want to keep you. Should I be back at four o'clock?"

"Four o'clock should be just fine," Brooke said, softly.

~ ~

As she and Sophie headed out to the beehives, Sophie asked her how the date with Janice, the sailing lady, went.

"That was weeks ago. How did you know about that?"

"Your nana told me."

"Of course she did. Well, I'm swearing off dating forever."

Brooke would rather embrace her single life and expect nothing from women. The disappointment of foiled dates clogged her creativity and sanity. Janice was a sailing queen who not only enjoyed eating food with her bare hands, but also kissed like a plunger, sucking Brooke's face into her mouth.

She'd rather hang with her honeybees than deal with another face-sucking cavewoman who trapped her in a sailboat the size of the backseat of her Corolla.

"So never again, huh?" Sophie asked, emptying a pollen tray.

"Never again. I'd rather toss myself in front of a speeding train than suffer through a date like that again. Well, maybe not a speeding train. That's a bit extreme."

"More like a scooter?"

"Yes, a scooter. Much more like a scooter," Brooke agreed.

"I'm not going to see boys anymore, either," Sophie said. "They act like idiots. Especially when you get them with a group of their friends. They turn into bullies. There's this kid Drake that likes me. He's nice when no one else is around. Almost to the point, I like him too. Then, the minute his friends come around, he turns into an imbecile. He laughs at people and tries to be funny, only he's not. He looks stupid. So, I'm done with boys for now. I'd rather read books than put up with their horseplay."

Brooke laughed. "You sound like my nana when she speaks about my pepe."

"Great, so it doesn't get any easier even when they're older?" Sophie flung her head backwards and groaned.

"I'm afraid not. I'm guessing they'd say the same about us girls."

Sophie nodded. "Probably. We're kind of hard to figure out. Especially Jacky."

Brooke placed a tray back in the hive and continued to work. "How so?"

"I don't know," she shrugged. "I guess sometimes I wish things could go back to the way they were before my mom died. It's like we have nothing in common anymore."

"Have you talked to her about it?"

"Nah."

"Why not?"

"We don't know what to say to each other because we always used to talk about my mother. Not in a bad way. We'd just joke around and try to get on her nerves. Those days are over now." Sophie spoke like an elderly woman looking back on her younger years, as if they were impossibly out of reach.

"Maybe you just need a new activity together."

Sophie played with a bee on her arm. "Yeah, maybe."

"We could invite her to spend some time with us here."

Sophie continued to focus on the bee. "I bet she'd like it if you invited her."

"Me?" Brooke morphed back into a teenager herself, riding out a flurry of giddy waves. "Why would you think that?"

"I can tell she feels comfortable around you. I haven't seen her smile and relaxed like that in a long time."

Brooke blushed.

"Just ask her," Sophie said. "I bet she'll say yes."

~ ~

Later that afternoon when Sophie returned to the greenhouse and worked on the plants, she played back her conversation with Brooke about Jacky. They needed to find something in common, otherwise whatever they had left in their relationship might soon become ugly and dried up like a dead hive.

She wished she could go back to their early days when she never considered herself a nuisance. She'd love to share a gigantic bowl of ice-cream with her at Friendly's, like old times. She'd even forfeit the sugar cone sticking out of the top of it. Jacky loved those, maybe more than the mountains of whipped cream oozing with hot fudge and caramel.

They shared some good memories, back in the day.

"Can you marry her?" she had whispered to her mother the night she first met her on the tennis court. "And, can I wear a pink flower girl dress with dandelions sticking in my braids. Pretty please. Oh and black, shiny shoes too! Pretty please with sugar on top!"

Her mother kissed her forehead, smoothing her hair back and whispered, "She even has a puppy named Rosy."

That sealed it for Sophie. No other second mommy would ever do. "Please marry her, Mommy."

For eight years, Jacky was her laugh buddy. They played jokes on her mother, stuffing rubber spiders in her bed to see her panic and catching her freak-outs on camera. Jacky showed her how to carve her first pumpkin and later bake the seeds. She bought her first pair of roller blades and took her to the park to teach her how to use them. Then later, they surprised her mom with her new skill.

Jacky also taught her how to master riding her Huffy bike, the one with the red and white tassels that hung from the handlebars. They'd pack a picnic basket and take off on rides through the neighborhood, landing in the park under some giant tree and stuffing their faces with peanut butter and jelly sandwiches and Utz potato chips, the barbeque flavor.

Jacky picked up the pieces where her mother left off. Her mother was a busy person. She had a lot of grand plans and goals. She needed to work extra hard to achieve them. She turned into a scrapper if anyone got in her way, too. Her mother didn't appreciate when anyone rained on her parade. No one crossed her path. Ever. Even strangers knew better. Her mother carried a certain attitude when she walked by trouble. She called it her *New York Tude*.

"You can't show fear," she'd say before pulling her along toward a jerk trying to cut her line. "You let them get away with an inch, they're going to eventually take a mile." She'd raise her head up, puff out her chest, and march forward. The air parted for her, as did people. What her mother wanted, her mother got.

Of course, this made Jacky very uncomfortable. They'd fight about it. They'd wait until they tucked her into bed and turned on the cricket machine – a noise maker that sounded like a forest of crickets lived under her bed – before battling out their sides.

Sophie would crawl out of bed and put a glass up to the door to listen better. Their voices sounded like they screamed right into the glass. Well, mostly her mother's voice. "No one is going to bully me," her mother yelled one night.

"You just have to think though," Jacky whispered. "You've got Sophie there with you. What if someone had a gun and decided to shoot you in front of her? People are crazy. You can't just walk up to a stranger and curse them out because he looked at you the wrong way. Look the other way for God's sakes."

"I've lived my life this way since the day I was born. I'm not going to change now. No one will ever walk over me or my daughter."

That argument ended on a slammed door.

Her mother could argue like no one's business. She should've gone to school to be a lawyer. She would've won every case, hands down. She excelled at getting people to quiet down and agree with whatever she had to say.

The nightly arguments always started out much the same, with her mother accusing Jacky of not supporting her and Jacky whispering to keep her voice down. Her mother didn't know how. No matter how many times Jacky asked her, even as nicely as she did, her mother didn't possess the ability to speak in a hushed tone, not when someone pissed her off and embarrassed her. Someone always seemed to do that to her.

Her mother didn't always walk around in fight mode. She had a soft edge to her that Jacky loved almost as much as Sophie did. Her mother was very generous. Not a week went by where she didn't stop by a dog shelter and drop off a twenty–five pound bag of kibble, high-grade at that. She also baked casseroles for the soup kitchen in Baltimore City.

Her mother was a wonderful momma. Each night, no matter how busy, she always took time to tuck her in and kiss her forehead. She wanted to hear every last detail of the day, then would read with her.

God, she missed her.

Sophie took a deep breath and rose from the ground. She headed over to the cucumbers and checked their water levels. Her mother loved cucumbers. She fingered one, and a flood of emotions filled her. She missed those summer afternoons when they'd slice one up and eat them as they talked about summer vacation plans.

She missed everything about her.

Sophie turned and spotted Brooke on the ladder, tending to a sick tree.

Brooke was beautiful. She smelled like earth after a nice refreshing rain. When she smiled, everything felt safe and warm. Her mother would've been jealous of such a woman so close to Jacky. She would've loved the apiary, but hated Brooke. She would've sensed Jacky's interest in her.

Jacky.

Reading that letter every night didn't help anymore. She couldn't stay mad at her no matter how hard she tried. That scared her because it meant she could get hurt again. Being mad at her made those hurtful words she had said easier to swallow. Before the shit hit the fan, Sophie had always operated under the pretense that Jacky adored her, supported her, and loved her like a daughter. Then, her hurtful words shattered that perception.

She'd give anything to know that Jacky wanted to be there with her heart and not out of some forced, obligatory legal contract that insisted she be. Jacky would never rip up a contract in spite of her own selfish desires. No. Jacky did as expected because that's what good people did.

Jacky would've been a great honeybee. She didn't know how to be selfish.

Jacky was a good person, and perhaps that's why Sophie feared losing her so much.

Brooke looked back over her shoulder and spotted Sophie staring at her. They shared a smile before Brooke focused back on the tree.

Maybe Brooke was right. Maybe she could invite Jacky to hang out with the bees. She'd probably like them, and might even be impressed with Sophie's ability to interact with them.

~ ~

When Jacky returned to pick up Sophie, Brooke waved her over. "Why don't you join us for a quick visit with the bees?"

"Yeah, join us," Sophie said in a small voice, kneeling down next to Bee. "You'll like it."

A part of Jacky feared the honeybees. What if she freaked out in front of them both? Some dog trainer she'd look like, running from a bunch of honeybees in a fit of fear. "You're out of your suits now. We can just do it another day."

"Oh come on, it'll be fun," Sophie said on a plea.

She's happy. If a fifteen-year old didn't fear them, why should she? "Okay. I'll try."

Brooke swiped her hands together and brought them up to her face, resting her beautiful dimples on them. "Excellent."

They ventured into the greenhouse, and Sophie went directly over to a cream suit hanging on a knob by some tomato plants.

Drew would be so proud of her in her first job. It beat the hell out of Jacky's first job as a busgirl at Louie's Bar and Grill where she'd come home stinking like day old food and needing three doses of shampoo to not smell like a walking French fry.

Brooke handed Jacky a jumper suit. "You'll have to tuck your pants into your socks first, then slide right into the jumper. I'll grab a net for your head."

Jacky placed the suit on a small table and began tucking her pants into her socks, and blurted out the first panicky question. "Do they sting much?"

"If you anger them, yes," Sophie said matter-of-factly.

Jacky's heart began to race. "How do I not anger them?"

She shrugged. "You just don't."

Brooke eased up to her side, placing her hand on her arm. Jacky waited on her wisdom. "She's right. You just don't." She winked and walked over to her suit.

Jacky climbed into hers, one clumsy foot at a time. "Is my heart supposed to beat like I just ran up ten flights of stairs?"

"Yup!" Sophie raised her arms up and wiggled into her suit. "That's the best part."

Jacky zipped up her jumper. "Will any bees be able to get inside of my jumper?"

Brooke and Sophie looked to each other and laughed at her expense. "Novice," they said in unison.

Panic rose, the kind experienced right before the roller coaster began its descent. "What if I've become allergic to bees over the years and don't know it, yet?"

"That's what the epinephrine pen is for," Sophie said, placing her netted hat on her head. "We'll just jab you in the leg with it and you'll breathe again."

Brooke brought out Sophie's jokester side, a side she'd missed way more than she'd realized. "Fantastic."

Brooke sashayed over to her. She guided the hat on her head. "Yup, we'll just stab you right in the leg and open up that airway." Brooke pulled on the net, bringing her even closer.

She smelled as fresh as spearmint.

"What's up with that twisted glimmer in your eye?" Jacky asked. "You're a beekeeper. Aren't you supposed to be pleasant and earthy instead of mischievous and sadistic?"

"Oh sadistic," Brooke said with swagger to her voice. "I never pictured myself in such darkness before. It's kind of cool." She circled her shoulders as if trying out a new body.

"You're both freaking me out." Jacky inhaled a nervous breath.

Brooke laughed and placed her hands on Jacky's shoulders. She stared straight at her as if talking to a child on a first day of school. "I'll be right there with you. You'll be safe. My bees are gentle, and they're going to adore you. Just stay calm. Don't make any sudden movements. Think slow motion. Just observe and stay in awe. And under no circumstance do you panic, okay?"

"Why would I panic?"

"Exactly." Brooke circled around toward Sophie. Then, the two of them headed out of the greenhouse entryway.

No. That question was not rhetorical. It requires an answer!

Jacky scurried up to them to stay close, as if somehow their bee suits would double and triple protect her.

They walked down the steep hill, which was layered in thick tree roots and random stones. They went to the edge of the property where yellow and orange wooden hive boxes lined the trees. Jacky's breathing quickened as they approached. She had been stung ten times in the butt as a child, not by honeybees, but by yellow jackets. Her ass had stayed swollen for days. She did not want a swollen ass again.

So, she stood a safe distance away from Brooke and Sophie as they practically hugged the hives.

"You picked a great day to get introduced," Brooke said over her shoulder. "The hives are happy today."

"What do you mean the hives are happy?" Sophie asked.

"The collective energy is in harmony. The air feels happy just like a playground full of smiley kids." Brooke lifted a cover off one of the hives and a bunch of bees flew out. "The communal nature among the bees is so tight that they are like their own breathing machine. Not one bee stands out from the rest. They work in tandem with the other. They're at peace right now, deeply engrossed in their tasks."

Jacky leaned in, careful not to get too close. "Sounds like a fantastic case study for MBA students."

"I'm sure someone has used them as a model," Sophie agreed.

Brooke cocked her head and gazed lovingly at the bees. "They are the most selfless creatures on the planet. They work to bring out the best in each other. The hive is their priority and they'll do whatever it takes to ensure its survival."

She picked up a tray and placed it in front of Jacky's chest. "It beats as one. It sleeps as one. It comes alive as one. It's its own body, with dedicated resources for various activities that need to happen to keep the hive happy and healthy. This requires honest communication amongst them. Each one needs to know exactly what the other is doing and thinking. It's that honest cooperation that keeps it functioning. Without it, the hive would die."

Just like with her and Sophie's symbolic hive, a breakdown in communication could shut them down.

Sophie looked at the tray with complete peace. "How do bees keep their hive happy?"

"Lots of love, nourishment, and of course, dance." Brooke winked. "Really, it's like with any unit, typically honest communication can restore it. The queen is the center of the hive, and her leadership can help guide the others to stay calm and focused in times of extremes."

Jacky continued to watch as Brooke and Sophie tended to the honeycomb and pollen trays. Not too long into her first trek into bee territory, she began to relax under their capable hands.

Jacky inhaled the fresh afternoon air. The entire esoteric experience from the lullaby of their energizing hum, to the sight of them taking nosedives and then rising back up on the edge of a wisp of air, to the spicy smell of the honey and wax brought all senses alive.

Peace rested on Sophie's face. Among the bees, she didn't have to put on a fake smile. She didn't have to fight the tension between her and Jacky or worry about her homework. In this paradise, life slowed down to a pace that allowed healing and nurturing to unfold. Sophie tossed her stress aside, easing into the paradise.

It was her second home.

"Ah, look the queen," Brooke said, pointing it out to Sophie.

"Yup. There she is. The only fertile female of the hive."

"Seriously?" Jacky asked.

"Yup. She emits this scent called a pheromone that tells the other female bees to stay sterile."

"What does it smell like?" Jacky stretched her neck to get a better view.

"Only bees in the hive smell it," Sophie said. "It's their communications system. The queen alerts that she is alive and well by spraying it, which keeps the bees happy and together like a family." She turned to Brooke. "Did I get that right?"

Brooke nodded and gave her a thumbs up.

"So no secrets," Jacky said.

"None," Brooke said, jumping into the conversation. "She's well taken care of by her court. That being said, the hive can turn on her quickly as soon as they realize she is no longer producing enough eggs to sustain growth in the hive. They begin a sort of search to replace her. They usually do this by way of emergency rearing."

Sophie arched her eyebrow. "Emergency rearing?"

"Let me explain."

"Please do. I haven't heard this, yet," Sophie said.

"The worker bees begin a process of building queen-size cells in the hive." She pointed to the honeycomb.

Jacky still remained a few steps back.

"You see, inside these larger, vertically-oriented cells, the bees know to feed these potential queens a special food called royal jelly. Ultimately, the developing queens raised in these cells might fight to the death to determine which one will become queen."

"What happens to her when they replace her?"

"She usually dies," Brooke said. She turned over her shoulder and glanced at Jacky. "Do you want to see the queen?"

Fascinated, Jacky moved in closer. "Sure, of course." She went in for a peek. She didn't yet advance three steps and bees already clung to her net, buzzing right above her left eye. They were probably planning who would sting her and where. She closed her eyes and tried to still her nerves.

Brooke held out a honeycomb tray. "Check it out," she said, pointing to a cluster of bees on the right hand edge. See, this is her court. They spoil her all day long, always reminding her that she is the queen."

Jacky poked her head closer. "Which one is she?"

"She's right here," Brooke pointed at her with the tip of her hive tool. "You see her body is longer and wider."

Bees began landing on Jacky's sleeves.

Brooke must have sensed her discomfort. "Just stay calm, and they'll just observe you."

"Right." Jacky nodded, then realized maybe she had nodded too quickly because a bunch of them buzzed around her.

"Here," Brooke said, handing her the tray. "You'll love the buzz at your fingertips."

"I don't know if that's such a good idea." Jacky backed up, and Sophie nudged her back forward.

"She'll loop a collar around a known aggressive dog with teeth the size of small sharks," Sophie said, "but she won't hold a two foot tray full of gentle honeybees."

"Oh?" Jacky turned slowly and caught Sophie's cocky grin. "You think I'm chicken?"

She arched her eyebrow. "You're not giving us anything else to go on here."

Jacky would stick her head in the mouth of a tiger if that kept Sophie grinning at her and welcoming her into their new team. "Give it to me." Jacky stretched out her gloved hand toward Brooke. Several bees crawled on it, so she pulled it back.

"Don't be afraid," Brooke said through a giggle.

She reasoned with herself that they were much smaller than her. She couldn't even conjure up a mathematical number to describe the amount of size she had on them.

Fuck it. Brooke had an epinephrine pen.

Brooke handed Jacky the tray of honeycomb. Jacky gripped it like she would a bomb. Her head spun, and her heart clenched. Suddenly, she fumbled it.

Bees flew everywhere. Jacky's reflexes took over and she began swatting at them.

Sophie came at her with the strength of ten bodybuilders, squeezing her hands around Jacky's wrists. "Relax," she said in a slow, authoritative voice. "Just breathe."

Jacky did as instructed. Sophie exaggerated her breathing. "In and out. Nice and slow."

She closed her eyes and imagined herself teaching a client how to relax in front of a dog. She breathed in and out, slow and steady until her heart finally caught up with her senses. Even the bees began to relax in her presence. They started to land on her arms and chest. They pinged the net in front of her face.

Jacky braved and reopened her eyes.

Sophie stared at her. "Better?"

"I think so."

Jacky looked over her shoulder at Brooke. She was kneeling, fixated on the blanket of bees on the ground. "I found her."

"Who did she find?" Jacky asked.

Sophie let go of Jacky's wrists. "The queen. Without her, the hive wouldn't survive."

"I almost killed a hive?"

Brooke and Sophie looked to each other as if enjoying a private joke at her expense. "If you could've seen yourself." Brooke began to laugh as she placed the queen back on the honeycomb.

"You looked like a baboon the way you were flinging your arms around," Brooke said in between laughter.

Sophie busted out laughing, too.

Soon, Jacky couldn't help herself either. She began cackling with them as the bees buzzed and danced around them.

After a few minutes, the laughing slowly rolled to a stop.

"Okay, let's move on further in our lesson here." Jacky brushed off her embarrassment and asked, "So are all the bees female?"

Brooke walked right back into professional mode. "The hives have males, too, called drones. Their one purpose is to mate with the queen. That's it. They're lazy little ones. They don't contain stingers to defend the hive or the ability to collect pollen or nectar."

"The females must get pretty upset with them," Sophie said.

"Well, they're the fathers, so no." Brooke laughed. "Females do all the work. They do one task, and one task only for a set time period, then move on to a new task."

"So no multi-tasking?" Jacky asked.

"Nope. Single-tasking only."

"Is that beneficial?" Jacky asked. She couldn't imagine focusing on only one thing at a time. She normally had five things on her plate on any given moment.

"Focusing on the task at hand is far more effective."

"So what are the typical jobs?" Jacky asked, intrigued.

"Well the first job a bee will have is housekeeping. They're immaculate and take their cleaning very seriously. They do this to prevent disease, to open up room for new eggs, and to store their pollen and nectar."

Brooke pulled out a tray and showed Jacky the empty cells. "Do you see how clean they are?"

Sophie moved in and put her gloved finger up to it. "Jacky would be so proud of me if I could be this clean."

They all laughed.

"I'm not much of a housekeeper either," Brooke confessed. "I'm lucky if my bed gets made once a week."

"Exactly!" Sophie said with vigor. "We're just going to mess it up again. I don't see the point."

Brooke nudged Sophie with her elbow. "We're on the same page, my friend."

Sophie's face blushed at the reference. She admired Brooke, and Jacky could tell she probably wanted to be just like her one day.

"So after they pass their proverbial brooms on to new bees," Brooke explained, "they take on the next role of undertaker."

"Ewe." Sophie crinkled her nose.

"Yeah. This is about when they are only three days to sixteen days old too."

"A lot for a little one to take on, no?" Sophie asked.

"They're resilient. They learn quickly to remove any bees who have died, taking them out of the hive and moving them as far away as possible. If a new brood is suspected of being sick, they remove them too so they aren't a threat to the entire hive."

"So no special care or attention when they're sick?" Jacky asked. "Poor girls."

"Nah, just a quick way to maturity," Brooke winked.

"Yeah." Jacky returned the wink.

Sophie stared at a few honeybees crawling around the tray. "So what next?"

"Well, they graduate to become nursing bees. They essentially become the babysitters only without the fringe benefits of junk food and video games."

Sophie laughed.

"They feed and take care of the young developing larvae, checking on them about thirteen hundred times a day."

"No time for junk food and video games. They must be exhausted." Sophie reached out for the tray.

"Some of them get a break from that and become part of the queen's court. They have the task of following her around the hive and taking care of her basic needs."

Sophie flipped the tray over like a pro and examined the underside. "That would be a pretty prestigious role."

"They're basically a glorified babysitter until they go on from there and get down to the nitty gritty of hive work."

"What role is that?"

"They collect nectar and pollen from foraging field bees that return to the hive after a day of collection. They deposit it into cells that are purposely set aside for food storage."

Sophie pressed on. "How old are they at this point?"

"About twelve to eighteen days old."

"Geez they sound like they've lived an entire teenage life by then."

"To them, they have. They are ready to do an important job by this time."

"Which is?" Sophie asked.

"Well, with all the fussing going on in the hive and all that food being stored, it gets hot. Someone has to keep the place cool. So, they turn into little air conditioners and fan the hive. They do this until they're about eighteen days old."

"Or else arthritis sets in?" Jacky joked.

"Ha, yeah, I guess eighteen days old would be our equivalent of getting up there in age."

"So what next?" Sophie asked, enthusiastically.

"Once they're eighteen days old, they're considered mature. Now the fun begins. They can begin to produce beeswax. This wax is used to produce new honeycomb and also to cap off the honeycomb once the honey has ripened."

Sophie handed the tray back to Brooke. "They become like artists."

"Yes, artists. Of course then they turn into something less artsy and more gutsy. They become guard bees."

Sophie fingered a bee. "Sounds serious."

"Their role is to protect the hive. They ensure that when a bee arrives, they have a familiar scent. If not, they're not permitted. Now just like in real life, there are always those who can be persuaded to let someone slip in, if the bribe is enticing enough. In this case, the bribe is usually in the form of nectar. These bees will typically come in, steal a little honey or pollen and then vacate."

Sophie laughed. "How clever."

"Well, remember by this time they've reached maturity and are quite clever. Guard bees turn to their last and most important task as field bees by day twenty two and spend their days foraging until they reach the ripe old age of forty two days."

Brooke pointed to the bees around them. "That's these little beauties flying around us. They're the ones that start off circling the hive and widening that circle to learn the landscapes that will serve as guideposts to and from foraging spots. These hard workers will visit roughly five million flowers. Do you know how much honey that produces?"

"A couple of bottles?" Jacky asked.

"Nope. One pint!"

"That's it?" Sophie asked.

"That's it."

Jacky observed field bees near the hive with a whole new appreciation. By comparison, she lived a wasteful and lazy life. She'd likely never look at a dust bunny on the floor quite the same way after considering the work ethic of housekeeping bees. Now if Sophie could be picking some of that up, they'd really be in a good place.

Sophie spent the next fifteen minutes explaining the pollen collection process and how she wanted to plant wildflowers in window boxes. She explained how important bees were to human beings, and how she would do everything she could to save them. She spoke with an energy that brought her to life. She reminded Jacky of a caterpillar transforming into a butterfly.

When they got back to the driveway near the greenhouse a few minutes later, Brooke pointed out that Jacky still had a bee on her net. It hung over her left eye.

"That's a guard bee keeping an eye on you."

"Remember those are the police force of the hive," Sophie added.

It buzzed and dangled from the netted string.

Jacky tried to be cool about it, not wanting to fly into panic mode again and knock over the tomato plants. "Cute, little girl."

Sophie busied herself climbing out of her suit when Brooke leaned over and whispered. "To think, you intimidated me at one time." Her breath washed over Jacky's face temporarily helping her to forget the guard bee. Brooke removed her net and shook out her hair. "It's a hot one out here today." She fanned herself.

Jacky stared right past the guard bee still hanging on her net, and straight at the charmer in front of her. Some women had no clue they were so sexy. "Yeah, it sure is a hot one."

Brooke giggled and glanced back at the bee. "She sure is a clingy one."

"How do you get rid of the clingy types?"

"I tell them to buzz off." Brooke scooted off toward the greenhouse. "Come get a drink of lemonade. That guard bee won't follow you in here," Brooke called out over her shoulder, then shook her ass just like she did the day at the school. *Shake. Shake. Shake.*

Sophie tapped her shoulder. "Just go after her."

Jacky looked away from Brooke's swinging butt. "What are you talking about?"

"What are *you* talking about?" Sophie arched her eyebrow again.

"Surely a way to get rid of a guard bee."

"Surely." Sophie elbowed her.

Jacky eyed her cautiously.

"She's interested." Sophie smirked. "And, you're happy around her. I think that's cool. So, don't be a dork. Just go after her." She waved her forward. "Go on, into the greenhouse. Get some lemonade. It's hot out here and you don't want to dehydrate."

Jacky eased into a laugh. "Of course."

Sophie offered her a knowing smile. Perhaps they had finally broken through that dam that had restricted the flow of communication. Maybe they would begin to share private musings once again as they once had before life twisted itself.

Chapter Thirteen

As time marched on, Bee rotated between being a well-behaved doggy and a total nut. That served Brooke just fine because it meant more one-on-one training sessions with Jacky. Brooke enjoyed her, and Jacky tiptoed between showing interest by flirting and taking it back by retreating to her professional, dog trainer demeanor. She obviously feared the fondness and getting involved in a romantic way. Justifiably so.

That kind of fondness could lead a person down serious paths, the kind where cute little mailboxes lined streets with cute little homes that housed adorable families with tail-wagging doggies and lunchboxes. Jacky didn't want to travel down that kind of serious road, not in the near future, anyway. Brooke could tell.

Brooke wouldn't push. She'd go about her normal life as usual, dating women she didn't care to be around and pretending she didn't mind Saturday nights spent on her grandparents' living room couch watching romantic comedies with them.

Brooke learned patience, silently praying that one day Jacky might be ready for something more than just dog training. Then, she'd make her bold move.

About two months into the hot summer season, Sophie surprised her one day by saying, "Jacky likes you."

"I like her too."

Sophie clipped new shoots from the tomato plants. "I mean she *really* likes you."

Brooke took a moment to wrap herself around what Sophie hinted. "No, she just enjoys being around the peace of this place." Brooke looked around the greenhouse with all its color and organic richness. "This isn't ordinary, being around all this beauty. Who wouldn't like it?" Brooke placed her clippers down and picked up the watering can.

Sophie kept watching her, all the time squeezing a fragile tomato branch between her fingers. "You're red."

"It's hot in here."

Sophie smirked.

Okay, work to be done. Chat break over. Let's get chopping and shearing. Brooke preferred keeping her feelings to herself, and to her bees, of course. They knew every little secret that she kept hidden, even the one of her fondness for Jacky.

"You're deflecting." Sophie released the branch from her clutch and squared off with Brooke. "Why?"

Brooke flushed. She stood before a very mature fifteen year old and kicked around nonsensical answers in her head. She shrugged and turned to her work.

Sophie met her at the plant she watered. "Want to know why I think she likes you?"

"Enlighten me."

"She looks at you in a way that she never looked at my mom. Like the way boys look at my friend, Ashley, when they're too shy to approach her. They sort of shuffle their feet around and look uncomfortable. Like they need to pee."

Brooke laughed. "Romantic!"

"It's true. They dart their eyes around, avoiding her, then when they think she can't see them, they gaze at her, like they've been stunned by landing on one of life's beautiful anomalies. Jacky does the same thing with you."

Brooke saturated the plant. "I'd have to see it to believe it."

"It's hard to miss. You just have to open up your eyes and you'll see what I mean."

~ ~

When Jacky returned to pick up Sophie just before four o'clock that day, she decided to have some fun and ring the doorbell.

She heard Brooke's footsteps, but no barking Bee. Brooke opened the door and beamed.

Jacky had never remembered seeing a daintier, more attractive smile before.

"One of these days," Brooke said, leaning her cheek up against the door, "I would love to see you live on the edge a little and be thirty seconds late. Could you do that for me?" She asked in a raspy, sexy voice.

Jacky stood before her, riding the waves of desire. "That's not possible." She braved a step closer. "I'm hard-wired this way."

Brooke inched the door open a little wider, cheek still resting on the edge of it. "That's okay. It's kind of a cute quality."

"Cute? No. Cute is Bee wrapped up in a circle on the couch snoring." She inched forward some more.

Brooke stood her ground, and the two faced each other. "You've got like five seconds to spare, and you can't stand the fact that you're not yet inside."

Jacky looked down at her feet. A mere two inches lay between her and the doorway. "Is this some sort of behavioral therapy?"

Brooke tapped the tip of Jacky's nose. "You're late."

Their eyes met.

"You're mean."

"You're itching to get inside," Brooke whispered.

"I am."

"What are you going to do about that?"

"Push you and take you with me?" Jacky asked, breathlessly.

"Is that a threat or a question?"

"I suppose a little of both."

Were they flirting?

Didn't she have a maniacal dog who should've been barking and causing chaos behind her? Wasn't Sophie supposed to be gathering up her things and rushing past them to get to the car, stopping only to thank Brooke, pet Bee, and shoot a funny look Jacky's way for being bold enough to flirt?

Brooke swung the door open wide and waved her in. "Come in. Sophie will be back in a few minutes. She's at the main house watching a short documentary my grandmother put together on ways to save the bees."

Jacky stepped into the living room, shaking off remnants of the flirts and collecting herself. "She made a documentary?"

"Yup."

"She just whipped one up, huh? Like baking a cake?"

"Like baking a thousand cakes and hand-delivering them to restaurants sprinkled all over the country. Sure."

Jacky laughed. "Impressive. Did you help?"

"I may have tucked myself into a few clips here and there." She cocked her head.

Jacky scanned the room, at a loss for what to do with the growing flutters. Brooke looked flushed and extra peppy. "So, you're in a playful mood. Let me guess. You were on a date recently?"

Brooke watched her as she shuffled her feet around. "I'm playful, so you jump to the conclusion I've been dating?"

"Well you do date, don't you? I mean some time ago you went sailing, right?"

"My nana has a big mouth." Brooke skirted around the room, picking up cups and straightening magazines. She looked up at Jacky. "To answer your question, yes, we went sailing."

"Did you like it?"

"It's a different world, for sure."

"A world you like?" Jacky couldn't stop plunging her line in to fish out more. She didn't want Brooke dating.

"I could get used to being in the open water, sure." Brooke walked into the kitchen. "Tea?"

Jealousy landed on her heart. "Sure."

Suddenly Latin music swept into the room through a set of speakers planted in each corner.

172

"She took me dancing, afterwards, you know?" Brooke yelled out from the kitchen.

More jealousy wrapped itself around her like a snake in full chokehold position. Dancing led to romantic innuendos.

Jacky tilted her head to get a better look at Brooke. She swayed to the sultry music as she spooned honey into teacups and drizzled cream as a follow-up. Her hips and shoulders swayed in unison, like a delicate swan. Mesmerized, Jacky strolled into the kitchen and watched her.

"Do you dance?" she asked, turning over her shoulder and meeting her eye.

"Not as good as you." Jacky's insides danced along with her words.

Brooke extended her hand. "Let me teach you."

Caught up in something outside herself, she reached out for her hand.

Brooke pulled her in close, gripping her right hand and placing her other on her back.

Instantly, Jacky's insides warmed. Her head swirled in a euphoric bath, heating her to the core. It teetered on the edge of reason, craving to swim on the side of ecstasy. She feared its pull on her heart. She could drown in that kind of unknown territory and never see the danger of an undertow until it knocked her off balance.

Warm ripples shouldn't have been traveling up and down her spine. Flailing like a rookie, she blurted, "Drew loved to dance, too. She wanted me to take dance lessons with her. She tried everything to get –"

"–Shh." Brooke placed her finger over Jacky's lips. "We're just dancing. Close your eyes. Let the music take you on a journey."

They hung out in a moment of silence, both widening their grins as the seconds passed between words. "I haven't smiled like this in a very long time," Jacky said. "I forgot how good it could feel."

Brooke closed her eyes, and Jacky enjoyed watching her expression change from serious to sensual, like she eased into a deep and intimate conversation with her soul. Connected to something deeper and more satisfying than the limitations of the physical room, Jacky entered this soulful place and followed Brooke's lead.

Brooke took her to the far reaches of the ordinary, out to where magic and bliss melded. To that place where rivers converged and vines weaved into the branches, creating a web of forestry that served as a playground for passion. Nothing else mattered in that moment but the soulful breaths of their entwined spirits, the light tapping of each other's hearts against each other, and the softness of her skin.

In the space between their movements, a mighty and powerful current swept Jacky away from all worries and heartbreaks and into a pureness that cleansed all residue and lifted her to mountaintops where no obstacle stood in the way of her view. From that vantage point, the world took on a pristine glow, wrapping her up in a sensual dance that sent her gliding like an eagle.

Free and safe from the perils of ordinary life with all its responsibilities and worries, Jacky tucked herself into the embrace of Brooke's sensual arms. She caved into the romance of the moment, closing her eyes and taking in the beauty of Brooke's strength and graceful moves. Their bodies danced as one, circling the kitchen with their imaginary flamenco dresses.

Brooke placed her cheek against Jacky's and continued to sweep her across the floor.

She felt like home.

Brooke placed her lips up to Jacky's ear. "You can tell a lot about a person by the way she dances," she whispered.

"What have you learned about me?" Jacky asked, dizzy.

"Well," she spoke softly. "You're reluctant."

Jacky became aware of the gate Brooke just opened up, and it beckoned her to go up to it and cross through. She imagined Brooke sitting on a stone wall, patting the empty spot next to her. Jacky wanted to sit and spill her soul.

She tempted her with her loving heart, exposing her to a danger that could destroy the status quo. Getting any closer to someone like her could cause irreversible damage. For the love of everything wholesome in the world, Jacky couldn't look away from her, though.

Brooke guided her to dance like a pro.

"You've certainly learned a lot from the bees."

She tilted her head and a confused puppy dog look sprang up on her face. "Elaborate on that, please."

"Well, clearly your bees have taught you how to communicate through dance. And," Jacky swung her with surprising grace, "I have to say, you're good at it. I'm not looking as clumsy as I really am."

"I guess Sophie's been educating you?"

"Oh, I've done my own homework, just as Sophie did."

"You've read up on the dance of bees?"

"More like I've listened up on the dance of them."

Brooke opened her eyes wide.

"Your voice is as exquisite as your dance," Jacky dared to whisper.

A twinkle rose. "You listened to my guided meditation on dance?"

Jacky leaned in closer, wanting to soar higher. She wanted to sit beside her on that stone wall and get drunk off her kiss. "Many of them."

Brooke stared at her lips, and Jacky couldn't resist. She moved in, tickled by the small puffs of air Brooke released on a moan, and hovered mere centimeters in front of her. Then, at the last second, she turned away, brushing up against Brooke's soft cheek instead.

They continued to sway to the sultry Latin beat, resting in the comfort of each other's arms. Brooke's body swayed against her, teasing that protective wall to wave like a silky robe. Jacky melted under her embrace, losing grip on the physical world and free falling into her mystical sphere.

Then, the front door opened and slammed shut. "I'm back," Sophie yelled.

They both leaped from each other's arms and looked around the room in search of something platonic and ordinary.

Sophie walked in with a bouquet of flowers. "These were delivered to your grandparents' house a few minutes ago."

Jacky turned to Brooke. Her face paled. She could only imagine they were from a recent date or admirer. The remnants of her protective wall hardened back to its original state.

"So are we ready to go?" Sophie asked. "I've got a lot of notes to transcribe for my presentation to the wildlife refuge."

"Yeah," Jacky said, still trembling. "We should go." *We should go very fast.*

~ ~

Sophie sat in the passenger seat on silent mode thinking about what she witnessed in Brooke's kitchen. She never should have let Bee go to the bathroom out back. She should have walked straight into the house with the flowers, then let Bee outside to pee.

Seeing them dance together brought on some strange emotions.

She looked over at Jacky. She glowed. Jacky was reeling. She had one of those faces where you could always see her emotions. That romantic dance looped in her mind, for sure. Yup. Jacky got stuck in a groove, just like any of her lovesick friends when crushing on someone.

She wanted Jacky to like Brooke. They clicked. They clicked probably better than her mother and Jacky did. That made her feel sad for her mother.

"I miss Mom," Sophie said, staring out the window.

Jacky lowered the radio and slowed down. She slowed a little too much. A car behind her began to beep.

Sophie snuck a peek over her shoulder. "That driver sure is angry." The car closed in on them, so close she couldn't see their headlights.

"I don't care." Jacky picked up the speed a little, but not enough to stop the beeping idiot behind them. "Let's talk about her."

Sophie feared the car would rear-end them. "I shouldn't have said anything. Just drive normal."

Jacky sighed, then pulled over and stopped the car. The other car passed her and honked the horn. She exhaled and bowed her head. "I miss her too."

Sophie chewed on the idea of not telling her what she saw. But instead, Sophie decided to act more like a bee. "I saw you."

Jacky swallowed hard, the kind where Sophie could see a small lump roll down the front of her throat. "You saw what exactly?"

"I saw you and Brooke in the kitchen. I was out back, and I saw you."

Jacky looked away, trying to hide the look of shame creeping on her face. She took a few out-of-control breaths, then bit her lip. "I don't know what to say."

"She likes you."

Pain stretched across Jacky's face.

Sophie felt bad for her. She liked her better happy. "I think it's really cool," Sophie said.

Jacky's pain smoothed instantly like someone pulled the string of a mini blind and pulled them up. "Really?"

"Like I said before, she makes you happy."

Jacky's eyebrows furrowed. "I still love your mom."

Sophie bit her lip and nodded, afraid the tears would come if she spoke.

An awkward pause ensued.

"We just danced," Jacky said so low Sophie barely heard her. "Nothing else happened."

Their roles reversed and now Sophie took the helm, listening as Jacky defended herself. Brooke was a good person, and Sophie really enjoyed how lighthearted she felt when around them together. But she still pitied her mother. She'd never have that second chance to fall in love again. "It's okay. It really is."

"We didn't even kiss. I couldn't bring myself to cross that line."

Sophie grappled with conflicting emotions. One part of her wanted Jacky happy and in love, the other feared how that would hit her whenever her mother came to mind in that context. "Even I kiss," Sophie said, staring straight out the front window.

"You kiss? Who do you kiss?"

Sophie laughed. "Boys."

"A lot of them?"

She shrugged. She had to have some secrets in life. *Time to change the subject.* "Are you ever afraid you'll forget Mom?"

"I could never forget her, kiddo."

"Sometimes I get scared because I can't remember what Mom looks like." She twirled a piece of her hair, seeking comfort in its constant presence in her life. "I can't remember the exact color of her eyes or how she smelled."

Jacky twisted her jaw. She did that often when uncomfortable. "We should talk about her more."

"I just wish she was here," Sophie said. "That's all I meant."

"What do you say we go visit your mom at the urn garden?"

Sophie massaged the memory bead Jacky had gotten both of them after the cremation. She hadn't gone to the urn garden in a while. Jacky invited her often, but she didn't want her staring over her shoulder as she talked to her mom. But in that moment, she needed her mother, and her mom needed them. It was a beautiful day, and the sun would be setting just enough to cast a golden light on her memory stone. She wanted to see that light. "If you want to, sure."

"She would like it."

"Yeah," Sophie said, easing into a careful smile. "I think she would too."

~ ~

Jacky pulled into Swan Cemetery and into her usual parking spot, alongside the small stucco chapel. She visited Drew every week since her death. She sat at her memory stone and told her everything that happened during the week. Well, everything except for her times with Brooke. She never brought her up except for the one time she talked about Sophie's new apiary and nursery job. Some things didn't belong in those moments, and a growing affinity toward a beautiful woman definitely topped that list.

178

"Isn't her spot farther away from here?" Sophie asked.

"It is, but the way they carved these narrow roads, I prefer parking here and walking. I always get in the way of a funeral procession."

"Alright." Sophie climbed out of the passenger seat and stretched.

They walked the narrow road in silence, Sophie likely uncomfortable and Jacky, well, contemplating the softness of Brooke's cheek against hers. Those flutters, very familiar to her now, were taking up flight in places they shouldn't. Especially when visiting the memory stone of her beloved spouse.

Jacky attempted to clear her mind so she could focus on Drew. She always liked to talk with her about a memory they shared. Reminiscing brought her back to the present moment, keeping her in her heart.

As they walked, Jacky remembered back to the day Drew baked her a birthday cake and dropped it as she walked over to the table. The cake glowed with thirty-five candles at the time. Drew was terrified of fire, so her eyes were glued to the flames. She didn't see the present from Marie and Hazel on the floor as she closed in on the table of friends. She smacked right into it and toppled over, landing right on top of the cake and extinguishing its flames. *Do you remember the icing smeared all over your face, sweetheart?*

Jacky continued to walk, hanging on to the lightness of Drew. As they got closer, Jacky noticed someone with a hat bent over at Drew's stone. She squinted to get a closer look at the person. Was she sobbing?

Did the woman have the correct spot? Did Jacky?

She stopped, spun around to catch her bearings. Everything always looked the same in a cemetery; same arched-shaped headstones, flowers, trees. Of course she had the right location. She knew the site like she knew her own home.

Who was that woman and why was she sobbing?

Sophie walked and texted, already ten paces ahead, unaware of the sobbing woman.

Jacky jogged to catch up, and suddenly, the woman looked up to the sky. Jacky recognized her profile. "Is that Ashley's Mom?"

Sophie stopped and looked up. "What is she doing here?"

"I'm as confused as you."

Kate looked up to the sky, face strained, hands folded in prayer, as if pleading with God. She sobbed, choked, and begged with the expansive cloudless sky.

"I guess she misses Mom, too?" Sophie asked in a strange little echo of a voice.

Kate entered heavily into Drew's life about six months before she died. They became quick friends and spent most every night together at the dojo. Her blood ran cold as they stood under the bright, blue sky and watched her fall apart. Jealousy corked its way through her sensibility.

Kate and her husband ended up divorced. Did Drew talk Kate into getting a divorce? Did Kate ever encourage Drew to divorce her? Did they talk about such intimate things? By the looks of her sorrow, Kate likely pulled Drew down the road of intimate revelations and tough decisions.

A friend who sobbed like her would've been privy to the inner folds of their marriage. Did Drew confide in her about everyday irritations like when Jacky left the toothbrush off the charger? Did she run to her every time they argued, telling her every last detail of her side and little of Jacky's? That's what best friends did. They whispered to each other in the corner of a dark room late into the night, venting about spilled juice and snoring. Did she know about the dishwasher argument when she yelled at Drew for piling everything on top of each other? Or what about the time Jacky wouldn't talk to her for three days because of a fight they had over how she folded her socks inside out and stretched them to the point they fell off her feet.

They could talk for years over Jacky's terrible habits and quirks. No wonder they grew close enough to merit sobs.

Kate's crying annoyed Jacky, suddenly. Her bowed head and jerking shoulders stunk of undeserved rights. What right did she have to mourn her after two and a half years? Did she hug Drew on those nights when she worried when her mammogram showed a suspicious spot? Did she cook her chicken soup when she got a cold? Did she place a heating pad on her tummy each month when her menstrual cramps proved too painful? Jacky earned that sobbing spot, not her friend.

Jacky panted and huffed air like Bee did in her front window perch. "I didn't realize she suffered over your mom like this."

"Me neither."

"Does Ms. Kate ever talk about her?" The irritation curled up around her words. Sophie blinked. "Sort of, I guess."

Jacky looked around, unsettled. What was it? Shame? Bitterness? Guilt? Perhaps a culmination of all three. How did she not know her wife had a best friend who would sob at her urn two and a half years later? How did a wife not know that? Drew would never be surprised to find Marie or Hazel at her site sobbing. Drew knew every nook and cranny of Jacky's life. She knew before Jacky sneezed. She knew when Jacky craved chocolate, when she needed a foot rub, hell even when she needed to be left alone. Drew only had to take one look at her and she knew.

Jacky screwed up in the feelings and perception department.

Was she not enough for Drew? Did Drew need more, more than Jacky had in her? Did Drew not view her as her best friend?

Did Kate know more of her secrets than even Jacky?

"Should we give her privacy? Let her finish up?" Sophie asked. She arched her eyebrow, still watching Kate's over-the-top mourning.

Jacky shrugged. "Probably." A gritty sadness rubbed itself all over her insides. "What should we do?" Jacky couldn't decide for them. "Should we get back in the car?"

Just then, Kate turned toward them. She jumped to her feet and wiped her eyes, fumbling for composure. "Oh, hello you two," she called out, waving a tissue at them. It flew out of her hand and floated to the ground. She chased it, attempting to stomp on it. It kept getting away from her, and she kept stomping. Finally, she succeeded and bent down to pick it up. She once again waved it at them. "I guess I got my exercise for the day." A strange guttural laugh followed her words.

Jacky walked toward her. "I didn't think anyone else visited Drew's site anymore."

Tears smudged her mascara. "I try and come once in a while." She sniffled and blew her nose on the tissue she just saved from blowing away, the same tissue that her shoe just stomped. Even with red swollen eyes, she was pretty. Her freckles dotted her cheeks, giving her face an innocent, youthful glow. She had perfect hair, too. It hung in long waves past her shoulders and flipped in all the right places.

"I knew you both spent a lot of time at the dojo together," Jacky said. "I guess I didn't realize that you were so close."

"We grew to be good friends as we punched and kicked each other at the dojo." Her eyes still sparkled despite the tears and smeared mascara. "I miss her punches and kicks."

"I can see that." Jacky wrapped her arm around Sophie's shoulder, staking claim to the only thing she could, her daughter.

Sophie leaned into Jacky as if sensing her fall down the hill of despair and regret. That little action might've gone unnoticed by many, but for Jacky, it saved her in that moment, like a life raft coming into view in an unforgiving, landless ocean.

"It's weird," Sophie said in a small voice. "You never told me you come to visit with her."

Kate placed her hand to her chest and collected herself. "I didn't want to add to the sadness."

"Even I don't cry like you were," Sophie said. "She meant a lot to you, I guess."

"No other friend cared about me like she did. She always knew how to turn a tough situation around. You know?"

"Like with your divorce?" Sophie stared her down.

The question rocked Kate off her feet. She braced against the memory bench of a Mrs. Camille Garner, a mother and wife who died thirty-two years ago.

Sophie's stare could cut holes in metal if the right answers didn't come out. Sophie protected her mother, and would mow anyone down who messed with her legacy. Just last month, a girl's mom from her soccer team commented about how Drew loved to gossip, and Sophie stepped up to that woman's shocked face, pointing her little finger at her and barked out a warning. When it came to her mother, Sophie was just as much a scrapper as Drew had been.

"Your mother told me to stick it out," Kate said, then looked to Jacky. "She told me to stay loyal to my commitment and work on my marriage."

Jacky blinked and looked down at her wife's stone. *Of course you did, Drew.* "That's the kind of person Drew was."

The three of them stared at the stone and bowed their heads, each caught up in their silence.

A wave of refreshing relief passed through Jacky, relief for putting to rest a silly knocking in the back of her mind hinting the unthinkable had transpired beneath her very nose. They were friends. Great friends. Drew talked her out of divorce, not into it. They weren't lovers. They were friends.

Everyone needed such a friend, the kind Jacky used to be for Drew before life took over and responsibilities bore down on their daily life.

Outsiders were lucky because they had a certain freedom with Drew that Jacky didn't have. They weren't the ones pressing on her to be home by five, to get the right apples at the grocery store, and to fold the clothes correctly. Friends like Kate came lint free, looking fresh and not reeking of the foulness that routine often put into a married couple's life.

Jacky imagined them having long talks over cinnamon tea, Drew's favorite, in the quiet corners of a café as their daughters practiced cheerleading moves in a nearby park. Drew knew how to carry on an interesting conversation, and she passed out great advice. Mainly to others. She rarely advised Jacky on anything because it always ended in a fight, usually by Jacky's doing. She hated being attacked or criticized, and dove into defense mode. How many intimate talks had she missed out on over cinnamon tea cups? How many had Kate gained as a result?

She gulped back a bit of jealousy and regret. More questions poked at Jacky as they stood around her stone. What secrets did the two of them share in those final months? Did she know Drew feared the dark and preferred sleeping with a nightlight? Did Drew tell her about the time she babysat and saw a ghost?

183

She regretted allowing life to cut away beautiful intimate conversations about philosophical things like love and marriage and commitments. Jacky unknowingly pushed Drew into those conversations with strangers, who later became friends, because Jacky lacked the confidence to accept the volley and return it.

"Well, I don't want to infringe on your time here. I should get going." Kate spun around to check the spot, like she'd forgotten something. "Okay then. I'll be on my way." She brushed past them, sniffling. "Oh, Hey, Sophie," she said, stopping and placing her hand on Sophie's arm. "Do you want hamburgers tomorrow after debate practice?"

"Sure," Sophie said with more reservation than usual. "That'd be nice."

"Great." Kate nodded to them and walked away, leaving Jacky alone to face the wave of jealousy pounding at her, threatening to topple her right there at the entrance to Drew's sacred memory.

A series of sobs convulsed somewhere deep inside of Jacky. She didn't want to lose it in front of Sophie, to let her see the regret for how she failed to appreciate her mother toward the end.

Sophie looked at her with pity, masked as sorrow. Pity sucked. It meant hope had long ago flown away and left her without any mechanism to set things right. Sophie had heard so many of their stupid quarrels about things that, in the grand scheme of life, didn't matter one bit.

Jacky caused this nightmare. If Jacky had kept her mouth shut that morning and acted like a normal human being instead of some rabid wild animal always trying to be the right one in the argument, maybe they'd be sharing a delicious pizza at their favorite restaurant and laughing about something simple and jovial that happened in Sophie's day. Something precious and undeniably refreshing.

In life and in death, she failed her wife.

She kneeled in front of the stone consumed with regret for being foolish enough to forget all the pain she had caused as she carried on with life. Drew was dead. She was alive. That notion reeked of absurdity.

She pictured Drew viewing her dance with Brooke, and saw sadness. Her heart ached. *I'm sorry I shunned you today.*

She began to cry. The tears rolled steadily down her cheeks faster than she could catch them.

"I wish I had been a better friend to your mom," Jacky managed to say in between sobs.

Sophie placed her hand on Jacky's shoulder. "You were always Mom's best friend. Don't ever forget that."

Sophie's maturity poked another hole in Jacky's strength, causing her to topple over on herself in a wave of hysteric bucks. "It's so unfair." Drew didn't deserve the cruelty of death while Jacky enjoyed soulful afternoons dancing to the beat of someone else's heart, someone as beautiful as Brooke.

Sophie wrapped her arm around Jacky and remained the stronger of the two, offering Jacky much more than she deserved.

Jacky placed her hand on Drew's stone. "I didn't mean to let you go, sweetheart."

Sophie cradled her shoulder. "She knows."

Did she?

Sophie continued to console her, standing in as the temporary adult.

~ ~

When they returned home, Sophie sat in her bedroom, staring at the letter again. It didn't mean anything to her anymore. The words sat lifeless, evoking no sharp blows as they once had. Instead of filling her with resolve, they hung about like meaningless dust.

Jacky was innocent. Her mother was the guilty one. Sophie had seen that with her own eyes. Over the years, Sophie denied that to herself, but the truth blinded her now. How dare Ms. Kate show up at her mother's urn garden? She didn't belong there, just as surely as her lips hadn't belonged on her mother's that night she caught them kissing.

Should she tell Jacky? Did she have the right to know? Would it do her any good to hear that truth now, after all this time? Would she turn into even more of a moral obligation?

She didn't want to be an obligation.

Sophie hated the secrets between them. They robbed them of what they used to have together, a solid, open relationship. The letter, the kiss, the fears, they all sucked the life from their home. How could they ever be healthy with that kind of deceit floating about? Just like a poisonous pesticide, it would lead to their ultimate demise.

Chapter Fourteen

Brooke ran to pick up her cell.

"Hey," Jacky said. "I need to… um… I need to cancel tomorrow's training session."

"Is everything okay?"

"Yeah. I'm just going through some things right now."

Brooke swallowed the first taste of distress. She had pushed too hard, too fast. "Do you want to talk about it?"

"It's just that things are going to get a little crazy at the school. We've got this big competition coming up, and a lot of our clients are entering. It's going to be a lot of hours for the next few months."

Brooke sat down on her couch, sinking into the disappointment. "Of course. I understand." She never should've asked her to dance. She never should've shushed her with she began to talk about Drew. She should've stuck with brewing the tea and not acting like a wild woman in the kitchen spinning and cajoling about like a Flamenco dancer. She had about as much Latin in her as an Eskimo.

Jacky sighed deeply. "The pressure of small business ownership is overwhelming. You know how that is, I'm sure."

No, she didn't know how that was. Her business never stressed her out. And, she had a sinking feeling, neither did Jacky's. "Are you sure that's all it is?"

Silence.

"Jacky?"

"I'm a confusing person, Brooke. My head is all over the place, right now."

"You can talk to me."

187

"I just need some time to sort through a few things on my own."

"Of course."

"Thank you for understanding."

Brooke cringed at the formality. "You're welcome."

"Do you want to arrange for one of the other trainers to take over with Bee for a while?" Jacky asked.

"No." She pushed the word out before ironing it over. She sounded so desperate.

She couldn't bear the thought of someone else pulling up to her house. Bee adored Jacky. Brooke trusted her. Jacky helped raise her confidence when dealing with Bee. Admittedly, Brooke enjoyed showing off for Jacky. She loved taking that leash and proudly prancing with her beasty dog down the street to face her fear. She did an internal happy dance whenever she managed to pass a couple with a dog or a jogger without as much as breaking a sweat. On those wonderful occasions when Bee didn't take notice of a person or dog, when she just walked on by them like they were blades of grass swaying with the wind, Brooke committed herself to not skipping for joy. She, instead, settled for that deep-dimpled grin that would appear on Jacky's face along with that streak of pride.

She shouldn't have cared so much what Jacky thought. But she did. She couldn't bear to open her door to a new trainer. She'd likely be a young girl with a perfectly polished ponytail. She'd likely sport one of those forced, smart smiles that served as positive reinforcement, much like with their canine counterparts. No, Brooke couldn't have it.

"My training associate Greg is really good with issues of protectiveness."

"I don't want a trainer named Greg." He sounded like a tax attorney with curly dark hair and beady eyes. Brooke's heart broke. Jacky dumped her before she could cook her a proper meal, bake her a cake or spoil her with love. In all of her natural, no-fuss ways, she was beautiful. She loved Jacky's relaxed look. It made her real and raw, comfortable. She could wake up next to her and not worry whether her mascara bled halfway down her face. Jacky wouldn't care if Brooke had a few gray hairs pop into her front wisps. "Please don't send me someone named Greg."

"I've got other trainers with different names." A laugh hung on the edge of her words.

"Ah, she jokes," Brooke whispered, resting her head against a pillow reminiscing about her cheek against Jacky's.

Jacky whimpered. "You know I don't want this either. I'd much rather be chasing Bee down the street than circling the training floor with a bunch of well-behaved Poodles pointing their pompom tails at just the right angle."

Brooke knew this had nothing to do with training Poodles. She pushed too hard and fast. She overstepped her boundary. She took it to the next level, when Jacky just wanted to stay on the ground. Her heart sunk. "Is this really about busy schedules?"

More gut-wrenching silence.

"I can't do this right now. I'm not ready," Jacky whispered.

Brooke winced.

"I'm sorry, Brooke."

Brooke leveled her breathing, fighting against the forceful ache pounding on her heart. Jacky obviously grappled with grief, but there was more to the story. "What happened, Jacky?"

"We visited with Drew at the urn garden after we left your house. I've got a lot of mixed emotions right now."

Brooke heard the sorrow and guilt in her voice. "You deserve to be happy, Jacky. I hope you know that."

She sighed. Brooke could imagine her biting her lip and clenching her strong jaw. "The jury is still out on that one."

Brooke wished she could hug her. "I'm here if you need me, okay?"

"Thank you." Jacky hung up on a soft cry.

~ ~

Sophie sat before her Auntie Marie and Auntie Hazel that Sunday night and confessed. "I know why Ashley's mom broke down at my mother's urn garden."

189

"Of course, because she misses your mom," Auntie Hazel said, sipping her tea.

"No." Sophie looked to Auntie Marie who eyed her with serious pause. She needed to tell someone before she cracked. "You have to promise me you won't say anything to Jacky."

Auntie Marie shifted in the chair, looking highly uncomfortable. "Now look here. You know I don't have it in me to keep secrets. I don't believe in them. So whatever you're about to say, you better know it's not safe with me."

"It's really not," Auntie Hazel whispered. "She can't lie or keep secrets."

"If Jacky knew, it would crush her."

"Then don't tell her or us," Auntie Marie said.

"Ms. Kate is going to ruin her relationship with Brooke. I overheard Jacky telling Brooke she can't be her trainer anymore. And, it's all because she saw Ms. Kate crying at Mom's memory stone and feels responsible. I don't want her to throw away something good over Ms. Kate's crying."

Auntie Marie frowned. "I'm going to wring Jacky's neck."

"She told Brooke she's not ready for the next step."

"Have they even taken a step?" Auntie Hazel asked.

"I caught them dancing in her kitchen. Then, we saw Kate sobbing at my mother's grave a few minutes later, and next thing you know Jacky called Brooke and quit on her."

"Hang on a minute." Auntie Marie shot her hands up as if balancing. "You're talking to two women suffering through menopause. You're going to have to slow down and feed us in small bites."

"Oh for God's sakes, Marie," Auntie Hazel scoffed at her. "It's not that complicated. Jacky's in love and she's feeling guilty. End of story."

Sophie loved how easily those two communicated together. They never held back. They unloaded whatever took up space in their mind. As it should've been. "I don't want Jacky to ruin something good, and I need you to urge her not to break it off before it has a chance to take off."

"She's entitled to her own feelings, dear." Auntie Marie sat back.

"Jacky doesn't know the whole story, though," Sophie said.

"There's more?" Auntie Marie's forehead creased.

"I caught my mom and Ms. Kate kissing not long before she died."

"Oh," they both said together. Their jaws descended.

"The Sunday before she died, Ashley and I snuck downstairs to get soda and they were in the foyer kissing. It was late, and they didn't know we were there. Ashley wanted to scream at them, but I held her back. I made her promise not to say anything because I was afraid what it would mean for everyone. What if Ms. Kate divorced Ashley's dad and they had to move away? What if Jacky left? There were too many variables, and thankfully Ashley promised not to say anything."

Auntie Marie slapped the chair's arm. "Jacky needs to know."

"What good is it going to do her now?" Sophie asked. "She'd never trust anyone again."

Auntie Marie latched onto that statement. "Ah, sweet Jesus." She tossed her hands in the air. "Why didn't you say something before now, dear?"

Sophie didn't want anyone hating on her mother. If they hated her, why not her offspring? "Because she can't defend herself. What if Kate kissed her by surprise? Maybe my mom didn't do anything wrong. Or what if she just goofed up and didn't have the chance to correct it?" She wanted her mom remembered for her humor and friendship. Not being a cheater. "I never should've said anything."

Auntie Marie and Auntie Hazel shared a look. Then, Auntie Hazel turned to her. "Your secret is safe with us."

Auntie Marie cleared her throat. "I agree that this would kill her. We need to let things take their own course."

Sophie frowned. "I was hoping you'd talk some sense into her. I don't want her to throw it away with Brooke."

"I'm not getting involved," Auntie Marie folded her arms over her chest. "Nope. You're going to have to figure out something clever for yourself on this one."

Clever? Sophie wasn't clever. She was too literal, rigid, an in-the-box thinker. "She'll listen to you, though," Sophie pleaded.

"You know what I think?" Auntie Marie asked.

"Enlighten us," Auntie Hazel said.

Auntie Marie looked her straight in the eye. "She'd listen more if it came from you, Sophie."

From her? No way. "I can't have this kind of conversation with her. We don't talk like that."

Auntie Marie scooted up. "You're the best choice here. So, quit the *Who me? I can't* crapola and go talk some sense into her because I really want to get into a bee suit and sip lemonade on Brooke's patio. You've painted quite a picture about that place, and now my chances are looking slim."

"You in a bee suit?" Sophie laughed.

"Why not?"

"Jacky fumbled a tray with the queen on it. I can't imagine what you might do." She giggled. "Maybe Jacky is actually saving a few thousand bees by keeping her distance from Brooke, then."

They all enjoyed a good laugh over that.

A few minutes later, Sophie realized all she'd revealed to them. She let her mother's secret out of the bag. Did that make her a horrible daughter? "I'm sorry I told you about the kiss. I feel kind of bad now. What if I got it wrong and Ms. Kate kissed her? That wouldn't be her fault. Maybe she's not a bad person because of it after all."

"Now listen," Auntie Marie said, scooting up in her chair and resting her elbow on her good knee. "I once kissed a married woman too. I'm not a bad person. Okay? I'm just human. Your mom was just being human."

The gravity of Auntie Marie's words brought her solace. "Thank you for saying that."

Auntie Marie opened up her arms. "Come here. Group hug."

Auntie Marie didn't often cave into mushy moments, but when she did, Sophie wrapped herself into it like her happiness depended on it.

It actually did.

~ ~

Brooke stood in front of her hives, hugging herself.

Jacky's call hurt more than she cared to admit, even to her bees. When she hung up, Jacky took a piece of her heart. "I shouldn't have gotten so involved," she said, talking to an undertaker bee who was clearing a dead carcass from the hive.

She leaned in closer to it. "I suck at this relationship thing. I pick the wrong people." Anguish flooded her. "It's so hard. I fell so hard and fast. How couldn't I? Her heart beat with mine. She melted against me. Her whole body caved. She surrendered, finally."

The bee dragged the dead carcass down the side of the hive box, diligent and determined to forget its own pain and challenges for the betterment of the hive as a whole.

"You are so lucky," she said to the bee. "You never have to guess what another is thinking."

Did Jacky spill the whole truth? Did she come on too strong? Did she hate the way she danced? Did her breath stink? Did her hair itch her face? Maybe she preferred blondes? Did she feel guilty? Likely. Jacky couldn't forgive herself for moving on. Many widows suffered like that, right? She lived and Drew didn't. That reality could definitely bring about regret and disillusions of undeserved opportunities. Survivor guilt, perhaps? Could she get past it? How?

The undertaker struggled with a divot in the side of the hive, but maintained balance and control over the carcass. Brooke could've just flicked the carcass off the hive and carried it to the underbrush herself, saving the undertaker some time. "I suppose that would be dishonoring you, though."

It followed a straight line down the side of the yellow-painted box diligently carrying out her role. If the bee didn't go through the steps, she might not evolve into a deserving being capable of moving on to her next role.

That's when it dawned on Brooke. Jacky struggled down the side of her proverbial hive, fighting her footing and balance before moving on to the next step in life. She had to go through the motions or she'd never find her peace. Steps simply could not be avoided because each step provided the know-how and guidance for the ones that followed. It would be too easy to take Jacky by the hand and lead her to that peace. She needed to find that on her own. She had to suffer and carve her own path toward it.

The undertaker finally landed on the ground and dragged the dead bee across the mossy rocks and toward the thick underbrush. She followed it closely, watching as the honest bee did her honest job, wishing she could have as much patience and faith in the process of life.

Chapter Fifteen

A whole week had gone by since Jacky spoke with Brooke. She never emerged onto her porch when Jacky pulled up to drop off or pick up Sophie on Saturday. She respected Jacky's need for space.

That space hurt. The wider it grew, the more Jacky grappled with its purpose. Without Brooke, life tasted bland and played out in gray tones. The music of life slowed to a hum. Brooke not only flavored and colored her world, but she added vitality to it.

Jacky propped herself on the couch and listened to another one of Brooke's stories that Sophie had lent her. She spoke about the honesty trait of bees and how without it, they'd never thrive as a society the way they did. With her enchanting whispers, she spoke about how just like with bees, humans wouldn't thrive without it either. Her voice softened Jacky's heart.

We'd never be able to fully invest in anyone, even ourselves.

Imagine for a moment, a world highlighted in honesty; where every person you met spoke only the truth. Immerse yourself in that world for a few minutes as we travel along a path brimming with an energy so powerful that your steps start to feel bouncy and light. You enjoy the refreshing sunlight warming your face as you spend your energy focusing on the things that really matter in life, things like love, friendship, and activities that nurture your soul.

Jacky breathed deeper, relaxing under Brooke's caring cadence.

Just like a honeybee, you are free to explore and focus on the beauty of knowing, without a doubt, that you are in alignment with your purpose and roles. You work with others in a fluid, cohesive manner, completely trusting in the overall dynamic that creates the powerful, life-affirming vibe known as collective spirit. All facts are out in the open to marinate and digest as needed for the overall betterment of community. You focus on the key elements that give lift to life, circulating informative, character-building messages that help everyone around you thrive.

Jacky wanted to stay in that soothing moment.

This is a special place where you don't need to worry about incidentals and what-ifs. If a question arises, you are free to ask without judgment or concern for repercussions, for everyone operates on the golden rule that honesty is sacred and thus nurtured. Life is more amenable in this place where the truth floats in the open airways for all to enjoy. Information flows freely. Constructive conversations take shape forming a new, brighter horizon. Ideas are explored without worrying of hidden agendas. Nothing relevant falls to the wayside. With all the facts on the table, real progress begins to happen.

Brooke's voice and beautiful message continued to swaddle Jacky's heart in a comforting hope. She remained relaxed on the couch with her eyes closed as Brooke led her through more vivid imagery and back to her living room.

Jacky opened her eyes after a while, staring at her ceiling fan.

Honest talks could fix everything, if only everyone played by the same rules. She'd be able to tell Marie how she hated when she nagged her. She'd state the fact, and they'd deal with it.

More importantly, she could tell Brooke about her fears, instead of hiding behind the veil of Drew's death.

She stood up and ventured to the kitchen to make some coffee.

Coffee.

Maybe she could invite her over for coffee, and ask about Sophie's work in the apiary that week. Or, she could extend her hand in friendship by sending a care package of treats for Bee with a pleasant note saying hello.

She stood with her hands on her hips. Yes, that would work.

She reached up to the top shelf of the cupboard and pulled down a mason jar.

Within five minutes, she had attached a ribbon to it and filled it with peanut butter cookies.

She pointed a pen to a notecard. *Just thinking of you* sounded too bold.

She looked down to Rosy, then back at the note she began.

Just thinking of you, and hoping you are well. Here's some yummy treats for Bee. Just don't let her bite off those pretty fingers of yours. (smile)

Too flirty.

Rosy glanced up at her as if on cue.

She tore it up and started a new one.

Just thinking of you, and hoping you are well. She hesitated, searching for a good hook. She looked back at Rosy who blinked. "You're right. This is ridiculous."

She went back to the living room and sat down. She flipped through a Cosmo magazine. Not long into an article on fall fashion, Sophie returned home.

"Hey kiddo. I thought you were going to Ashley's for a sleepover tonight?"

"I am. But not until later. First I have some research to do." She wheeled her laptop case over to the couch and then plopped down.

"That hard of a day?"

Sophie propped her feet on the coffee table. "I went over to the apiary after school and was surprised to find Brooke with a new trainer. Did you know she hired a new one?"

Pins pricked up her spine, like someone squeezed a voodoo doll and stuck her with hundreds of needles. "I had suggested Greg."

"He wasn't Greg."

"How did Bee act around him?"

"She humped his leg."

"Really?"

Sophie nodded as if numbed by the news herself. "And that happened at the end of the training session." She climbed to her feet and wheeled her case off to her bedroom, leaving Jacky with a rabid bite of jealousy and longing.

197

~ ~

Halfway through her plate of mashed potatoes, Brooke's phone rang.

It was Jacky. Her heart soared.

"I hope this isn't a bad time?"

"Your call saved me from eating a whole plate of lumpy mashed potatoes."

"Mashed potatoes? Lumpy at that? Oh, geez, I'm sorry I interrupted."

Brooke giggled.

"Would you settle for a cup of coffee in lieu of lumpy potatoes?"

Brooke loved hearing her familiar voice. "I can have it brewing in five minutes," she said with a skip to her heart.

"That's the best thing I've heard all week."

~ ~

Just as the sun started to set behind the carriage house, Jacky pulled into the driveway. When Jacky rang the doorbell, Brooke had just finished pulling chocolate chip cookies out of the oven. She ran out of the kitchen to grab the door. Bee went crazy on the ledge of the bay window.

When Brooke opened the door, she didn't try to stop Bee from jumping. She wanted Jacky to see how her absence affected them both.

"I've been a terrible student," Brooke said, closing the door behind them.

Jacky bent down to pet Bee. "Some students require lifelong learning."

Brooke nodded. Jacky had summarized her perfectly.

Bee sniffed the bag Jacky carried. Reaching into it, she pulled out an adorable mason's jar filled with treats the shape of hearts. Jacky handed the jar to her. "I almost mailed them to you." She pulled in her lip. "I suck at writing though. I couldn't come up with anything clever to say that would clear my jerk status for backing out on my commitment to you and Bee."

Brooke opened the jar and handed Bee a treat. "Trying to mail anything to a carriage house is impossible. My grandparents would've signed for it and forgotten about it. It happens all the time. Once they forgot to hand over a Christmas package for my ex. Her parents had mailed it to her, and it sat in my grandparent's foyer for weeks. She cried thinking they had forgotten about her. Probably served her right to suffer a little."

Jacky chuckled.

"I'm rambling."

Jacky remained fixated, dispensing a yearning. "I missed you."

"I'm glad you finally called," Brooke whispered.

Jacky pulled in her bottom lip, looking shy and vulnerable. "I heard about Bee humping your new trainer's leg. I guess I'm not Bee's only one anymore."

Brooke laughed. "What are you talking about?"

"Your new trainer."

"What new trainer?"

"Sophie told me you have a new one, and Bee humps his leg."

"Is that why you called? Were you jealous of this new trainer?"

Jacky opened her mouth, and closed it. Then, reopened again. "I guess I am."

"I wouldn't hire a new trainer." Brooke warmed at the idea that Sophie wanted them to spend time together. "I think your daughter pulled a fast one on us."

Jacky blushed, and blossomed into a relieved smile, one that spread through her entire being. "It would seem so."

Brooke placed her hand on Jacky's arm. "Come in. I baked some cookies to go with that coffee."

Jacky followed her into the kitchen, over to the same spot where Sophie caught them dancing.

"So what else besides a little jealousy brings you by?" Brooke asked.

"I wanted to thank you for taking Sophie under your wing as you have. She's loving this whole beekeeping thing."

Brooke wanted more of a reason. "She's great at it."

"She's opening up again. Little by little."

"Little by little is good." Brooke walked toward the coffee pot.

Jacky followed. "I worry about her, you know?" She fidgeted with the bottle of peppermint oil on her counter. "For so long she just hung out in her bedroom and read books. Since coming here, she regained a part of her innocence and zest for life. I suspect you have a lot to do with it."

Brooke reached for the peppermint oil and added a drop to each of their mugs. "We have the bees to thank for that." She stirred one of the coffees.

"You're too humble."

"I can't take credit for what they teach us." Brooke circled toward the living room.

Once they sat on the couch, they sipped. "So how have you been?"

"I've been fine," Jacky said.

Brooke scanned her face and it told a different story. She sat before a woman who was sinking into a well of loneliness. She had shame and regret written in the fine lines around her eyes. Her left eye twitched, indicating lying didn't come naturally and the weight of all she carried began to take its toll. Just like her bees, Brooke learned to read body language. It offered a lot more information than did words. Words often misguided reality. They said one thing but meant an entirely different thing. "Really?"

Jacky sipped her coffee. "Yeah." She bounced her head up and down as if convincing herself of that lie. "I'm doing fine."

Brooke braved forward. "I don't believe you."

Jacky scoffed, then hid her resistance in another long, drawn-out sip.

"Do you want to talk about it?"

Jacky eyed her and labored for air. "I wouldn't even know where to start."

"How about at the beginning?"

"Do you have all night?"

She had the rest of her life. "Tell me what's on your mind."

Jacky rubbed her eyes. She looked exhausted and beat down by life, like she'd been in the ring for too long and took on too many punches.

"Go on. Just let it out."

Jacky inhaled deeply. "I lied to you about something."

"Oh?"

"I haven't been busy at the school this week."

"I know. Sophie fills me in."

Jacky winced.

"It's okay." Brooke placed her hand on her knee.

"I've got a lot of baggage, even for a friendship."

"Baggage can be unpacked."

"Mine is awfully wrinkled."

"It means you've lived," Brooke said.

Jacky's jaw tensed, and her eye twitched again.

Instinctively, Brooke delicately smoothed her finger along Jacky's lid, easing the twitch into submission. "Talk to me."

"Our dance." She met her eye. "It opened my heart again, and that scared me."

"Of course it did." Brooke placed her hand on the side of Jacky's blushed face, trying to soothe her.

"You don't understand."

"Then, help me to."

"The reason goes deeper than my desire." Jacky paused. A reservoir of silence permeated the space between them. Then, she spoke again. "It's my fault Drew died."

Brooke cradled Jacky's cheek. "Tell me what happened."

"We were having a fight. It got ugly. I said things I never should've said. And it kills me that I can't take them back. There's no rewind and erase buttons."

"Every couple fights. It's natural. It's conflict." She dropped her hand and caressed Jacky's wrist now.

"I can tell Sophie blames me. Hell, I blame me. When Sophie looks at me," Jacky groaned, "well, I wonder if she wishes I had died that day instead."

Jacky's face took on a fresh layer of agony. Brooke tightened her grip on her wrist, urging her to continue.

"I know we're all in this to die. I get that. Maybe we're all in line to die on a certain prearranged day, even. Maybe she died that day because the day belonged to her. I want to believe that because that's the only way I can forgive myself."

Brooke didn't agree. Fate didn't work that way. Living constituted a series of choices and those choices dictated life, not destiny.

"I said many things to Drew that I shouldn't have. God, we could argue. But we loved each other. Couples fight. Right? I mean, that's what we do. What we did. We'd argue our sides, stubbornly at best, and eventually we'd forget why we stopped talking for a time. We'd just pick up one morning where we left off before a fight. She'd pour me cereal, I'd pour her milk. We'd crunch, pass the paper to each other, and carry on with our lives. We learned to forgive and forget, just as much as we learned to hide our feelings. Only the words I tossed at her that day weren't meant to be the last ones she heard. Why did the universe decide those had to be the last words she'd ever hear and the last words I'd ever speak to her? It's so unfair."

Brooke had a pretty good idea of the nature of those words. She'd tossed them to Penelope a few times herself. They were like bricks in a foundation. They weren't the entire foundation, just a part, woven into the whole, not as support, but as a component. Not a very important component. Just a part of the sum.

"If you truly loved her, she knew it."

"I did. I loved her with all my heart. And it sucks that I get to carry on and she doesn't."

"You can't think that way."

"I can't help it."

"You realize that by carrying that regret around you're doing her a great disservice, don't you?"

Jacky sniffed. "I don't know about that."

"By not getting on with your life, you're saying to everyone around you that she ruined you. That her death destroyed you."

Jacky gasped and nodded.

Brooke continued, "You and Drew built a beautiful life together, and her spirit still lives on in that world and in the love you have for your daughter. To fall to the ground in defeat over some words, that in hindsight meant nothing, isn't honoring her legacy the way I know you want to honor it."

Jacky's chin quivered. "You're so right."

Brooke paused, thinking how best to help her. "Most of us have been taught that we need to be strong, always moving forward no matter what. But that's not always easy, is it?"

Jacky shook her head. "It's the most difficult thing I've ever attempted."

Pain etched on her face, and all Brooke wanted was to wipe it away with something clever and wise; something her Nana or her meditation teacher would've said.

"If we never give ourselves a break from trying to be strong, we welcome disaster to come in and destroy everything we're working so hard to maintain."

"I just want to feel at peace, but reminders pummel me down whenever I open up to it."

Jacky equated strength with peace. Brooke didn't see it that way. "We have to get beaten down from time to time. That's part of the human experience. We have to fall to the ground and learn to accept defeat and mistakes we've made."

"So just give up?"

Brooke half-smiled, taken in by Jacky's need to make things right with Sophie, with Bee, with her obvious struggle. "No. You don't give up. You allow yourself to feel those emotions, but then, you have to climb back up on your feet and move on after you've learned the lessons. You have to get back up because there are victories waiting on you."

Jacky searched her eyes. "How do you know just what to say?"

Brooke released a soft sigh. "I've had my share of disappointments in life. Of course, nothing compared to yours. But, nonetheless, I've suffered heartbreaks that have brought me to my knees; my parents uprooting without inviting me along and my girlfriend leaving and taking our dog. My nana helped me through them. She's wise and her advice sunk in I guess."

"To look at you, I'd never know you suffered heartbreak," Jacky said. "Your positivity gives me hope."

"You have to believe that only the best of all the love, pain, suffering, and healing will stay with you. From there, you'll have new shades of colors to draw from."

Brooke paused again, watching as Jacky absorbed what she said. She desperately wanted Jacky to release her pain. "Sometimes it takes a while for the dust to settle. Trust that it will shortly, and when it does, you'll find your new building blocks somewhere in there."

Jacky teared up.

Brooke placed her hand on top of Jacky's. "You need to forgive yourself."

"How am I supposed to do that?"

"You turn to those who love you and let them help you heal. Support systems are vital."

Jacky drew a deep breath. "I wonder if I'll ever get to the point when I'm not trying to get somewhere. When I'll look around and be happy right where I finally am."

"You'll have plenty of time to slip into that peaceful pocket. You deserve it. Life will continue to tumble around you, it always does. That's the ebb and flow. That doesn't mean you should stop and let it suck you down and drown you."

Jacky wrestled with pain. "It's hard to inhale air when under the water."

"I would imagine so." Brooke paused and took in the recognition surfacing on her face.

Jacky fidgeted with a string on her shirt.

"It's time for you to get back up."

"I feel it, too." Jacky swallowed hard.

Brooke stepped onto the ledge of boldness. "I don't think Drew would want you to stay down like this. She'd want you to get back up on your feet and live your life."

Jacky squeezed her eyes closed for a few emotional seconds, then met Brooke's eyes again.

Brooke continued, "If you stayed down, I would imagine she'd be very upset with you. She wouldn't want you to fall to the ground and let life flush you away."

"I wouldn't want that for her, either."

"Exactly." Brooke paused, allowing for some breathing room. "I also don't believe she'd want to be the cause of a great life wasted. You've got time left. What if it's another fifty years? You can't go on carrying this weight for the next fifty years."

Jacky swallowed hard. "I'm tired of carrying it. It hurts."

"Let it go."

Jacky frowned. "I sometimes wish I never met her so I'd be ignorant to the pain of it all."

"If you knew ahead of time that you'd suffer this way, would you really have walked away from her?"

Jacky blinked. "Impossible. I fell head over heels the first moment I met her."

"Every woman dreams of being loved with such passion." *I sure as hell do.*

"I did love her with every part of my soul."

"That doesn't have to stop for you to move forward."

Jacky ran her fingers through her hair, then rested her chin in the palm of her hand. A peaceful glow began to surface.

"Keep honoring her as you do. Keep those pictures hung on the wall and continue to love her. And, know that it's okay to be happy. She would never want to see you live any other way, just as you wouldn't want that for her if the situation was reversed."

"Yeah." Jacky nodded, still visibly struggling.

"You're very tense."

"Hm. Yeah, I am." She released a half beat laugh. "Maybe what I need is a set of earbuds and one of your guided meditations."

"I can do better than that." Brooke placed a pillow on her lap. "Here. Lay back."

"A personalized one?"

Brooke reached out and caressed Jacky's hand. "There's a first time for everything."

Jacky smiled, then did as told.

Brooke ran her fingers through Jacky's hair, easing her into a relaxed state. "Take a nice deep breath."

Jacky inhaled deeply and a lopsided grin grew.

"No giggling," Brooke whispered.

"No, ma'am."

"No calling me ma'am, either."

Jacky chuckled, then nodded. "Okay, I'm ready."

"Good. Now inhale again. Let it penetrate all the way down into your belly. Enjoy the gentle expansion as you inhale."

She voiced her words slowly, carefully.

"Let go and surrender all worry and stress as the breath glides in." She paused. "Now let it out."

Jacky exhaled, slow and steady.

"Inhale again and allow your breath to travel through your body, cleansing all the fears and pains."

"You're good at this," Jacky said.

"Shh. This isn't about me. This is your time. So enjoy it. Ease into it. Let it dissolve your negative emotions."

Jacky nodded and swallowed hard, tensing her jaw.

Brooke whispered slowly, "Imagine that you're holding in the palm of your hand, a big problem." She rested for a few seconds, then eased ahead. "Make it the one big problem that is getting in your way every day as you wake up, as you brush your teeth, as you stare in the mirror at your reflection." She rolled out her words one easy beat at a time. "The one that sits on your shoulders and presses them down. The one that pinches your heart and tears you up inside."

Jacky tilted her head as if searching her mind for the right problem.

"Do you have it?"

"I have it."

"Good, now squeeze that problem in between your hands with all the power you have within."

She gazed down at Jacky's hands. They pressed against each other.

"Take control over it." Brooke hesitated, letting the exercise sink in. "*You* have the power. It has no power."

She nodded.

"Jacky," she spoke softly. "You need to forgive yourself so you can move forward." She dropped her voice by a few tones. "The fields of change are upon you, calling out to you from the far reaches of the deepest forests where all sadness and regret live. That is their home. This is your home," she punctuated. "Right here, where your friends and family are."

Jacky's breaths relaxed.

"You're free to explore the opposite side of regret and sadness. You must. It's your right to experience all the emotions you're outfitted to receive."

Jacky sighed, as if struck by disbelief.

Brooke swept forward. "You're free to tiptoe into the landscape, and when you do, you'll remain safe. All you need to do to come back is turn over your shoulder, and you'll once again be right here in this spot, under the sun, and in the pocket of friendship and love."

Jacky's shoulders rose and fell - a good sign she discovered her safety spot.

"Your life is made up of a series of hills and valleys. Everyone experiences both of them. You're not alone. Everyone who has ever walked by your side, in front of you or behind, has also entered into a journey that has hills and valleys similar, but unique to their own experience."

Jacky sniffled.

"These hills and valleys can teach us important things if we're willing to stay open to their lessons. Sometimes you're the teacher of them and other times the student. We're all connected. We all matter. You matter, Jacky."

A single tear rolled down Jacky's cheek.

Brooke began to speak slower and even softer. "You're glowing. Your entire body is vibrating a new energy, one that radiates hope and peace to you and to everyone within your reach. It's a vital energy because it heals. It heals your heart, blessing it with an empathetic connection that smooths over all callouses caused by mistakes and hardships."

A peace swept across Jacky's face.

"You're filled with a gratitude for all life has gifted you with. There's so much to be thankful for. You have many gifts and you share those with so many. You're a teacher and a mentor. Where your heart bleeds, it will heal and be able to stay open, letting in the love and forgiveness you deserve."

Jacky's eyelids trembled.

Brooke lifted her voice to match the joyful emotion she wanted Jacky to experience. "See yourself happy. Stay open and loving. Embrace the day and all its lessons, taking them into your heart as nourishment for your revived soul."

A small cry escaped from Jacky.

"It's time to forgive yourself, Jacky."

Brooke drew a restful breath to deliver the next important point. "You are meant for a great life, and Drew wants that for you."

"Hmm." Jacky's mouth lifted ever-so-slightly into a smile.

"Today is a new day. You've got a clean slate ready to be filled with the flow of everything good in this world. You're tapped into the power of the universe, to the healing light that refuels your spirit."

Brooke enjoyed the peaceful veneer on Jacky's face. "Whether you're sitting in the valley or on a hill, you can connect to this light. It's yours."

She nodded.

"You're safe here. You're here in the warmth of this room. Your mind is clear and peaceful now. Your breathing is calm and your heart is open. You're back here in the safety and comfort of this space where you're free to be you, a woman who loves deeply, cares immensely, and projects an enormous amount of good energy."

Brooke massaged her hair back for one last sweep.

"When you're ready, open your eyes and enjoy the freedom."

Jacky blinked, opening them ever so slowly.

Brooke gazed down at her, enjoying the look of peace in her warm, moist eyes. "How do you feel?"

"Like I could cry."

Brooke wiped the tears from her cheeks. "That's good. Set the emotions free."

They shared a thoughtful gaze.

"How did you get to be so good at this?" Jacky asked in a sleepy voice.

"Lots of observation." Brooke learned how to offer herself and others slack through her bees and then by listening to her healthy share of successful meditations by others, which helped her to be more patient and understanding in life. Was she a Zen queen? Hell no. Was she a student willing to open her mind and learn? A million percent yes.

Jacky sought out her hand, and cradled her fingers.

The room disappeared around them.

~ ~

Brooke's dark hair hung in loose curls down the sides of her shoulders, dangling around Jacky's face. Her spirit curled up around Jacky. She reminded her of a rose, soft and gentle to the touch, vibrant and soothing to the spirit.

How sweet of Sophie to nudge them together as she did.

Jacky looked up into her warm eyes, cradling her beauty. Her dimple widened across her petal soft cheeks. Jacky indulged in the delicate hint of her feminine, musky scent. Her stomach flipped and fluttered, teasing her into a state of pure elation.

Brooke's hand brushed against Jacky's waist.

Jacky continued to gaze into her soothing eyes. Braving all, she brought Brooke's hand up to her lips, brushing it in lingering sweeps and indulging in its softness.

She wanted nothing more than to keep on caressing her fingers, inhaling her beautiful scent.

Brooke leaned down and kissed her forehead.

Jacky could lay there all night and never tire of her lips on her skin. The world stilled in that precious moment, temporarily blanketing her in comfort.

Brooke traveled to her right eyelid and feathered it with kisses, stilling over it for a few indulgent seconds. She moved to the left eyelid and offered equally concentrated attention to it, taking away the twitches and nerves that capsized her for so long.

Jacky opened her eyes a slit to find friskiness layered in her beauty, and relaxed into the melodic reverie that sang from her soul.

They stared at one another, saying nothing with words and everything with their spirits.

Jacky looked to her soft lips.

An exquisite longing took over Brooke's face, the kind a child might have when wanting a cookie, but being afraid to reach out and grab it.

Jacky contemplated making the first bold and intimate move into a kiss. She wanted to so badly. She wanted to touch Brooke's succulent lips against her own, to have her warm breath tickle her. She exhaled her powerful craving. "I really want to kiss you."

Brooke placed her finger on Jacky's bottom lip, and slid it back and forth gently. They trembled under her caress. Brooke stared at them with a look of love for their trembling truth. No words were exchanged. They weren't necessary.

Brooke leaned in a bit closer, and her breath caught. When she exhaled, Jacky smelled the delightful scent of peppermint oil. Sweeter than any candy, it caressed every sensory nerve in Jacky's body, teasing her to continue on that delicate journey.

Brooke moved in closer. Jacky lifted to meet her. Just as their lips were about to touch, Brooke shifted toward her cheek. Entranced in the subtlety of it all, of the softness that glided against her skin, Jacky closed her eyes to take in the stroke. A moment later, she opened up and took in the full view of the face staring down at her.

210

Then, as natural as could be, Jacky sat up and faced her. She sought out her gentle cheeks and planted soft, loving kisses on each one as if they were the most delicate things in the world. They fluttered under her touch.

Jacky pulled away to gaze at her once more.

Brooke smiled, a teasing smile, one Jacky realized she loved and never wanted to miss. She wanted to caress her, to connect with her soft skin. When she cradled her hand, Brooke moaned, feathering her fingers around Jacky's palm.

"You're safe with me," Brooke whispered.

Love swaddled her like a warm blanket. "I feel safe with you. Since the first day you came into my school fifteen minutes late and smiled at me, you've been my safety."

The fresh summer air filtered through the window on a gust, filling the room with the scent of flowers and freshly cut grass. Everything teased her senses, illuminating all earthy pleasures. She bridged the splice of their existences by tracing Brooke's beautiful face and plucking up one of those gorgeous loose curls between her fingers and twirling it. When she did that, Brooke moaned, and Jacky's breath hitched. She loved being so intimately connected with this beautiful woman.

If she just braved forward and kissed her, she knew the gap would be joined and the connection would be permanent, unbreakable. Not only would their breaths connect, but their entire beings would.

Almost on instinct, Jacky began to fidget with the loose curl.

Brooke watched her closely as she pulled in her lip, moistened it.

They stared intently, and Jacky's breathing shallowed.

Brooke moved in, and Jacky enjoyed the steady rhythm of her breathing. She stared at her lips, beckoning for hers to land on them. They were in sync as Brooke's breath became hers and Jacky's became Brooke's. The air between them circulated with a magnetic and powerful energy.

Finally, Jacky couldn't take it a moment longer. She needed Brooke. She had to become one with her. So, she sought her out. When her lips brushed Brooke's, on a touch so soft and tender, she wrestled with a small cry at the back of her throat.

Brooke offered up feathery passes, and Jacky responded in reciprocity easing into the softness, then pressing on with more passion.

Their breaths quickened and deepened, matching each other's. Jacky teased open Brooke's lips with her tongue, using its soft tip to flirt with hers. Its indulgent touch, velvety and warm, resisted in a beautiful dance against hers. They swayed in beat to the tantric rave of their passion as they swirled and tasted each other, kissing with an electric intensity; one born out of a sheer desire to become one. Brooke danced to the rhythm of sensuality, tempting Jacky to indulge further.

Soft rapturous murmurings turned into a pleading demand for release, and Jacky rose up and guided the weight of herself on Brooke in a flux of blissful abandonment. Much to Jacky's delight, Brooke pulled her closer, luring her deeper into her heart. Jacky eagerly responded, feeding her desires with the nutrients her heart needed. All too soon, the pinnacle of joy began to exert dominance, calling off all bets to turn away.

Jacky hungered for her. Ever downward, she leisurely ventured across contours, restless in joyous response. She kissed the curve of her neck, the delicate landscape of her shoulder, and in return Brooke pressed her arched torso against her receptive body.

Jacky was in ecstasy. Her shallow breaths were her only evidence of reality. She looked at Brooke's slender body offering a golden glow in the chandelier's reflection. A hint of her mounting passion danced in the intricate beauty of her soul. She planted a kiss on her love-hungry lips, and she released a moan. Jacky kissed her ever so slowly, lazily. Her left hand traced her neck and hair as she breathed her in. The other hand slipped under her shirt and traced her spine, relishing the softness of her skin. Jacky's fingers sank into her flesh, as the waves of love grew stronger.

The sensual kiss led them to her bedroom where they slipped into that peaceful pocket of bliss, making love under the glow of a moon full of light and promise.

They fell asleep in the enchanting lull of the early night, tucked in between a place where life opened back up and allowed love to grow.

When Jacky woke at eleven o'clock that night, she couldn't keep herself away. She moved in to wake her with butterfly kisses. Brooke opened up with a smile. Jacky could live ages in the highlights of that smile. Brooke seemed to enjoy the tickling and let out that charming giggle that Jacky adored. Jacky once again indulged in her breath brushing against her lips. It tickled, and it caused her heart to flutter.

They spent the next hour, curled up in each other's arms, kissing and cuddling, exploring those innocent parts of their bodies that allowed them to savor remaining mystery for another time. Holding hands, they lingered on the afterglow.

Chapter Sixteen

"I need to talk." Jacky stood in front of her best friend, clinging to herself, drenched.

"Well, get in from out of the rain, you damn fool." Marie pulled her into the foyer. A pile of shoes awaited her soggy ones. "This better be good."

"Something big happened."

Shock zapped across her wrinkles. "Oh my God." She grabbed Jacky's arms and shook her. "Is it Sophie? Did something happen to our Sophie?" she cried.

"No. God no." She pushed Marie's hands off her. "It's not like that kind of big." She placed her hand to her chest. Her heartbeat still hadn't slowed. "I came over to tell you something giddy, not terrifying."

"At one in the morning?" Her face contorted.

"Like I know the protocol for such things."

"Such things?"

"I just left Brooke's."

They stood staring at each other, each calming their respective hearts, letting them catch up with the rest of them.

Marie released a chuckle first. "You had sex." She spoke calmly, allowing her words the freedom to fly. "You did, didn't you?" A squeal trailed the question.

Jacky remained straight-faced.

Marie narrowed in on her. "Please don't tell me you knocked on my door to tell me you winked at her."

"It started off as a kiss, and then grew from there."

215

Marie stood in her foyer, jaw dropped. "Well, how do you feel?"

A happiness from deep inside grew. "Alive."

~ ~

Brooke brought Jacky back to life. Her hunger for passion grew again, whetting her appetite for new experiences and ones long forgotten. Everything tasted delicious again and shone brighter. In the weeks that followed, Jacky snuck over to Brooke's early in the morning for walks and more kisses. She woke up each morning with a zest that desired more flavor and teasing, and then later at night, retired to her bedroom and to the soothing placations of Brooke's velvety voice whispering peaceful lullabies through her earbuds and straight to her heart.

They took it slow. Continuing their romantic courting without clouding it over with promises or heaviness. They slid into a natural, safe, and friendly peace.

"One step at a time," Brooke would murmur and walk away, leaving her longing for more.

Brooke brimmed of intrigue, always arousing Jacky's attention and supplying her with endless bursts of sunshine. It filtered through the shadows of her broken heart and shed light on the new infantile chambers that ultimately took on beats of their own.

She inspired a new confidence in Jacky; one that fell upon her most vulnerable points and nullified them, lifting her up to a new level that allowed her the wonderful space to try out the new buzz.

Jacky's entire being lit up with joy. She wore the resulting smile like a new outfit. It lifted her shoulders, widened her stride, and raised her confidence. She beamed, and that excitement caught on to those around her. Her clients eased up their pretentious demands. Vendors offered her better deals. Servers offered her extra bread and paid closer attention to filling her water and coffee. With happiness came a certain quality to living that Jacky had not realized she'd been missing.

Sophie even noticed. "You're glowing," she'd say, then quickly dart out of the room.

About three weeks after their first moment together, Jacky returned home from work and got her mail. She sifted through the pile of bills and oversized postcards from retailers, layering them into a pile. She paused and reflected on Drew's name on the cellphone bill.

She stared at her name, swiping her finger across the bold letters.

It was time.

She hugged herself, imagining Drew's arms around her.

"Would you be terribly upset?" Jacky whispered. "You know this doesn't mean our end. You're always going to be here with us."

Jacky looked to a picture of them on the fridge, the one of them in front of the fire pit in their backyard eating ice-cream. "You know, it's been forever since we've had ice-cream by the fire pit? We haven't since Sophie's championship game, remember, when she hit that ground ball to center field and tied the bases?"

She released a painful hum. "God, I miss you."

She stared at her name again. "You always had all the answers, didn't you? You knew when to take action on things. You knew when to fight a point and when to use silence. You would know when the time arrived to fix this bill. You wouldn't have let Verizon have this extra money all this time. You were always smarter and stronger like that."

She began to rip open the envelope with her finger. "Give me a sign sweetheart. Let me know you're okay with this. Will you?" Her chest rose and fell. "I hate that I have to decide."

Her words crumbled. "I know it's time for me to do this. I just wish you were here to do it for me," she said with a crack in her voice. She fell to her knees and rocked back and forth, clutching the bill.

~ ~

217

A few more weeks had passed with Drew's name still not changed from the bill.

Then, Jacky was walking beside Brooke and Bee when she spotted a patch of overgrown grass. A four-leaf clover stuck out from the long blades. It stood taller and prouder than the other clovers, as if it wanted to be found. She bent down and touched her fingers to it. "Drew had spent her entire life seeking a four-leaf clover, and here one grows at our feet."

Brooke cradled her hand on her shoulder. "That's her way of telling you she's still with you."

Tears welled up as Drew's warmth still passed through her. She plucked it up and stared at it. "Many years ago, Drew read *The Power* by Rhonda Byrne. It instructed her to select something personal and memorable that would serve as a sign that personal power did lay within her. It had to be something unique that she would recognize right away as her sign. A four-leaf clover popped into her mind first. But, she squashed that idea right away. She didn't believe she'd ever see one. She worried she'd spend the rest of her life without her personal power. So, she decided a rainbow would be her sign. Surely, she'd find a rainbow at some point and be able to say that she did in fact have that power Rhonda talked about. Well, we drove through storm after storm seeking a freaking rainbow for an entire summer. Not one."

"Not one?"

"Nope." Jacky rose to her feet, and twirled the clover. "She felt doomed. Of course, keep in mind, up to that point she never told me about her initial clover choice. I just knew about the rainbow. So this one day a client comes in and hands me this laminated four-leaf clover and says to me, I found this on a walk and I laminated it. I keep it in my wallet, and just now, something's telling me to hand it over to you, to pass it on. So I take it from her, thank her, and chuckle at the weirdness. I go home later and I pull out the laminated clover and hand it to Drew, laughing about the weird client. Well, her eyes doubled in size and she started to cry and shake. The universe found a way of giving her a sign."

"Through you no less."

Hmm. "Yeah, I suppose so."

~ ~

The next night, with Sophie hanging out at Ashley's house, Jacky called Marie and asked her to come over for moral support. She would call Verizon and transfer the account to her own name, then cancel Drew's cellphone service.

She arrived with a six-pack of Angry Orchard Hard Cider.

Jacky walked over to her laptop sitting on the kitchen table. "I've got the website pulled up right now."

Marie pulled out a hard cider for them, then put the rest in the fridge. "Let's drink first."

Marie popped off their caps with a bottle opener.

They clinked bottles. "To Drew," they said together.

"I charged her phone so I can download the rest of her pictures to my laptop before I donate it."

Marie's face blanked. "I can do that for you." Marie grabbed the laptop and spun it towards her. "Give me the phone."

Jacky stole the laptop back. "I can do this. I need to do this."

"There are going to be lots of memories." She shook her head side to side. "Taking her off the cellphone plan is going to be enough for you to deal with for one night. Let me download them for you, and you can walk through them after you've had a chance to deal with this hard task first."

"Okay." Jacky walked up to the kitchen counter and picked up Drew's cell. Too afraid to turn it on, she handed it to Marie.

Marie inhaled deeply before turning it on.

Jacky watched as Marie untangled the cord and plugged it into the laptop. "Drink your Angry Orchard." She pushed the bottle to Jacky.

Jacky watched every one of Marie's moves, including the slight, but very obvious arch to the eyebrow as she meandered the computer.

"This is silly." Jacky stood up. "I can download my own pictures."

219

Marie's face turned red, and she tried to cover up the screen with her body. "Let me do this for you."

"Hell, Marie. I can do this myself. I want to see." She squared off with her. "I'm ready for it."

Marie nodded, still red faced.

Jacky pulled her chair in close as Marie began downloading the five hundred plus pictures from Drew's camera roll. They flashed in front of them, mostly of Sophie and Rosy. She noticed a few of herself, some of the dojo, and a whole slew of them of Kate smiling and taking what looked like selfies.

Marie fidgeted, as the images continued to funnel into the photo library.

Then, a few provocative images flashed by.

Jacky's heart began to doubt its pacing, knocking around as if wanting to flee the scene. The pictures stopped flashing on the last one. Jacky stared at a set of a boobs she didn't recognize. "Why are there boobs in her cellphone?"

Marie squirmed. "I have boobs in mine too. Doesn't mean anything."

"Drew wasn't a fan of soft porn as you are. She finds… *found* it degrading. So why are we staring at perky boobs with hardened nipples?"

"I'm sure it's just a joke or something."

Jacky's legs began to tremble. Then, the tremors swam up into her stomach and chest, rendering it very difficult to breath. "Can you scroll backwards please?" Jacky asked.

Marie cupped her hand on Jacky's knee before following her order. Jacky braced for heartache. "I can't take a full breath."

"Relax. It could be just a joke picture."

"I'm not laughing."

"Me either."

Marie sighed then hit the back button, scrolling through images of Rosy in the front yard, Sophie performing a cheer, Ashley and Sophie giggling in the backseat of the minivan, Jacky walking in front of Drew with Rosy, Drew taking a selfie with a strawberry dangling at her lips, another of Drew in a selfie in front of a mirror where she's posing rather sexy. "I've never seen that picture. Why would she take this picture and not share it with me?"

Marie's breath rattled. "I'm sure she just wanted to edit it a bit before sending, and then forgot about it. It happens."

Disgust crawled on Marie's face. Or was it shame? Or was it fear? Jacky couldn't tell anymore. Nothing made sense.

"Keep scrolling."

Marie continued to scroll, slowly clicking to each one, seemingly as scared as Jacky to see what the next would reveal. Then, Kate appeared in a picture that stopped Jacky's heart. "Why is Kate naked? Oh God, why does my wife have a naked picture of Kate on her cellphone?" She gasped for air, punched her chest, and bent over.

Marie rubbed her back and didn't say anything. She just rubbed.

Jacky looked back up at the picture of Kate leaning back on a staircase Jacky didn't recognize, legs spread open, fingers playing with her swollen clit, a look of ecstasy on her face as she leaned her head backwards. Her hair flowed and flirted with her toned arms and shoulders.

Marie yanked the phone out of the cord and sat on it. Then, slammed the laptop cover shut.

"Give it to me." Jacky extended her hand. "Come on, give it to me."

Marie slowly pulled the phone out from under her left leg and handed it to Jacky.

She stood and looked at it again. "She didn't even try to hide it with a passcode. It's like she wanted me to find out."

"She didn't know she was going to die."

"Are you defending her?"

"No." She ran her fingers through her steel gray head of hair. "Geez. No."

Jacky viewed the apps on Drew's phone. She waved her finger over the Messenger app. "I'm going to dread opening up this app, but I need to see if there's more evidence." She clicked into it and scrolled through to find a new, unopened message from Kate from the morning of the crash.

"I need to see you. Please get over here."

Her heart dropped to the ground. The chair sat too far away. She landed in a heap on the floor. Balled up, she squeezed the phone so hard, her fingernails turned white. "Oh my God, they were having an affair."

Marie bent down to her level and hugged her. "Let me see."

Jacky clicked back into Messenger, and stared with blurred eyes at the conversation trail. She scrolled, trying to get to the beginning of it. "My God, it's endless." She saw emoticons with kisses and winks and hearts, red ones not pink, and xo's, and hugs, and heart bubbles coming out of cute cartoon puppies mouths, and enough baby's and sweetheart's to fill a freaking novel.

"She couldn't erase them?" Jacky asked. "Did it not dawn on her I might find these?" She continued to scroll way past the three month mark prior to her death. She stopped on a random one where Kate blew a kiss. "Hey sweetheart. I'm craving you."

Jacky tossed the phone. "I can't."

Marie hugged her tighter, rubbing her head and telling her some nonsense about how everything would be okay.

"She was at the cemetery."

"I know. Sophie told me."

"Do you think Sophie knew?"

Marie kissed the top of her head. "If she did, it just means she loves you too much to have told you. That's what we do when we care for someone. We protect them from things that can't be changed."

Jacky pictured Kate sobbing at the stone. "She looked right at me at the cemetery. She acted like she had every right to sit at Drew's urn and sob over her."

Marie just rocked her more.

After an eternity, Jacky lifted her head. "I need to be alone."

"That's not a good idea."

Jacky stood up and walked toward her front door. "Please. I need to be alone right now."

Marie twisted her lip and bit down. "Okay. I get it. Just don't do anything stupid, okay?"

Jacky didn't agree to that promise.

~ ~

Brooke opened her front door and found Jacky shivering and crying. "Oh my God, what's wrong?"

Jacky stared at her with mascara smeared down to the apple of her cheeks. "She cheated on me."

"Drew?"

Jacky nodded, and her teeth chattered.

Brooke wrapped an arm around her and led her into her warm living room. The crackling fire roared a bright orange. She placed a blanket over her shoulders and eased her backward against the couch.

She explained the whole story in shallow breaths, choking down sobs and wrestling with trembles.

"I'm so angry." Her temples visibly throbbed. "I just got my life back."

Brooke lifted her hand and brought it up to her lips.

Jacky pulled it away. "I can't." Agony ripped apart the peace she had worked so hard to create.

Brooke saw their future fold up into the heart of that anger. "I know you're scared. You don't know who to trust now," Brooke said.

"Trust!" Jacky laughed. "How am I ever going to trust again? Everyone comes sugar-coated. None of us show our true colors. We put on a mask, our best one, and over time it begins to fade away. The sparkles disappear. The colors fade. The fibers start to break apart."

She paused and shook her head.

"Then one day you wake up and the mask is gone," she continued, "and what you have before you is the real deal. The face that can't lie and hide. The one that gets discarded. Perhaps someone will eventually pick it over, examine it and decide that maybe this one is worth cleaning up, repainting, and adding sparkles to again. Or maybe not. Maybe they see the grime and layers of problems that would take a thousand lifetimes to chisel away. I'm afraid that's what I've turned into here."

Brooke hated what Drew did to Jacky. Drew acted like so many other ungrateful people, people like Penelope. People discarded each other like trash, leaving each other for others to pick over. Jacky got that right. Some got picked, others lived out their lives isolated in a pile of leftovers.

Anger corked its way through Brooke. "I really hate your wife right now."

Jacky groaned and nodded. "Me, too."

"How dare she get to do this to you? To Sophie? To us?"

Jacky buried her head in her hands.

Brooke stood up and paced the floor, livid with a dead woman.

"Love is such a gamble," Jacky mumbled.

Brooke stopped in front of Jacky and absorbed her despair. That very moment could define their future. Brooke needed to remain calm.

She lifted Jacky's chin with her finger. "Not always."

"There's no control over the process."

"Love isn't a process," Brooke said.

"Which makes it difficult for people like me who love processes. I need to know where I'm going and what I'm doing. If I can't plan for the future, how can I trust the present?"

"By letting go of the future," Brooke whispered, "and joining in the dance right now while the rhythm beats strong and provides all the nourishment needed."

"You speak like you're experienced."

"I hang with the best dancers of them all. If there's one thing a beekeeper learns in life, it's awareness." Brooke let her finger slip from her chin. "That and lots of patience."

Jacky reached out for her hand. "I just need time to process all of this."

Brooke squeezed her hand. "Of course."

Jacky leaned in and brushed her lips against Brooke's forehead. "Please be patient with me."

Brooke nodded and swallowed a sob.

~ ~

When Jacky arrived home, she drank three more Angry Orchards in a matter of minutes. She wrestled over Kate in her mind, and all she wanted to say to her. She wanted to tell her what an ugly, disgusting person she was for ruining their marriage. She didn't deserve to sit in peace thinking she had gotten away with making a fool out of her. She needed to know the damage she caused.

On a huff, Jacky marched through the living room, past all the pictures of their family, and out the front door. She bolted down the street wearing nothing but a pair of boxer shorts and a tank top without a bra, no less. She ran barefoot in the street, stepping on stones and crunching the first of the fallen leaves. The pain of the pebbles digging into the soles of her feet soothed her by comparison to the pain ripping through her heart. She pressed on, passing streetlights at a blazing speed. Her legs turned numb under her.

A surge of rage rose. She wanted to punch her. She wanted to wind up her arm and punch her right in the gut to let her experience the piercing pain too. How dare she walk around with her head raised, wearing her chic sunglasses and sporting her expensive highlights after what she did? Who flung herself on a staircase and snapped photos of her spread legs? Who did that?

How did it begin? How did one start an affair?

She and Drew quarreled a lot. Did their fighting do Drew in? She flung those insults just as harshly.

Maybe Jacky should've paid her more attention. But how much? She massaged her neck, cleaned out the gutters, gave up watching *Survivor* because Drew couldn't handle the scenes with bugs. Hell, she even bought her a car for her birthday.

How did Kate slide into the equation? Did they partner up at the dojo for kicks and end up sipping from the same Margarita at happy hour later on? Who came onto whom first? Drew knew how to flirt. She excelled at it. That's how she got Jacky, that damn sexy quality and raspy voice she used in the beginning. Did Drew invite her out for a drink? Did they sit in a dark booth sharing laughter and winks? When exactly did Drew decide at what moment they should kiss? Maybe she wished Jacky never entered her life. Did she wish Jacky would roll over and go away so Kate could slide into their family unit instead?

How many times did she fall asleep unknowing that Drew stared at the back of her head possibly weeping because she'd have to spend the rest of her life with someone other than her new lover Kate? Had they slept together in their bed? Did Kate take her side? Did they roll over mid-nap and cuddle and kiss under the same blankets that Jacky wrapped herself in each night?

The questions kept shooting at her from all different angles, relentless in their pursuit of destroying her sanity.

She ran around the corner to Kate's street, blinded by tears and rage, powering her stride with her arms. Her feet barely touched the ground by the time she arrived in front of Kate's house. It hung in dim light, but one light in the living room casting cozy shadows across leather furniture and another toward the kitchen in the back.

She trusted Drew. She gave her everything. She valued their love. She would've taken a bullet for her. She would've donated one of her kidneys had she needed one. She would've confessed to a crime if it meant keeping Drew safe and out of jail. She would've moved to Alaska if Drew dreamed of it. She would've done anything for her because she loved her beyond anyone else. She viewed her as a soulmate. She always cherished the moment of their first meeting as kismet, where the universe sprinkled magic in the air and nudged them together at just the right time and place.

All that trust shattered in a matter of nanoseconds.

She stood at the foot of Kate's perfect home with its beautiful sparkly windows, surely triple-paned, and curtains pulled straight out of a home décor magazine. The lawn had just been groomed. It smelled fresh and pure, a complete contradiction to what went on beyond that red door with its welcome wreath.

Little gnomes and frogs with cute hats and signs with witty sayings blanketed the kidney shaped flower beds with their azalea bushes and healthy hostas. How did someone with so much still need to take? Did her husband know and that's why he divorced her? Did Ashley know and not tell Sophie?

Did everyone know but her?

Kate deserved to suffer. She deserved to have all those pretty flowers ripped up from their roots and strewn all over the front lawn. Jacky imagined herself ripping blades of grass with her bare hands, clawing her way up to the flowers beds. Along the way, she'd toss pebbles from the sides of the path into the grass, chucking them high into the air so they'd rain down on every possible inch of the manicured lawn.

Kate deserved to have the tires of her Escalade slashed so she could be inconvenienced and unable to drive to her mistress's urn garden. She imagined gutting all four tires until they lay against the gravel like pancakes. A nice, long, deep key groove along the shiny black paint would top the night. She'd love to dig at that polished black until paint chips bled into the driveway.

Jacky wished she had eggs. Lots of eggs. She'd like to toss them at all those window panes.

Kate didn't deserve pretty flowers and fancy cars. She didn't deserve to be happy.

Jacky cried out in pain. Kate wormed her way into their lives and ruined it, and she stood by like an idiot unaware of any of it.

Jacky picked up one of the stone frogs and eyed the window.

Think of the consequences she could hear Marie whispering to her.

Sophie entered her consciousness. Poor Sophie.

She placed the frog down and stared into the living room window. She saw Kate at the far end of the house, fiddling with something in the kitchen, unaware of her presence.

All those getaway trips for the dojo and silent nights made sense now that Jacky knew the truth. They had stopped having fun a long time ago, and Kate stood in as the filler.

Had Drew ever loved her?

Yes. She did. Jacky trusted that much. That trust in her love hurt her the most; the trust that you could love someone with all your heart one day and fall just as quickly to the love of another in a blink.

She walked back home without tossing one stone or plucking one plant, and gritted her teeth with the sting of every single pebble that time. They stuck in her feet like needles.

Chapter Seventeen

When Sophie returned from Ashley's the next morning, she smelled apple cinnamon. She tossed her bag on the couch and ventured into the kitchen where she found Jacky wiping crumbs off the counter. "Hey kiddo. Hungry?"

The smell of apple cinnamon reminded Sophie of happier times, back when her mother filled the home with laughter. Every Sunday morning, Jacky would bake them apple cinnamon muffins and together they'd lounge in their bedroom, reading the newspaper, petting Rosy, and devouring them. "What's the occasion?"

Jacky poured a handful of crumbs into the sink. "I thought we could use some apple cinnamon muffins for a change."

A calmness surrounded Jacky as she placed the plates down on the kitchen island. "Everything okay?" Sophie braved to ask.

Jacky looked up at her. "Everything is okay, kiddo. So tell me about this presentation coming up. What are you going to talk about?" Jacky plopped down on the stool adjacent from her, and pulled the baking wrapper from a muffin.

Sophie picked up a muffin from the baking pan, unwrapped it, and sank her teeth into it. The spiciness tickled her senses, watering her mouth. "I'm going to talk about all sorts of fascinating bee facts, like the waggle dance."

"Talk to me about the waggle dance." Jacky bit into the muffin and crumbs dropped to the island.

"Well, okay, it's how bees talk to each other. Did you know they are experts in solar compassing?"

Jacky devoured another large bite and spoke with her mouth full. "What's that?"

"They know the sun's exact position at all times, and its relationship to food sources."

"Fascinating," Jacky said, and more crumbs fell to the island.

"They did a study with a colony where they set up two food sources in opposite directions of the hives. Then, as bees began to find the source, they marked the ones who were in one food source with a red mark and the others at the other food source with a blue mark. Then, they observed as the bees came back to the hive. They watched them perform what's known as a waggle dance, which means they dance in a figure eight, using the sun and the food source as their directional points. Here's where it gets interesting. The red ones started their figure eight at a different point than the blue ones. They discovered the bees were dancing to show the other bees the location of the food. Even though the bees were in a dark hive, they could still understand the position of the sun in relationship to the position of the nutrients and their home. They're true map readers."

"Sounds like they could have fun with outwitting each other."

"No, that's just it." Sophie sat up on her folded legs. "They don't deceive. They say it like they see it."

Jacky shoved more muffin in her mouth. "I'd like to be a bee."

"Me too." Sophie licked her fingers, just like she used to as a little girl.

They met on a smile.

"You're happy with beekeeping, huh?" Jacky placed the rest of her muffin down on her plate and gazed at her with the same awe she used to when she'd win cheerleader competitions or debates.

"I feel alive when I'm with them."

Jacky cupped her hand over Sophie's wrist. "You have no idea how happy I am that you, my beautiful daughter, have found such a love for life."

Sophie caught her breath, then clenched her jaw to hide the rush of emotions. She put the other half of her muffin down and fingered it until it became a pile of crumbs. She could feel Jacky staring at her. When she looked up, Jacky's eyes were filled with tears.

Sophie's cell rang and saved her from an uncomfortable segue into a mushy moment. "It's Auntie Marie." Sophie jumped off the stool and answered, "Hey Auntie."

Jacky whispered, "Tell her I said hey."

Sophie continued staring into Jacky's watery eyes when she said into her phone, "Momma J says hey."

Sophie turned away just as Jacky broke out into a soft cry. She cleared the room before Jacky could see her own tears, too.

~ ~

A few hours later, Marie and Hazel sat with Sophie and their dog, Zen. "Is Jacky okay?"

Marie couldn't lie. "Maybe it's time you and Momma J have an honest to goodness conversation."

"She was acting weird this morning. Is she sick?"

Marie and Hazel shared a look.

When Marie turned back, she noticed panic took over the poor girl's face. "Oh, God, no. It's nothing like that. Though, I guess it kind of puts what I'm about to say into perspective."

Sophie looked directly at her with the maturity of an adult. "She knows about Ms. Kate."

Marie squirmed. "I'm not going to lie to you, so yes. She discovered some text messages."

"When?"

"Last night."

Sophie cupped her hands around her face. "We ate muffins together this morning." Realization played out, as if she dug around her beautiful brain for details on something important. "That means she doesn't hate me."

"Oh, for God's sake, why would she hate you?"

Sophie lowered her hands to her lap. "I'm not her real daughter, and so I was afraid she'd leave if she ever knew about my mom and Ms. Kate."

"Just what kind of person do you think she is?" Marie asked, defending her best friend to an agonized teenager.

Hazel slapped her clear across her arm. "Marie, give her a break, will you?" Her eyebrows arched high.

"No, she's right," Sophie agreed. "Jacky's been through a lot, too, and I've been so worried about how that would affect me that I didn't wonder about how it affected her."

"You've both been through hell and backwards on the slow train," Marie said. "It's time to get off that one and find a new way."

Hazel rolled her eyes. "Always talking in analogies."

"Well, do you have a better idea?"

Hazel faced Sophie. "Ask her what she saw and tell her what you saw. Simple. Tell the truth. Hiding it doesn't help. It blocks you from bonding."

Hazel leaned in toward Marie. Then she did something out of the blue, something Marie had waited their entire life together to experience. She lifted her chin with her finger and planted a kiss on her lips right in front of Sophie.

Sophie gasped, then giggled. "Well, it's about time."

"Yes," Marie whispered and winked at Hazel. "It sure is."

~ ~

"Jacky?" Sophie whispered.

Jacky woke up from a nap with a giant gasp, as if she'd just taken her head out of a plastic bag. She'd been dreaming of being in the bee apiary and thousands of bees attacked her, causing her throat to swell and air circulation to cease.

"Sophie." Jacky rose up in the bed, bracing herself with her wobbly arms. She composed herself by smoothing over her hair and licking her dry lips.

Sophie sat down. "I have something to confess."

232

"Okay, kiddo. You can tell me anything."

"I saw them kiss once."

Jacky froze. "You saw who kiss?"

"My mom and Ms. Kate."

Jacky drew a deep breath.

"Ashley and I were getting some soda and they were in the foyer. They didn't see us. We saw them. I didn't want you to be hurt, so I didn't tell you. But," Sophie wrestled with her fingers, "more importantly, I didn't want you to leave us. That's why I never told you." Giant teardrops leaked down Sophie's cheeks.

Jacky pulled her into her embrace. "Oh, kiddo," she said, rocking her gently. "Even if your mom and I didn't work things out, I'd never leave you." She hugged her tighter. "You're my daughter. I could never imagine my life without you in it."

Sophie leaned into her shoulder. "Aunt Marie told me about the text messages. Mom ruined everything."

Jacky continued to rock her. "No. She didn't ruin everything. She's your mom, and despite whatever she did, she's still a beautiful person who loved you and in her own way, I suppose maybe loved me too. What she did was wrong and hurtful. She made a mistake." *And mistakes, just like her own, needed to be forgiven so they can lay to rest.*

"Will you ever be able to forgive her?"

Jacky blew out air, attempting to balance without much success. "I've already forgiven her."

Sophie relaxed in her arms, crying softly. "You're such a good person. You make it impossible to stay mad at you."

"Why would you want to be mad at me?"

"Self-preservation, I suppose," she muffled.

Jacky backed up, and Sophie lifted her head. A sadness sat on Sophie's face.

"I don't understand," Jacky said.

"I've got something to show you." Sophie rose from her bed, took Jacky's hand, and led her to her bedroom.

233

She pulled out a Taylor Swift CD and opened it. "I wrote a letter to myself right after the funeral." She pulled a piece of torn paper out of the CD jacket.

Jacky took the letter and sat down on the bed.

I'm the only one who drives Sophie to every cheerleading practice, student council meeting, and slumber party. You can come home and take your own daughter to the eye appointment. Yes, she's your daughter!

Jacky's blood turned cold. "Oh my God."

"I wrote this letter to myself the day of the funeral. I wrote it because I needed someone to blame. You were that person."

Jacky couldn't look at Sophie. The shame ran too deep. "I'm so sorry."

"I also wrote it out of fear. I was so afraid that you wouldn't want me anymore. So, I needed to be mad at you in case you sent me away. The anger that came from reading it, protected me. So, each night for months, I'd read that letter. Every once in a while, when I let myself get too close to you, too comfortable, I'd read the letter again."

"Those were just words I tossed out because I was angry."

"I know that now."

Jacky met her eye, and in them she saw love and the gift of forgiveness.

"I'm sorry I kept this from you for so long," she said. "I didn't understand it all until I finally learned what family meant. The bees showed me that. They taught me that honest talks are necessary to the family unit. Without connection the hive is in danger of dying." The tears kept flowing. "I don't want our hive to die."

She hugged Sophie, hugged her with all the love and power she possessed so it could fill her and let her know without an ounce of doubt that she loved her and could trust her.

"Can we start a fire in the pit right now?" Sophie asked, not letting go of her embrace.

"Roast a few marshmallows?"

"I hate marshmallows."

"I thought you liked them," Jacky said, pulling away.

"I only pretended to because you liked them."

Jacky laughed. "What other secrets have I to discover?"

"No more secrets. Just one important task."

Sophie reached for the letter, and Jacky gratefully relinquished it. She followed her daughter out of her bedroom and out to the fire pit. Together they built a grand fire, one mighty enough to help them move forward together in harmony.

Sophie handed the letter to Jacky. "Would you like to do the honors?"

"No. I'd prefer that act be saved for you."

Sophie tossed the letter into the flickering flames. "The bees taught me a valuable life lesson."

Jacky put her arm around Sophie's shoulder. "What would that be, kiddo?"

"That most problems can be solved easily if we just learn to talk about them openly and honestly."

Jacky watched the flames grow larger. "It's that simple."

"Yep," Sophie said, leaning her head against the crook in Jacky shoulder. "It was that simple all along."

They stood in silence for a while, each caught up in their telling moment when they learned that the truth could set a person free.

"By the way," Sophie said, "Auntie Hazel kissed Auntie Marie this morning."

"How is it you keep catching people in these kisses?"

"I've seen you kiss Brooke, too." Sophie smirked.

Jacky turned her foot up and patted Sophie's ankle with it. Together they stood in silence watching the flames dance as their goofy smiles grew bigger.

~ ~

It took Jacky some time before she could face Drew.

She stood before her memory stone and inhaled a long thoughtful breath.

Guilt no longer pinned her down. Granted, she never should've used those two bitter words in the end. She would never use them again. She'd learned her lesson.

235

She was human, and she made a grave mistake. Just as Drew was human and made her grave mistakes.

Drew needed to be needed. She craved attention the way a flower craved the sun. She loved new things and experiences, and so Kate offered that to her. If Drew had lived, Kate would have realized soon enough that she had failed too. Drew needed nourishment from them both to stay alive and perky, smiling like a sunflower in a summer garden. Such life needed new tilled soil and constant conditioning. It needed the crafty and clever hands of a creative gardener who understood the necessity in its rotation. Drew needed to feel alive. Routine sucked the life right out of her.

And so, she caved and made a mistake.

Knowing Drew, she would've kicked herself for the pain she caused, trudging over the sad fact in her mind that if she could've done it over again, she would never have indulged in that first sip, that first kiss, that first regrettable step into adultery. If given the chance to peek into the future, she'd love more and hurt less. She'd act out of civility and omission instead of rage and despair. She'd gamble on the good faith of selfless surrenders rather than cling to the false promise of an ego feed.

Drew didn't set out to be a cheater. Jacky trusted that. Drew didn't want to fall out of love with her and tangle up in the web of deception with Kate on any conscious level. Her body and soul craved the unknown. The lure at the edge of reason dangled in front of her like a chocolate bar covered in the sweetest of sugars, tempting her, teasing her, falsely promising her that with just one hit, she'd be able to walk away and settle back into her routine with a grateful heart.

She was not able to.

Drew could not be satisfied with a life lacking euphoric highs. Jacky was no more capable of producing those than desiring to do so. Jacky preferred stability over mystery. She enjoyed quiet evenings in front of the fire over a dance fest in a crowded club. They survived as two polar opposites wanting to change the other to fit their mold of what perfection stood for only to find themselves in a rat race of sorts. The only option out was to follow the intended path, opposite each other.

Jacky would never know the logic or lack thereof behind Drew's cheating. She'd never know if Drew loved her to the moment she took her last breath or not. She would never know whose face she saw last, besides Sophie's of course – hers or Kate's. The one and only constant was the unknown of it all. Life was one big unknown, tossing temptations and untamed knee-jerks around like glitter in a snow globe. Jacky tired of being a victim to the shake of that globe. She tired of chasing those flecks of circumstance and running out of space to put them all. No matter how much of the mess she cleared, more showed up out of nowhere and cluttered her life.

That was life. Take it or leave it. Wallow or rise up with it.

She refused to continue swallowing the bitterness of regret. Focusing on the mess didn't do her or anyone else any good. She needed to start pinpointing new ways she could turn those flecks into something more purposeful.

Knowing the truth changed everything. She couldn't get back on the same track once knocked off it. She would have to find a new track and dig into it until it worked. Jacky didn't know where that track sat, what it looked like, or how she'd get there, but she knew it would be worth exploring.

Before she began that new discovery, she needed to forgive both Drew and Kate, just as Sophie had forgiven her. The anger would eat away at her future if allowed to fester any more than it already had.

She placed a pink carnation on Drew's stone. She loved pink carnations. "I hope you can forgive me, too," she said, then walked away down the path she had traveled so many times before that, on her way toward freedom.

She climbed back into her car, drove the ten miles to her next stop, and braced for the next step.

She walked up the long walkway with the pretty statues, flowers and bushes, past the black shiny vehicle with no markings, thankfully, and knocked confidently on the front door.

Kate opened it. "I've been expecting you for some time now," she said. "Sophie told Ashley you found some text messages, and Ashley asked me for the truth."

"Text messages and pictures, yes."

She groaned. "I'm sorry."

Jacky hated to ask the next question, but she needed to know. "Did you love her?"

Despair hung on her face. "I didn't mean to."

Jacky believed her. Just as surely as she didn't want to say those hurtful words about Sophie, Kate truly never set out to maliciously fall in love with her wife. Love was not malicious, even though the biting end of it could cut deep.

"When did you first know?"

"The moment she asked me how to do a roundhouse kick."

First moments could never be forgotten. "She had my heart at *what's your dog's name*."

A funny thing started to happen as they gripped their memories. Jacky could feel Drew with them, and the anger that took up company in Jacky's heart since finding out thinned into vapor and began to float away. Their regrets disappeared and opened up a new path to the future, one that hinted of new beginnings and an earnest desire to learn from the mistakes of yesterday to help balance out the mistakes that would undoubtedly come into the swing of the future.

"So we both loved her," Jacky said, accepting the truth of the matter with as open a mind as possible. She and Sophie needed closure, and Jacky relied on the faith that facing and accepting the truth would give it to them.

"We did," she agreed. "But, she loved you more."

Jacky whimpered.

"You were her home and life. I was more of a joyride that got old fast." Pain etched in her eyes. Standing in her doorway, Kate wrapped her arms around herself, losing her battle against the tears.

Together they shed them, sobbing over their losses, losses equally as painful and everlasting.

"Can I ask you a question?" Jacky asked, wanting to understand the hollowness in Drew the night before she died.

"Of course."

"Did you have a fight the night before she died?"

Kate looked to the ground. "She told me she couldn't do it anymore. She wanted to end it. The morning she died, she was on her way to my house."

A new blow struck Jacky. "She said you had a dojo full of kids."

"She was coming to explain to me why she had to end it."

"You never got to find out?"

"She didn't have to say it. I already knew. She loved you more."

Chapter Eighteen

Brooke took out a honeycomb tray and stared at the capped honey-filled cells. The process would always mesmerize her. The bees born in the autumn would likely live four to five months through winter, surviving on the stored honey. They would have plenty of it to see them through to springtime. Soon, it would be time to cover their hives and ride out the winter without them.

She dreaded the lonely months ahead of her, trying her best to get past the bitterness. Would Jacky and Sophie have been better off had they not learned about Drew's secret? No. They would have lived under the shadow of a lie. The truth hurt, but at least a person could do something constructive with the truth. They could rebuild and grow. Without growth, there would be no momentum, no exhilaration, and no joy for what the open field had to offer.

The truth always outshone a lie.

To hide in the shadows of ignorance and deception only undermined the future. It extinguished the very flame that brought magic to the banality of routine and rigid definitions for what life was supposed to be instead of embracing what life could be.

Someone like Drew never learned the value of intentional rest, to be in that place of harmony when life breathed in sync with her. She preoccupied herself so much with trying to get somewhere else that she forgot to look around and enjoy the present.

Brooke put the tray back and sealed the lid on the hive. "I need to take my own advice and be patient with life." She patted the lid and warmed at the love and harmony of her bees, trusting in the process of life. "All in good time."

~ ~

241

Around dinner time, Jacky returned home and found Sophie cooking chicken and rice.

Jacky sat down on the stool. "I paid Ashley's mom a visit."

She paused in her stirring of the rice. "How did it go?"

"Better than I expected."

"So you didn't smash any windows or punch her in the face?"

Jacky smirked. "I wanted to. But, then she opened the door and I saw a look on her face that caught me off guard."

Sophie wrinkled her nose. "What do you mean?"

"She loved your mom."

She continued to stir. "You're okay with that?"

"I'm sad that your mom loved her too. It's sadness, not anger. I felt sorry for her."

"Ashley's still embarrassed." Sophie poured Adobe seasoning into the rice. "She's afraid this is going to ruin our friendship."

Enough destruction had already been done. "Don't let it destroy you both."

"I won't." She stirred, angling toward Jacky. "Do you love Brooke?"

"Of course. She's awesome. Who doesn't love her?"

She put down the spoon. "No. I mean *really* love her."

"Yeah." Jacky rested on that admission. "Yeah, I do."

"Then don't let their affair destroy you both, either."

Jacky took in her earnest plea. "I don't intend to. I just need a little time to process it all."

"Good thing she's patient," Sophie said picking her spoon back up. "But, she's not a honeybee. Her patience will eventually run out if you wait too long."

"Spoken like a true beekeeper."

Sophie winked and took out two plates from the cabinet. "Hungry?"

"Starved."

~ ~

Jacky took Sophie's advice and didn't take too long. The heart knew what it knew.

She drove the long way around town, past the busy streets and onto the quieter, country roads where the colorful foliage met the bright blue fall sky. She rolled the window down and let the fresh air filter in, filling her with new vitality.

As she closed in on Brooke's neighborhood, she spotted the crazy, fun-loving beast, pulling Brooke along behind her like a twig.

There was such beauty in imperfection.

Within the noise and chaos lived a rawness that created action and surprise, jolting the predictability of the mundane off its axis and freeing one to explore what lay beyond the ordinary. *The truth in chaos frees the soul. Yes, it frees it and helps it see past the grooves and dents and into the heart of its flame.* Jacky blinked back joyful tears. *Into that part deep within. The part that craves to be swept up in its rapture. Where real passion ignites. Where the real dance of the soul comes alive.*

She watched Brooke struggle for control as Bee lunged toward the adventure of life, one passionate bark at a time. When she neared Brooke's driveway, she pulled in and waited for them to return.

She waited for them under the mighty oak tree in the side yard, looking up at its thick and knotty branches. She inhaled and took in the earthy aroma of the fallen leaves at her ankles, enjoying the rustle of them as she kicked them with her feet.

She listened to the squirrels play in the branches above. She connected to the simple and grand undertows of the moment. For the first time in a long time, silence comforted her. Her heart reflected back a wishful, thankful beat.

When she opened her eyes, Bee bolted toward her. She bent down to pet her, then looked up and noticed Brooke standing with her hands tucked into the front pockets of her jeans. Everything in her pose told her to move forward, to embrace that small pocket of time where nothing else mattered but the silence of her mind and the openness that silence created in her heart.

Jacky had lived so long under the blanket of her mourning and guilt that when she finally looked up and took it all in, every detail she had missed, she wanted to embrace and enjoy the life and love dancing around her.

Life happened whether orchestrated or not. No matter what life tossed at her, she knew now that she'd be okay.

The love on Brooke's face told her that she didn't have to go through any of that alone.

If a bee could live up to forty something days and thrive in its richness without care of its demise, she could surely change her life and trust in its new direction.

She walked toward Brooke one slow step at a time, taking in her loving eyes. Meanwhile, Bee jumped and pranced around her. "I hear you might be in need of a dog trainer?"

A gleam rested in Brooke's eye. "She's a beast."

"A beast?"

"A total beast."

They stood within arm's distance, smiling and taking each other in. "I hope I'm not too late," Jacky said.

Brooke cradled Jacky's hand. "Better late than never."

Embracing the energy flowing between them, Jacky stepped in closer and planted a soft kiss on her forehead. "I see someone has been a very bad student."

Brooke giggled at Bee as she frolicked around their feet, whining for attention. "She has been."

Jacky planted another soft kiss on her forehead. "You and I both know I'm not talking about Bee."

Brooke warmed under her touch, folding into Jacky's arms. "I guess we should get started then?"

Jacky cradled Brooke, enjoying the beat of her heart against her own. "I'm not in any rush."

They cuddled under the tall oak tree for a long while, wrapped up in the earthy aroma of the fresh fall day. Jacky trusted in that moment, the moment when grace swept in and offered her the gift to dance with life again.

The Following Spring

On a beautiful April morning, the whole gang met up at the park along with a hundred other people. At the helm of their crowd stood Sophie and her best friend, Ashley.

Many were there to take part in their first ever community Save-a-Bee project, including Marie and Hazel with their matching bright yellow bee sweatshirts, Tom and Elise, and of course Brooke.

Sophie and Ashley called for the crowd's attention with megaphones. They stopped and giggled, likely at the sound of their voices as they echoed off the trees.

"What on this God's green Earth did you feed those girls for breakfast?" Marie asked. "They're going to wake the bears from hibernation with those cackles."

"Oh shush." Hazel elbowed her. "Marie's just grouchy because she's drinking decaf again." Hazel rolled her eyes.

"Not by my choice." Marie pointed her finger. "She's on her health kick again, worried I'm going to have a heart attack because some magazine article told her caffeine was bad. Next month, it'll be good again and she'll be pouring me ten cups of coffee."

Elise nudged Jacky. "Do they always do this?"

"Relentlessly."

Tom curled up around Elise and placed his hands on her shoulders. "They sound just like us."

"You all bicker too much, if you ask me," Brooke said. "Sounds like they need a trainer."

"I stop at dogs." Jacky said, matter-of-factly.

"Hazel and I are just looking out for their health," Elise said. "They're the ones who bicker and make us look like the bad ones."

Hazel nodded. "You're damn right about that."

"Hey, you two," Sophie called out over the megaphone. "With the matching yellow sweatshirts."

Marie and Hazel both pointed to themselves.

"Yeah, you." Sophie's voice curled up around them. "Stop bickering."

Hazel and Marie nudged each other, muttering under their breaths like a couple of teenagers caught cheating on a test.

Jacky put her arm around Brooke and took in the view. What a spectacle her new Inner Circle had become. Sure they quarreled and groaned along the way, but one thing remained true – they all cared deeply for the person who stood at the helm of their hive, and would do just about anything to protect her wonderful, trusting, and giving heart.

Since meeting Brooke, she and Sophie both learned the trick to moving on. They had to find something outside themselves, something far more purposeful than their sum.

Jacky listened to her daughter educate the crowd about honeybees. She talked about their value to the world, and simple ways to help save them by doing things like planting wildflowers in window boxes, avoiding the use of pesticides, supporting organic farmers, allowing weeds to grow, and taking action by signing petitions banning the use of chemicals in farming and public landscaping.

"The cool thing about bees," Sophie said, "is that they work together for the betterment of society. They are the ultimate role model for a collaborative, healthy community. Their communication skills keep them alive and thriving. They're the perfect exchangers of information, trusting and attentive to each other in a way that enriches their relationships and offers them a deep connection to the environment in which they live. They're the keystone to our world as we know it, and it's imperative we protect them as if our life depends on it, because it does."

Jacky and Brooke held each other tighter, absorbing Sophie's profound speech. Her words offered Jacky courage and hope that together they could weather anything life tossed at them, as long as they stayed open to honest communication, forgave each other for their mistakes, and danced with an open heart and mind through all of life's ups and downs.

The End

NOTE FROM SUZIE CARR

As with all of my books, I enjoy giving a portion of proceeds back to the community by donating to the NOH8 Campaign www.noh8campaign.com and Hearts United for Animals www.hua.org. Thank you for being a part of this special contribution.

A SPECIAL REQUEST

If you enjoyed reading this story, I'd be so grateful for your honest review of it. Just a sentence or two will help others discover *The Dance* and help me to serve you better with future books!

(www.amazon.com/author/suziecarr)

ENDNOTES

Winston, Mark L. (2014-10-06). Bee Time: Lessons from the Hive. Harvard University Press.

Made in the USA
Middletown, DE
08 February 2016